# THE RIOT

# THE RIOT

*A novel by Frank Elli*

**NEW YORK** *Coward-McCann, Inc.*

To
Professor Harold J. Alford
University of Minnesota

# THE RIOT

CHAPTER 1

ON the surface it was a lazy Monday morning in the State Penitentiary. The only motion in sight was smoke spiraling from the towering powerhouse chimney and gliding over the southeast gun tower. The only sound in the air was the listless drone of machinery. It was early; the thirty-foot east wall still shaded the lawn in front of Cellhouse Eight. But it was hot; the glowering July sun was already sweltering the twenty-two walled-in acres of earth.

Cully Briston, a tall muscular man in his late twenties, stood alone on the shopline walk. He was stripped to the waist, his sweat-damp T-shirt hanging from the hip pocket of his faded dungarees. There was a motionless struggle going on. He was aware of being watched by the gun tower guard forty feet behind and thirty feet above him. He, in turn, had his eyes fixed on the three denim-clad figures perched on the ridgewall of the messhall roof—the roof-tarring gang of which he was one. It was a three-way stalemate, for the men on the roof had the guard on the tower walk under sidelong surveillance.

Cully's next move hinged on the hoped-for sound or movement which would distract the tower guard behind him, a beefy-faced man in goggle-size sunglasses with a rifle in his hands and a pistol on his side. The moment the guard turned his head, a nod from one of the men on the roof would send Cully into action. Twenty feet away, stashed in the window well below the bakery, was a two-gallon jug full of day-old potato beer. In a matter of seconds, after the guard turned his head, the jug would be in the empty tar bucket and, via the block and tackle suspended from the roof, on its way to consumption above and beyond the eyes of the gun tower guard. Cully would follow by way of the extension ladder under guard behind the building, and the roof-tarring gang would spend the morning under the blazing sun, far above the ubiquitous eyes on the ground, where the four of them could get peacefully and groggily sick on green potato beer. Anything to break the gnawing monotony.

But the stalemate dragged on, and Cully was on the verge of trying it raw-jaw, of making his play on the chance that the eyes behind the sunglasses were looking elsewhere, when a brow-wiping gesture came from the roof, a gesture signaling trouble— The Man is on the scene. He made a casual move toward the dangling tar bucket as the scuff of feet caught his ear.

Sergeant Grossman, the shopline sergeant, was coming up the walk. Narrow-shouldered and potbellied, he was a middle-aged man with a bony nose and vein-webbed face, referred to behind his back by both convicts and guards as Andy Gump. Although there was nothing humorous about the man, he did bear a physical resemblance to the comic-strip character of that name. As usual, he was scowling.

"Who moved that block and tackle, Briston?"

Cully turned, grinning. The prominent, slightly marred features of his face were arranged in such a way as to stir geniality in a bartender, hope in a panhandler, and perhaps curiosity in a woman who wasn't looking for anything permanent. But in a man like Sergeant Grossman, a man who had spent thirty-five years of his life zealously performing the thankless duties of a punisher, the feeling aroused was obviously suspicion.

"Lieutenant Becker gave me the okay," Cully said. "If I send the tar up in back, the boys'll hav'ta walk the length of the buildin' with it. It's hotter than hell up there."

"Makes no damn difference. Besides, Becker's not runnin' the shopline—I am. You take your orders from me around here. Grab that bucket and get goin'." He cupped his hands around his mouth and shouted to the roof, "Get that block and tackle back where it belongs."

Still grinning, Cully unhooked the tar bucket and started up the shopline walk—a block-long strip of concrete flanked by the greenest grass behind the walls, shaded in the morning by the decrepit two-story building partitioned into shops and, in the afternoon, by the so-called hub of the prison, a block-square structure more than seventy years old, which housed the Control Room; several upstairs offices; four cage-type cellblocks, including Isolation; and the messhall and kitchen. The outer buildings—the powerhouse, cannery, hospital, and three modern cellhouses—were comparatively new.

Cully cast a farewell glance at the window well under the bakery as he passed and decided he'd try his luck at the power-house later on. The juiceheads on the coal-unloading crew should be straining off their weekly ten-gallon batch of raisin-jack sometime before noon. And if that fell through, he'd hustle up enough cigarettes to go halves with someone on a tube of cotton. Damn Benny inhalers were expensive—three cartons for a lousy cigarette-size roll of smelly cotton, same price as a fifth of top-shelf booze on the streets. Even so, if a man wanted to stay alive in a graveyard like this, he had to jack up his wig on something once in a while or he'd turn into a zombi. Hell, if he couldn't score for a chunk of cotton, he might even go the goofball route today. Anything to break the goddamn monotony.

As he passed the carpentershop, he caught the eye of a stocky Negro beyond the door and tweaked his nose at the man, a familiar signal, meaning Andy Gump was on the prowl. Ahead, the walk was deserted. The men on the free-moving maintenance crews, all but the roof-tarring gang, had found a shady spot to work, away from the fiery glare of the sun. The stationary work crews were under guard inside the cannery, shoeshop, tailor shop, and laundry. More than half the seventeen hundred men confined behind the walls were locked in the cellhouses. Since the license-plate factory had burned to the ground the previous summer, work had become a privilege.

Cully was passing the laundry, tweaking his nose at the men beyond the windows, when Grossman's nerve-grating voice came ripping through the drone and whir of machinery.

"Get back there, Briston!"

Grossman was standing near the window well. The two-gallon jug of potato beer sat on the grass beside his feet.

Cully dropped the tar bucket and started back past the shops, slowly, his mind racing ahead. There was no way in hell the old creep could pin the jug on him. The jug had been planted there before daybreak, passed from the spud cellar to someone in the bakery. He had got the word from one of the coffee pourers at breakfast: "There's two gallons of hooch in the regular spot." He hadn't touched the jug, hadn't walked within ten feet of it. Hell, he'd scream bum beef loud enough to be heard in the warden's house.

Grossman was gloating—a tight grin on his face, his jaundiced eyes smirking. "How'd this get down there, Briston?"

"Got me, Sarge."

"Y'damn right I got'cha! *You* put it down there."

"Why me? There's over two hundred guys besides me on this shopline."

"I saw you hide it down there when I rounded the corner."

Cully started to call the man a liar. Instead, he said, "Crissake, Sarge, I've been under the gun all mornin'. I haven't been within ten feet of this spot. Ask the tower guard."

Since the new deputy warden, an out-of-state man, had taken over inside the walls the previous month, some of the old-line guards had been ignoring rule infractions; a few had even softened to the point where they were on gossipy terms with the hardnoses—the guard haters and wheelers and dealers who spent most of their time in Isolation. Only yesterday more than half the men in the cannery crew had got so drunk on fermented apricot juice that they had had to help one another back to the cellhouses. Lieutenant Becker's shakedown squad hadn't even bothered to search the building. The night crew had gone out and drunk up what was left. Still, Cully decided as he caught the twist of Grossman's mouth, if the old-line guards were hoping the joint would blow up in the new deputy warden's face, it sure as hell looked as if Andy Gump wasn't in on the play.

Grossman picked up the jug and said, "C'mon, boy, we'll hash this out in the Control Room."

Cully just stood there, feet planted, arms folded. He was a head taller than Grossman, thirty years younger, and perhaps forty pounds heavier, all bone and muscle. Sweat blistered the tattoos on his chest: twin bluebirds flying toward each other. A chain-entwined anchor with u.s. NAVY inscribed below it was tattooed on one shoulder. Tattooed on the other was a leggy nude bathing in a champagne glass. When he spoke, the friendly tone of his voice disguised the impulse he had to spit in the man's baggy-eyed face. "Let's talk it over right here, Sarge. If you take me to the Control Room, I'm goin' to The Hole on a bum beef—and you know it. I haven't touched that jug."

"I saw you hidin' it down there when I came around the corner."

Again he refrained from calling the man a liar. Instead, he said, "I've been in this zoo over four years on a lousy beer joint burglary—most of it in The Hole. It took me until now to score for a work assignment. If I go to Lockup on this phony beef, I'll blow it."

"That's your tough luck, boy. C'mon." He made a grab for Cully's arm.

"Keep your hands off me, Grossman!"

As Cully jerked his arm away, Grossman stepped off the walk, flagging an arm at the gun tower guard, who moved quickly along the railing, his rifle trained on the walk.

"Get movin', boy," Grossman snapped. "That fightin' you do in the ring around here might scare some of these guards, but those big fists of yours don't mean nothin' to me."

Cully cast a contemptuous glance at the gun tower. There was one creep he'd like to meet in a bar outside. Always looking for a chance to point his rifle inside the walls. The same type of gutless stooge that Eichmann used to dump the rat poison in the air vents at Auschwitz. He glared at Grossman, letting his face show the contempt he had for the man. There stood the daddy of them all, Andy Gump. The sadistic potbellied old creep would rather sniff out a jug of potato beer than hit the sack with a sexy broad. Hell, the stir-simple old bastard acted as if he personally had been the victim of every crime committed by every con behind the walls. "Look, Grossman," he said, "why don't you play the game straight? Catch me clean. I never squawk when a guard catches me clean. Hell, don't panic; it's early yet. You'll catch someone doin' somethin' before the day's out."

"Keep your trap shut, boy! Just get movin'. You're up to your neck in trouble right now."

Cully decided to play it cool. The new deputy warden wasn't a bad guy; he might believe Grossman; then again he might not. But if he cussed the old creep, he'd get twenty-nine days for sure. A minute's pleasure wasn't worth twenty-nine days in Isolation. Grinning, he reached for the jug in Grossman's hand. "Want me to carry the evidence, Sarge?"

Grossman swung the jug behind his back. "Get movin', boy!"

Cully started down the shopline walk, sneering up at the gun tower guard. He didn't really give a damn. Actually, a few days in The Hole would break the monotony, reverse the routine. He'd sleep the days away and spend the nights jabbering out of his cage, low-rating the prison officials along with Big Red Fletcher, Bugsy Matthews, Joe Surefoot, and all the rest of the stir-crazy hardnoses, who seldom saw the sky more than once or twice a year. He'd find out what was going on in there, the scheme behind the Molotov cocktails and the coil of rope that Grossman had dug out of the pipe closet in the shower shed behind Isolation the day before, the ten homemade shivs rumored to have found their way in. No, he didn't really give a damn one way or the other. At least a trip to The Hole would break the goddamn monotony.

He was moving along the prison's front walk, past the Control Room windows, Grossman with the jug of fermenting potato beer a few steps behind him. The smell of the sanitary buckets in Isolation, as though seeping through chinks in the seventy-year-old brick building, was livelier than usual this morning. As he caught a sickening whiff, he visualized the familiar primitive-looking cellblock inside: Isolation, The Hole, a pile of rusty paint-chipped steel which seemed to sag under the weight of the ponderous black padlocks hanging from the steel-latticed cage doors, twelve cages to a tier and four tiers facing each side of the cellhouse, and always, especially in the summer, the suffocating stench of human excrement in the air.

As he shoved open the solid-steel door to the Control Room, the foul smell swirled around him, and he heard a gravelly voice from Isolation yell, "Hey, you lazy bastard! When ya gonna change these stinkin' buckets?"

He glanced to his right, toward the heavily barred door leading to Isolation. The guard on duty inside, a gaunt man in his early forties, his tired face accentuated by a thin receding widow's peak, was leaning in the fan-shaped wicket.

"Say, Sarge," the guard called, motioning to Grossman, "when am I going to get some help? These guys in here want their buckets changed."

"People in Hell want ice water," Grossman snapped. "See Lieutenant Becker. I got my hands full."

Cully had started toward the doorway to his left, the doorway leading to the waiting room and offices, but stopped now, and leaned against a radiator in the entrance area as Sergeant Gallaway, the Control Room sergeant, caught Grossman's eye and asked, "Got any idea where Becker is? Have you seen him out there?" He was sitting at the window in the screened-in area, where the cons' institutional records were kept in filing cabinets and the count boards lined with name tabs hung on the walls.

"Damned if I know where he's hangin' around," Grossman said. "Probably in the kitchen havin' coffee. I got—"

He was cut off by a wild commotion in the Isolation cellblock. Hoots, whistles, and shrieks came gushing into the Control Room. Grimacing, the Isolation guard withdrew from the barred fan-shaped wicket as the cellblock behind him, out of view from the Control Room, exploded with noise. The cage doors rattled, and the steel floors and steel cage walls buckled under a savage barrage of pounding and stomping. The whole building seemed to thunder and vibrate. Then, as suddenly as the racket had erupted, it died, and a high-pitched voice yelled, "That phony screw likes the smell. It reminds him of home."

"Damn animals in there need a good snootful of tear gas," Grossman said. "That'll shut 'em up." He noticed the grin on Cully's face and flicked his eyes. "Get movin', boy! You know the way."

Deliberately swaggering, dragging his feet, Cully turned through the doorway and started across the waiting room toward the deputy warden's office. The boys in The Hole were in rare form this morning, really rare form. And with his luck, it looked as though he'd be getting in there just in time to help sniff up the tear gas. One hell of a way to break the monotony.

He jerked his arm away, glaring, as Sergeant Grossman prodded him with the jug of potato beer.

CHAPTER **2**

DEPUTY Warden John Fisk, a balding heavyset man of perhaps forty, in charge of treatment and security behind the walls, closed the Manila folder on his desk and rose slowly to his feet. "I'm going to let you off with a warning, Briston. Go back to your work assignment now—and consider yourself lucky."

Cully felt neither gratitude nor relief, only a bitter satisfaction. For the past ten minutes he'd been denying the charge, hanging onto his temper as Grossman kept insisting that he'd seen him hide the jug in the window well. As he started up from the chair now, Grossman gripped his shoulder, holding him down.

"I want this man taken off the roof-tarrin' gang, Mr. Fisk. He's a troublemaker—always shootin' angles."

"We'll discuss it later."

"I'd like to get it settled right now. If he goes back to work, he'll be struttin' all day. He's got a loud mouth, Mr. Fisk. He called me some pretty nasty names this mornin'."

Fisk was frowning. "You didn't mention profanity in your report."

"I thought the boy was in trouble enough without sayin' he called me a son of a bitch—and worse."

Cully was on his feet before he knew it. "You're a goddamn liar!" He was straining to keep his hands from Grossman's face; the baggy eyes, the bony vein-webbed nose, the thin purple-splotched lips. Stifling an impulse to spit, he turned to Fisk.

"This lyin' ol' creep wouldn't last fifteen minutes in a dog pound—the Humane Society wouldn't allow it—but in this crummy zoo nobody cares how he gets his kicks—and you know it."

Fisk's face reddened. "Take him to Isolation," he said, and turned away from the leer on Grossman's face.

Cully was still bristling when they reached the door to Isolation. Grossman called, "Key up," then reached through the wicket bars, and rapped on the inner ledge.

The Control Room sergeant, watching from his swivel chair behind the table at the opening in the screened-in area a few yards away, caught Cully's eye and winked. "What for this time, Briston?"

"Same as last time, Gallaway—bum beef. Andy Gump got hard up for a pinch."

"Keep it up, boy!" Grossman said, glaring. "You'll get yourself in some *real* trouble."

"Go to hell, you silly old bastard. Once I get in there, I'm as bad off as I can get."

Grossman pressed his face against the wicket bars, shouting, "Key up! Key up! Open this goddamn door!" He pushed past Cully and headed for the opening in the screened-in area. "Let me have your key, Gallaway. I'll be damned if I'll wait for that greenhorn in there to get done makin' his rounds."

Gallaway shoved his chair away from the table. "Help yourself. You're on your own. You know damn well that door isn't suppos'ta be opened from this side."

Grossman leaned through the opening, pulled open the table drawer, and came out with the key. "I've been openin' doors around here for thirty-five years," he said, as he rammed the key into the lock. "I don't need no out-of-state college man tellin' me how a penitentiary should be run."

He swung open the barred door and was prodding Cully inside when the mesh-steel gate on the second-tier landing crashed open, and a shirtless redhead came vaulting over the rail, yelling, "Grab him, Cully!"

Momentarily stunned, Cully glimpsed the action: Big Red Fletcher hurtling through the air; the gate on the main floor flying open and a swarm of wild-eyed faces crowding out; Bugsy Matthews and Joe Surefoot brandishing shivs. Then, as if his limbs were acting of their own volition, he whirled and pounced on Grossman, who was plunging into the sunlight, one stride away from the outer door.

There was a grunt, a smothered shriek, and then he was on the floor, knees straddling Grossman's chest, one hand squeezing his stringy neck. He was staring down at a stranger. He had never seen Grossman without a guard's hat. The man was bald, and his face was livid and contorted now, his eyes wide and glassy. Cully released his grip as the solid-steel door slammed, shutting out the sunlight.

He knelt there, gaping. Familiar faces, the pasty-white faces of cons seldom seen in General Population, were bounding past. The Hole was wide open. Cons were crowding into the Control Room, running wild; shirtless, glittery-eyed, sweat glistening from their backs and faces; some in stockinged feet, some barefooted, some armed with crude prison-made shivs. Inside the screened-in area, Bugsy Matthews had Sergeant Gallaway backed against a row of filing cabinets. The table in front of the opening was overturned, and a gangling shaggy-haired con was climbing inside. Beyond the entrance area, in the waiting room between the guard captain's office and the office of the assignment lieutenant, others were crowding through doorways. Then, as abruptly as the scramble had started, it began to subside. Perhaps one minute had passed since Grossman had unlocked the door to Isolation.

Cully moved to his feet. Grossman began scoonching toward the wall, flat on his back, his breath coming in gasps.

"Hey, Cully, drag him in here," Red Fletcher called. He was leading Deputy Warden Fisk toward the janitor's closet in the corner of the waiting room.

"You heard the man," Cully said. "Get up and get in there."

"Please, boy," Grossman croaked between gasps, "I can't make it. Please! Let me out in the air. I won't say nothin'. I give you my word."

Joe Surefoot, a dark sinewy Chinookan Indian, came rushing into the entrance area. Sweat streamed from his face, with its hawkish nose, jutting cheekbones, piercing black eyes. His knuckles and wrists were blood-raw. Smears of dirt and blood crisscrossed his bony chest. His coarse black hair was streaked with concrete dust. He had a long sharpened piece of steel in his hand. He passed it in front of Grossman's terrified eyes. "Get up from there! We're giving the orders now." His voice was high-pitched, almost feminine; his diction, precise.

Cully was scared. He looked around for help. Only a few cons—old-timers and those who had spent time in The Hole—knew the Indian by sight, but every con in the prison had heard the story. The Indian was snaky with a shiv. Seven years ago he had nearly gutted Lieutenant Becker over a sackful of wooden chess pieces, and he'd been in The Hole ever since—seven years. The cords in his neck stretched as tight as harp strings now as he leaned over the frightened form on the floor. "Get up! Do as we say! I'll cut your head off!" He was screaming, waving the shiv in Grossman's face.

Cully backed away, relieved, breathing again, as a tall broad-shouldered con with a boyish face and a mop of rusty hair came trotting toward them.

Big Red Fletcher was The Law in The Hole, the schemer, the undisputed take-charge guy. Three times since his transfer from the Reformatory five years ago, he had engineered a take-over in the Isolation cellblock, holding the Isolation guard hostage while he dickered with the warden. The last time, more than a year ago, he and the cons who had backed him up, including Cully, had held out for thirty-six hours, demanding clean mattresses and library privileges. He had surrendered on the warden's promise to fulfill the demand; but more than a year later the straw-stuffed mattresses in the cellblock were still dirty and lumpy, and no library cards had been issued. He stepped in front of Surefoot now, his thigh against the shiv. He was a head taller and a foot wider than the Indian. "Cool it, Joe," he said. "Get back in Isolation and help dig out the rest of those bricks." He took a cautious swipe at the Indian's hand, the hand that gripped the shiv. "G'wan, get going. We've got to get through that wall back there. I can't find the key to the door. If we don't get into the shower shed, we're screwed. G'wan."

Surefoot had ducked around him and was glaring down at Grossman, who was lying flat on his back, his hands clutching his chest as he stared glassily at the ceiling, his furrowed face corpse-gray, his livid lips half open and twitching, as though he were trying to dislodge a gag. Surefoot kicked him. "Let's kill him! He's got it coming." The Indian's voice rose, thin, hysterical. His eyes flitted over the sweaty faces in the gathering crowd. "I say kill him! If he had a gun, he'd shoot us all." He made a threatening move with the shiv and was making another when Fletcher grabbed his arm.

"Dummy up! You're screaming, man."

Cully took a step to the side, away from the shiv in the Indian's hand. He shifted his weight, set to throw a punch. He had made up his mind to swing if the Indian tried to knife Grossman. He wanted no part of a murder rap.

"Who's giving the orders?" Surefoot said, his eyes sliding away from Fletcher's. "Let's vote. I say kill him!"

Fletcher moved closer, his chin nearly touching the Indian's forehead. "Who let you out of your cage, Joe?"

"You did."

"Okay, then *I'm* giving the orders. I say leave him alone— at least for now."

"Why should I? He didn't leave me alone. Just last week he shook down my cell while I was in the shower and took those chess pieces I made out of soap."

"Dammit, Joe! Forget those chess pieces. G'wan, get those bricks out back there." He began steering Surefoot toward Isolation. "Coupla you guys go with him. The rest of you get away from the windows—stay out of sight."

The crowd broke up, shoving, jabbering. A few followed Surefoot into Isolation. The rest followed Fletcher into the office-section waiting room, leaving Cully and Grossman alone in the entrance area.

"Bring him in here, Cully," Fletcher called. "Put him in the mop closet."

"Please, boy," Grossman gasped. "In the name of God, open that door and let me out."

Cully looked down at the trembling old man and felt a moment of pity. Then he noticed the wetness around the crotch of Grossman's pants. Pity turned to contempt. "Get up, you ol' creep, before someone decides to cut your throat."

Inch by inch, Grossman lifted his head and looked around. Then, groaning, his trembling hands groping for the radiator, he caught hold and began dragging himself up.

Deputy Warden Fisk and Sergeant Gallaway, the Control Room sergeant, were already in the janitor's closet when Red Fletcher snatched Grossman's arm and shoved him inside. "Get Malaski out here," he called toward the guard captain's office. "Hurry up! Let's get moving."

Bugsy Matthews came to the doorway. He was stripped to the waist, slick with sweat, and the legs of his dungarees were ripped off above the knees. He had a square jaw, a bull neck, deepset eyes, and a shaggy mop of wavy blond hair. The lean, heavily veined muscles of his arms, legs, shoulders, and chest were covered with crude hand-inked tattoos, mostly pornographic. Cully had passed many nights in The Hole listening to the story of Bugsy's life—Training School, Reformatory, Penitentiary. He'd been Red Fletcher's yes-man since Training School days and would do just about anything the big redhead told him to do. His muscles were his pride and joy. He held the push-ups record in Isolation—one hundred and twelve without stopping. His nickname had been picked up several years earlier when the newspapers had carried an account of his extradition from a neighboring state back to the Reformatory for parole violation. According to Fletcher, Bugsy was scared to death of riding in an airplane. When the parole authorities had sent a plane after him, he had put up such a fight that a rope and cattle chute had to be used to haul him aboard. He stepped from the captain's office now, shaking his head. "Man, I ain't gonna touch that fat slob. He's havin' a heart attack or somethin'. They'll get me for murder."

"What happened?" Fletcher asked.

"He flopped out when that crazy Indian told him he was gonna lop his head off."

"Is he breathing?"

"Man, can't'cha hear him? He sounds like a steam engine. He's layin' in there like he don't know what's goin' on."

"I advise you men to send to the hospital for the doctor," Deputy Warden Fisk called from the closet. "If something happens to Captain Malaski, every one of you will be held responsible."

"Get screwed!" Fletcher said, and slammed the closet door. He slid the locking bolt in place and started toward the entrance area.

Cully caught his arm. "What's the score? How'd you guys get out?"

"Bugsy conned that half-wit screw into opening his cage to change the bucket. Told him it was leaking."

"Should've seen me," Bugsy said. "Huh, Red? Soon as he opened my cell, I grabbed his keys and slung him inside. I let Big Red out, and he let the rest out. Huh, Red?"

"Thirty-two besides Bugsy and me," Fletcher said. "Everyone on the Isolation side. I left six locked up on the Segregation side. Four stoolies in there for protection and two nuts. The nuts don't even know what's going on. One's that lifer—that weird-looking character who always spends summer in Lockup."

"Y'mean, Hardnose?" Cully said.

Fletcher nodded. He was looking toward the screened-in area. "Get that phone off the hook in there," he called. "In the offices, too. Coupla you guys keep an eye on the front walk. And someone see if the guys in back are getting those bricks out."

The noise and commotion had abated to jabbering, aimless moving about, the occasional slam of a desk drawer. A few cons were still prowling the offices, rummaging through the desks, but most, as though wondering now why they had left their cages, were drifting into the waiting room, forming huddles or just standing alone, looking worried.

Cully nudged Fletcher and said, "What's the deal? Why are they diggin' the bricks out in back?"

"Parole, man. Over the wall."

*"Thirty-four guys in broad daylight?"*

Fletcher grinned. "Why not? Only most of 'em don't know it yet. Just me, Bugsy, and Surefoot."

The cons standing nearby had overheard. One, the oldest con involved in the Isolation breakout, a wiry, surly man in his early forties, hacked out a laugh. His name was John Kelly, an outspoken guard hater with a record of four felony convictions and five parole violations. According to his own diagnosis, he was suffering from cage fatigue. He was the only con in the prison who was always given two Nembutals before making a parole board appearance. He was also the world's worst escape artist. Over the years a tangled rope, two caved-in tunnels, and a broken ladder had landed him in Isolation, instead of on the freedom side of the wall. His latest flop, the cause of his having been in Isolation for the past six months, had been due to a miscalculation. He had burrowed out of the ground too soon, four feet inside the west wall. Scowling now, he stepped up to Fletcher and said, "I'm game. How d'you figure on goin' about it?"

"First we've got to pick up something in the shower shed. Then through the messhall, out the kitchen, and over the wall behind the powerhouse."

"And what if we make it over?"

"There should be some trucks in the outside garage."

"And what if there's not?"

"We'll run for it. Must be less than two miles to the mountains."

"Never make it," someone said. "If ya don't get shot goin' over, they'll get ya on the other side."

"I'll take my chances," Fletcher said. "I'd rather get my brains splattered over the wall than rot in a stinking cage."

The cons in the waiting room began crowding around Fletcher, everyone talking at once:

"Man, I didn't know the score. I thought we were gonna wreck the joint."

"Yeah, I'm all for raisin' hell, but I ain't ready to commit suicide."

"Christ, I know I'm nuts, but I ain't nuts enough to go over the wall at nine in the mornin'."

"Hell, we'll never get outta this buildin'. What if—"

"Not so loud!" Fletcher snapped. "There's a gun tower out there. Besides, nobody's twisting your arm."

A skinny ferret-faced kid, perhaps eighteen years old, with a blue dot tattooed on his cheek, said, "I ain't chicken. I'll go if the rest go."

"Count me out," someone said. "I'm only doin' five years."

"Same here," said a husky young Negro, called Coolbreeze. "I'm with you studs as far as the kitchen, but I ain't goin' near that wall in daylight."

"Sounds like suicide," someone muttered. "There's two gun towers behind the powerhouse."

"They'll be on fire," Bugsy said. "Huh, Red?"

As Fletcher started to speak, a con hugging the wall beside one of the windows in the entrance area hissed, "Cool it! Cool it! There's a bull on the walk."

Except for the labored breathing coming from the captain's office, the room was silent. The cons stood motionless, all eyes on the solid-steel door.

"Get ready to put the arm on him," Fletcher stage-whispered.

He was moving toward the entrance area when the con at the window turned, with a grin, and said, "No sweat. He's not comin' in. He's walkin' toward the hospital."

Fletcher turned back to the silent onlookers in the waiting room. "Okay, you guys, make up your minds. The ones who want in on this break get back in Isolation and help Joe dig out those bricks." He grinned at Cully. "Might as well go for broke, man. You just signed up for another hitch when you grabbed Andy Gump."

Cully grinned back at him. "How do you plan on settin' fire to the back gun towers? Molotov cocktails?"

"That's right. We got a little help from the boys on the construction gang this time. We got six jars of gas and a rope with a grappling hook stashed in the shower shed."

"Had," Cully said. "You *had* the stuff. Andy Gump found it

yesterday. I was watchin' from the messhall roof when he carried your stash out front."

The cons within earshot who had started toward Isolation began moving back into the waiting-room. Four or five came drifting out of the offices. The rifling of filing cabinets in the screened-in area stopped, and a few more cons joined the silent circle forming around Fletcher and Cully. For what seemed a full minute, the only movement was the shuttling of eyes, along with a trickle of sweat on the anxious faces; the only sound, a spasmodic gasping and grunting coming from Captain Malaski's office. Then Bugsy let out a halfhearted laugh and said, "Big Red'll think of somethin'. Huh, Red?"

Fletcher swung around, scattering the circle as he charged into the assignment lieutenant's office. He looked out the barred window which faced the front wall, forty feet away and almost directly in line with the heavy steel door leading to the administrative offices at the front of the prison. Two gun towers could be seen from the window.

"Nothing happening on the wall," he said as he returned to the waiting room. "We still got a chance to come up with something." He started toward the screened-in area. "Put the phone back on the hook in there. Some of you guys get over by the door. Grab anyone who comes in."

Everyone began talking at once:

"Maybe we missed somebody."

"Who?"

"What about the assignment lieutenant?"

"He wasn't in his office. Probably didn't come to work today."

"How lucky can you get?"

"What about upstairs?"

"Yeah, that new headshrinker's got an office up there."

"So has the resident parole officer."

"Some of you guys get up there," Fletcher said. "No rough stuff, though."

"Hey, Red, now that you're runnin' the joint, is it okay to smoke in here?"

Fletcher looked over his shoulder. Two cons in blue, mattress-striped shirts were squatting in the corner, grinning. "What're you guys doing here?"

"We were waiting to see the deputy warden," one said. "But it looks like you canceled his interviews."

Before Fletcher could speak, a telephone rang. Motioning for silence, he hurried into the screened-in area and picked up the phone. He held the mouthpiece against his chin. "Control Room, Gallaway." He stood there grimacing for several seconds, then said, "Yeah, send him over."

"Who was it?" Bugsy asked.

"The bull in Cellhouse Four. I'm suppos'ta give number twenty-three five eleven a pass to the hospital. He's got a gut ache. Hey, that reminds me, somebody check on Malaski."

Cully was standing near the captain's office. He stepped inside. Two shirtless barefooted cons were kneeling beside a gray-haired man who was stretched out on the floor, staring at the ceiling. Captain Malaski weighed at least two fifty, and every pound was quivering now, as his hands clenched and unclenched to the rasping convulsive rhythm of his breathing.

"He's in bad shape," one of the cons said. "I gave him one of the little pills he's got in his pocket, but it didn't help much. He says it's his heart."

Cully backed out of the office, remembering the previous winter when he'd been picked on the prison's all-star football team and the man on the floor had released him from Lockup to play in the annual New Year's Day game. He looked for Fletcher. The waiting room was crowded and noisy again. Another mainline con in a mattress-striped shirt had joined the two who were still sitting on their haunches in the corner. Two civilians in shirt sleeves were being escorted to the janitor's closet. One, a tall stoop-shouldered man in his late thirties, was the resident parole officer. The other was the recently hired psychologist, the first in the history of the prison, a chinless crew-cut blond, perhaps thirty, built in the shape of a pear, all hips and buttocks. Both looked as if they were in shock.

Cully spotted Fletcher. The big redhead was standing in the doorway to the assignment lieutenant's office. Bugsy and Joe Surefoot were inside. As he neared the doorway, he heard

Fletcher say, "Neither one of those guys ever harmed you, Joe. The fat guy just started working here a month ago."

"Makes no difference. They're all the same." Surefoot's voice was shrill. He was sidling toward the door, his dark deepset eyes flicking from Bugsy to Fletcher. He had a shiv in his hand. "They'll hang us anyway. The stash is gone. We'll never get away. Let's kill 'em! We'll never get another chance."

"For crissake, Joe, quit screaming," Fletcher said, moving into the room. "We're not sunk yet. The Population goes to the yard pretty soon; so do most of the bulls. As long as the tower guards don't know we're loose, we still got a chance."

"*Bull lovers!*" Joe screamed. "You guys turned into bull lovers." He made a lunge for the door.

Bugsy and Fletcher grabbed for him and missed. Cully was standing in the doorway. Instinctively, with no intention other than that of protecting himself, he swung. The blow landed solidly on the side of Surefoot's head. The scrawny Indian spun back into the room, crashed against the desk, and slid to the floor. He scrambled to his knees, crawled a few feet, then flopped on his stomach, and lay still. The shiv had fallen at Fletcher's feet. He picked it up and handed it to one of the cons crowding the doorway.

"You'll hav'ta watch him, Cully," he said in an undertone. "He'll bury some steel in you the first chance he gets."

"Don't worry about me, man. I can handle myself. Besides, I'm in this, too. He's not gonna put my neck in a noose." He jabbed a thumb over his shoulder. "Malaski's dyin' in there. Somebody better call the hospital."

Surefoot was moving to his feet, his dark angular face twitching with hate, his eyes on Cully. "Who hit me?"

"Nobody," Fletcher said. "You slipped and hit your head against the desk."

"Okay, that's all right with me. You guys go your way, and I'll go mine. I'll settle up. When the time comes, I'll settle up." Glaring through the hair hanging in his eyes, he pushed past Cully and out the door.

"Hell with him," Cully said. "What about Malaski?"

"What about him?" Bugsy said. "It's not our fault he's got a bum ticker. We didn't touch him. All we're worried about is gettin' outta here. Huh, Red?"

"That's right, Cully. We can't risk alerting the towers. We still got a chance."

"We can get the doctor without alertin' the towers. Hell, man, if Malaski konks out, we're facin' a murder rap."

Fletcher spread his hands. "Go ahead, but if you get the doctor over here, he stays. He's not running back and forth—and Malaski's not leaving the building."

"Hey, Red!" someone called. "We got into the basement. Kelly says there's a pipe tunnel down there."

There was a rush for the staircase in the alcove beyond the deputy warden's office. Joining the noisy gallop was one of the three convicts from General Population, the one who had reported to the Control Room for a hospital pass.

Cully started toward the screened-in area. They'd never make it. If by some miracle they did get beyond the walls, every farmer in the county would be out with a shotgun. They'd be back in Lockup for the noon meal. He glimpsed the two cons guarding the solid-steel door in the entrance area. He knew the husky young Negro, Coolbreeze Clark, but the skinny kid with the blue dot tattooed on his cheek was a stranger. Probably a Reformatory transfer, he thought. He found the telephone directory card on the floor beside the overturned table and looked for the hospital number. As he started to pick up the phone, he caught a familiar smell—Benny. Three shirtless cons were hunched over a filing cabinet a few feet away. One held a shiv and was slicing up the cigarette-size roll of medicated cotton from a plastic nasal inhaler. The con glanced at Cully and winked.

"Let the good times roll!" He tossed Cully a piece about the size of a cigarette filter. "By the time they lower the boom, we'll be too high to give a damn."

Cully grimaced and gagged as he swallowed the piece. It burned his throat and left a sickening taste in his mouth. "Where'd you guys score?"

"Fisk's desk drawer."

"How many?"

"A handful, man. All wrapped up in cellophane and sealed with Scotch tape. Fisk must've busted a packhorse."

"Yesterday," Cully said. "The rumor is that he nailed Shaky Jake's connection comin' in with a load. That old whiskey-nosed bull that used to have the laundry crew."

"Must've been a finger job," the con said, and flipped a piece of cotton in his mouth.

Cully picked up the phone. As he started to dial, someone called, "Hey, Malaski's sittin' up. But he's still breathin' funny."

A door rattled, and heavy pounding came from inside the janitor's closet.

"Dummy up in there!" someone shouted.

Cully motioned for silence as a voice came over the phone: "Hospital, inmate Cummings."

"Send the doctor to the Control Room right away. Captain Malaski passed out."

"His heart?" the voice asked.

"I don't know. Send the doctor." He set the phone in its cradle, then took it back out, and let it drop on the floor. If a caller got the busy signal, he'd wait and call again, but a wrong answer would alert the gun towers. Not that he really gave a damn. Wrong answer or not, the party wouldn't last much longer. As soon as the morning yard rang out, Lieutenant Becker would come into the Control Room to check the count, and if he didn't return to the rear of the yard line and follow it to the yard, the tower guards would know something was wrong. Christ, he ought to have his head examined. Grabbing Grossman wasn't bad enough, he had to slug that knife-happy Indian. He noticed two barefooted cons in front of the deputy warden's office. They were drinking from his jug of potato beer. The con who had made the Benny score was in the center of the waiting room, surrounded by outstretched hands.

Cully sucked at his teeth, swallowed, rubbed his tongue over the roof of his mouth. The bitter taste of medicine stuck to his gullet like paste. He glanced at the wall clock, then glanced again. The red second hand was sweeping the face, yet it didn't seem possible. It was only twenty-five past nine. Less than half an hour ago he'd been on the shopline scheming to get his hands on the same jug of homemade beer that two Isolation cons were now guzzling right in front of the deputy warden's office. Christ, what a day this turned out to be!

He glanced over his shoulder as the outer door swung in and a tall young man in a knee-length white smock coat moved a few feet into the room and stopped. He was followed by a con hospital attendant. They stood there for several seconds, staring, their mouths slack; then the heavy door thumped shut behind them, and the doctor started toward the opening in the screened-in area.

"He's in the office back there," Cully said, pointing.

He met the doctor in the waiting room. Several shirtless cons, smirking, a few flaunting shivs, had already formed a gauntlet in front of the door to the captain's office. The two barefooted cons who had been drinking from the jug came swaggering across the room.

"Hey, Doc," one called, "got any goofballs on ya? My nerves are killin' me."

"Yeah," the other said, "give us some goofers."

The doctor ignored them. At least outwardly, he had composed himself. He glanced about as if the room were unoccupied. His lean face was expressionless. His eyes, clear and gray behind a pair of shiny black-rimmed glasses, were alert but impassive. He nudged the gaping hospital attendant and said, "Get the emergency stretcher off the wall over there, we'll need it."

"The captain's not leavin' here, Doc," Cully said, as he followed him into the office.

Malaski was still on the floor, glassy-eyed, legs sprawled, his back against the wall. His heavy-jowled face was limp, grayish blue, and wet with sweat. His shirt and pants were unbuttoned, and a sweat-soaked T-shirt was twisted into a wadded roll across his hairy chest. The fat of his belly lay in his lap like an overflow of dough. He was breathing in grunts.

"He'll have to be taken to the hospital," the doctor said. "He needs immediate treatment."

Cully shook his head. "Sorry, Doc, but the guys runnin' this show don't want him leavin' the buildin'. You neither."

Beyond the doorway someone called, "He's fakin'. Ain't nothin' wrong with the tub-a lard."

"He needs immediate treatment," the doctor repeated and glanced toward the door, where the con hospital attendant, a slender blond effeminate-looking man in his late twenties, was standing. "Bring the stretcher in here."

"I can't, Doctor Saunders. They won't let me take it off the wall."

Cully glanced at Malaski and quickly away. The dull watery eyes were staring up at him. "Christ, Doc, can't you call up and have 'em send somethin' over?"

"I need a respirator. It would be quicker and safer to carry this man to the hospital."

The huddle in front of the doorway broke up as a heavy pounding came from inside the janitor's closet. There was a bang as someone rammed open the bolt, a moment's silence; then Cully heard Fisk say, "We can't breathe in here. I advise you to either move us or leave this door open."

"Leave it open," Cully said loud enough to be heard in the waiting room. "You guys can keep an eye on 'em."

"Big Red said to keep it locked," someone called back.

"I said keep it open! And someone bring that stretcher in here." He turned to the doctor. "I'll level with you, Doc. Some guys involved in this still hope to make it over the wall. There's a chance as long as the tower guards don't know what's goin' on. Will you give us your word that you won't tip off the towers? Otherwise nobody leaves here."

The doctor glanced from Captain Malaski to the cons crowding back into the doorway. "I don't have much choice. I'll give you my word."

"Big deal!" a sneering voice drawled. "I don't trust him. Anyhow, what about Malaski? He knows what's goin' on."

"He's helpless," Cully said. "But he'll hav'ta give his word, too."

The captain nodded groggily.

"Who's gonna pack the stretcher?" someone asked.

"The attendant and I can manage," the doctor said.

"No dice," someone said. "I trust the doc, but not this fairy."

"I have a number just like you fellows," the attendant said indignantly. "What you do doesn't interest me a bit."

"Shut up, freak!" someone growled. "You're the biggest snitch in that crummy hospital. I oughta crack your skull right here."

The attendant darted into the office.

"Knock it off!" Cully said. "The fruiter stays here. There's two guys out there from Population. They can carry the stretcher."

As Cully helped the doctor steer Malaski onto the stretcher, the captain found his hand and gave it a limp squeeze.

With forced roughness, Cully freed his hand and turned away, wondering if the cons in the doorway had seen. Christ, what must they think? Playing nursemaid to a goddamn bull! He must look like a fourteen-carat ass kisser. Not that he had anything against Malaski—in fact, he kind of liked the guy—but the man was a guard, and he was a con. He was repaying a favor, he told himself, not building goodwill for the future. When the party was over, he'd take his lumps with the rest.

"C'mon, coupla you guys help haul this fat bastard as far as the door. And remember, Doc, if the towers get tipped off, somebody's gonna get hurt. We still got five more in the closet out there."

The stretcher was being maneuvered from the office when the sound of scuffling came from the waiting room. Cully sidestepped the doctor and shoved past the cons in the doorway. "Who hit him?" he asked, and started toward Grossman, who lay sprawled on the floor in front of the janitor's closet, clutching his chest.

"Nobody hit him. He just crapped out."

"My heart!" Grossman croaked.

A lanky con wearing a guard's hat acted as if he were about to kick him. "Get up, you dog! You ain't got a heart."

"C'mere, man," someone called. "Lookit Andy Gump. He oughta get an Academy Award."

"Nice try, Andy," the lanky con said, "but we ain't issuin' any more hospital passes."

Cully noticed that the four men in the closet were watching

Grossman with undisguised disgust. As the doctor, drawing a stethoscope from his smock coat pocket, dropped on one knee beside him, Grossman raised his head and whispered something.

"Wha'd he say, Doc?" Cully asked, but the doctor was bending over, adjusting the stethoscope to his ears.

"I heard what he said," the lanky con wearing the guard's hat said. "He said, 'In the name of God, take me to the hospital.'"

After a thirty-second examination the doctor rose and started toward the entrance area, where the two cons in mattress-striped shirts had set the stretcher bearing Malaski.

"What's wrong with him, Doc?" Cully asked.

"With the captain?"

"No, with that phony ol' creep on the floor."

"He's frightened. He'll be all right."

There was a sudden commotion, the rush of feet, and a hoarse voice yelled, "What the hell's going on? Shut that goddamn door."

As Cully turned, his heart gave a lurch. At first glance it appeared as if the whole guard force was pouring into the room from the alcove beyond the deputy warden's office. Then he glimpsed the faces: Fletcher's, Bugsy's, Kelly's. All the cons were dressed in guard uniforms. A few were swinging canes—the heavy lead-tipped canes the yard guards used to carry. "We found the stuff downstairs," he heard someone say.

Red Fletcher was blocking the doctor's path to the stretcher. "Where d'you think you're going, man?"

"He's takin' Malaski to the hospital," Cully said. "He'll keep his mouth shut. He gave his word."

"Can't risk it. We're in business with these uniforms. If we use our heads, we can walk right out of here." He glanced toward the janitor's closet. "Hey, you guys, shove Andy Gump inside and lock the door."

"They can't breathe in there," Cully said.

"That's tough, man. I've been living in a rusty steel box with a stinking bucket for years, and nobody ever asked me if I could breathe." He gave Cully a sidelong look. "Man, you sure turned into a Boy Scout all of a sudden."

Cully stood there looking guilty, flushed, sweating, too embarrassed to defend himself. Then, angered by the cocky grin on the big redhead's face, he felt his temper rise. He started to speak but checked his voice when he became aware of the silence. He and the doctor were standing alone. The cons from Isolation—at least fifteen of them wearing guard uniforms—were ganging up behind Fletcher.

"We ain't runnin' no health resort," Bugsy said. "Huh, Red?"

"That's right, man. I don't claim to be bad, but until someone shuts my mouth, I'll give the orders."

Fletcher was the tallest man in the room; Cully, an inch or so shorter. They were standing face to face, smirking at each other, when the crowd parted and someone called, "Hey, Doc, more business."

A squat, jolly Mexican had a guard by the arm, guiding him through the crowd. The guard was hatless, and the side of his face was streaked with rivulets of blood. He was shuffling along as though dazed.

"Hey, that's the messhall bull," someone said.

The Mexican grinned. "He tried to commit suicide."

"What happened?" Fletcher asked.

"He ran into a door. He was trying to get away."

"From who?"

"From Surefoot and Gigolo. They got through the shower shed wall and took over the messhall. Somebody must've got to a phone. The bulls know what's going on. They're running out of here like mad."

There was a rush for the window in the assignment lieutenant's office. At first glance it was obvious that the prison was being abandoned. The two-hundred-and-eighty-pound sergeant from Cellhouse Six was waddling wildly across the lawn. The heavy steel door to the front of the prison was open, and several guards were crowding out, shouldering past Lieutenant Becker, who stood in the doorway, pointing a double-barreled shotgun at the Control Room door. A few men in shirt sleeves and T-shirts were running along the gun walk atop the wall. The two gun towers in view from the window were double-manned, and the wall above the door leading to the Administration Building, directly in front of the Control Room, was lined shoulder to shoulder with motionless rifle-armed men.

Becker swung the shotgun toward the window, and the crowd, packed sardine-tight in the ten-by-twelve office, scrambled back into the waiting room. The doctor and stretcher were gone; so was the messhall guard. The door in the entrance area was open. Cully and Fletcher started toward it.

"Becker won't come inside with a gun," Cully said. "Somebody might snatch it. And I doubt if they'll fire from the walls as long as they know we got Fisk."

"You guys ain't goin' out there, are ya?" Bugsy asked. "Better play it cool. Better wave a white rag or somethin'. Huh, Red?"

Fletcher was stripping off the guard uniform. He flung the coat and hat on the floor and joined Cully in the doorway. Becker was no longer in sight. The door to the front of the prison was shut tight; even the peephole shutter was down.

They stepped out on the walk in front of the Control Room and faced the downpointed rifles on the wall above them.

Fletcher cupped his hands around his mouth and shouted, "We got hostages. Fire one shot inside the walls and you'll bury them."

His voice died like a whipcrack in the sultry air, and then there was silence. The grim-faced men on the wall stood motionless, their rifles pointed downward.

# CHAPTER 3

CULLY felt the Benny take hold: a tingling scalp, a relaxing to-hell-with-everything feeling. About half an hour had passed, he judged. It was five minutes to ten on the messhall clock, and he'd taken the first piece around nine-thirty. His throat still burned from the second piece of amphetamine-soaked cotton, the piece he had just washed down.

He took a sip of steaming coffee, arousing the sickening medicated taste in his mouth. Christ, he thought, what a lousy way for a man to get his kicks. He wouldn't give two bits for a ton of the stuff in the free world, but if a guy wanted to get off the natural in a zoo like this, he didn't have much choice. He glanced at the sweaty faces around him—flushed, glary-eyed, everyone talking at once. Christ, it looked like the whole joint was turned on. Six hours from now they'd be cutting each other's throat for a few strands of the stuff.

"Hold it down!" Red Fletcher shouted from the center of the messhall.

He was standing on one of the long benchlike tables which filled the room, row after sagging row, from the four battered steam tables in front, to the barndoor-size archway, which led to the kitchen in the rear. Messhall swampers in sweaty T-shirts were watching from a distance. Some were drifting along the aisles between the tables. A few cooks in soiled aprons had ventured into the center section and were mingling with the noisy gang from Isolation. Several Isolation cons still wore guard uniforms, a few still carried lead-tipped canes; others were now armed with cutlery: butcher knives, French knives, meat cleavers. Bugsy Matthews was carrying a sledge-size steak tenderizer.

"Dammit, hold it down!" Fletcher shouted again, and kicked a pair of dented aluminum salt and pepper shakers from the table.

Bugsy, wild-eyed, stripped to the waist, his veiny muscles glistening with sweat, began beating the steak tenderizer on the table, shouting, "Dummy up! Dummy up! Big Red's got somethin' to say."

"C'mon, you Benny-heads, hold it down," Fletcher said, and the voices around him abated, jabbered on for a moment, and finally grew still. "We've got the inside, and they've got the walls; so let's figure out our next move before they decide to rush us."

Cully glanced over his shoulder. He hadn't seen Surefoot since their clash in the Control Room, and the Indian's absence bothered him. He'd feel more comfortable with his back against a wall. He took a sip of coffee. Then, as the voices rose up again, he set the cup down and started toward Fletcher. "Hey, Red," he called, "who's keepin' an eye on the hostages?"

There were eight hostages locked two to a cell on the main floor in Isolation: Deputy Warden Fisk; Sergeant Gallaway; Sergeant Grossman; George Hicks, the Isolation guard; Miles Murry, the psychologist; Fred Campbell, the resident parole officer; Peek-a-boo Perkins, the assistant steward, who, instead of joining the scramble for one of the three exits, had unwittingly locked himself in the vegetable cooler; and Dirtyneck Dugan, the messhall guard, who, for some unexplainable reason, after having his head wound stitched and bandaged, had left the hospital and returned to the Control Room. Captain Malaski had been taken to the hospital in town, and Doctor Saunders, the young part-time prison surgeon, was going about his business as if a breakout from Isolation were a daily occurrence. Everyone else behind the walls had a number.

"I've got the padlock key," Fletcher said, "and there's a coupla guys on guard over there. Why?"

"Just checkin'. As long as they know the hostages are okay, they won't come bustin' in here."

A double-tough twenty-three-year-old lifer, nicknamed Gigolo, a big good-looking blond, said, "Guess we'll hav'ta settle for a riot. Superman couldn't crash outta this joint with all those rifles on the walls."

Everyone began talking, shouting:

"A tunnel! What about a tunnel?"

"Man, you're crackin' up."

"Hey, that's an idea! It might work at night."

"Hell, yeah, we can come up fifty yards from the joint."

"Let's make the finks and baby rapers dig us a tunnel."

"A riot sounds better to me," Gigolo shouted over the clamor.

"What're we gonna riot about?"

"About the conditions, man. The goddamn conditions!"

"Yeah, how about them stinkin' buckets?" Bugsy shouted.

"Somebody make up a list."

"Y'damn right! We got plenty to bitch about."

"Like what?"

"Like those stinkin' buckets, man!" Bugsy yelled.

"And the food. The goddamn food is rotten."

"And the parole board. Don't forget the parole board. That half-assed outfit oughta get investigated, too."

"Crissake, man, there's a million things wrong with this joint," Gigolo shouted.

"Yeah, and the public's got a right to know."

"Hey, Freddy, cut me off another little piece. Ya act like ya paid for the stuff."

"Yeah, hit me too, man. Ya gave me just enough to get hung up."

Bugsy was hammering on the table again.

"Cool it! Cool it!" Fletcher was shouting. "We can hold out for a coupla days. We'll draw up a list of grievances, and while they're listening to our gripes, we'll be digging a tunnel."

"Good show!"

"We'll get the finks and baby rapers to dig it," someone shouted.

Kelly came shoving through the crowd, his hairy chest matted with sweat, his face scowling under a growth of black whiskers.

"How's it look?" Fletcher called. He was still standing on the table, straddle-legged, arms akimbo.

Kelly waved a hand, the thumb and forefinger shaping a circle. "We're in like Flynn. They must have orders not to shoot. I've been walkin' all over the joint—right in front of their guns."

"Are the cellhouses locked?"

"Five, six, and eight are wide open. The guys are ganged up at the windows inside. They're a little leery yet."

"What about four and seven?"

"Seven is locked tighter than a drum—inside and out. Four is open, but the screw clamped the bull locks on the cell doors before he shoved off. Coolbreeze and that kid from the Reformatory, the one with the pachuco mark on his cheek—what's his name?"

"Rick."

"Yeah, him and Coolbreeze Clark grabbed some sledgehammers from the carpentershop, and they're in there smashin' the locks."

"Lotta unnecessary work," Cully said. He was standing directly below Fletcher, still scanning the crowd for Surefoot. "Holler up to the screws on the wall out front, and tell 'em to throw in the keys. They'd rather give us the keys than have the cellhouses wrecked."

"Who gives a damn what they'd rather have?" someone shouted. "Let's wreck the goddamn joint."

Cully flushed, straining to control a flaring anger. A man couldn't make a sensible suggestion around hardheads like this without some loudmouth twisting it around to make it sound phony, like the guy making the suggestion was a stoolie or, just as bad, an ass kisser trying to build up points for the time when the bulls would be back in the driver's seat. He glared over his shoulder. "If you dumb bastards want to break your backs, go ahead. But you don't need a sledgehammer to get rid of the locks. Take 'em off with a key and dump 'em in the furnace at the powerhouse."

"Cully's right," Kelly said. "Anyway, we'd hav'ta use an

acetylene torch to open the cells in Cellhouse Seven. That's an eight, ten hour job."

Cellhouses seven and eight—separate buildings—along with the powerhouse, the officer's dining room, and the fenced-in softball field behind the powerhouse, on which a new kitchen and messhall were sporadically being built, were located on the east side of the prison. The auditorium, Cellhouse Six, and the hospital were located on the west side. The cannery ran lengthwise along the central section of the rear wall, the wall which separated the prison from the recreation yard. Concealing the one-story cannery from the tower guards on the front wall and taking up the entire center of the prison were the two largest and oldest buildings: the narrow block-long two-story brick building partitioned into shops, and the block-square brick building (in which all the activity up to now had taken place) which housed the feeding facilities; four antiquated cellblocks, including Isolation; the hall-like vacancy left by the demolition of Cellhouse Three; the Control Room; and the offices above. These two buildings, separated by the grass-flanked shopline walk, had originally made up the entire prison.

Of the six still-occupied cellhouses spread out behind the thirty-foot-high walls—Isolation being Cellhouse One and Cellhouse Three having been demolished—three were modern, and three, like Isolation, all housed in the same building, were part of the original territorial prison, five-by-seven steel boxes with steel-latticed doors secured by heavy padlocks. These cellblocks were without plumbing. Two men occupied each cage and shared the same bucket. Cellhouses six, seven, and eight—large airy buildings on either side of the prison—had roomy four-man concrete-walled cells, modern plumbing, and intricate locking systems, worth thousands of dollars.

"We'll get the keys," Fletcher said. "But right now let's get someone to type up a list of grievances. What's that egghead's name who's always writing that rehabilitation crap in the prison paper? I think he's the editor. You know him, Cully."

"Yeah, I know him—Skinny Burns. He's good people. As solid as any con in this joint."

"Man, you're jumpy. I didn't say he wasn't."

"He sounds like a phony to me," Bugsy said. "Huh, Red?"

Cully flicked his eyes at him. "How would you know, Dumbo? You can't read."

"Forget it," Fletcher said. "How about finding him, Cully? Tell him we need a list of reasons why we're rioting. And tell him to hurry. We've got to pass it out front, so they know we mean business."

Cully nodded. The Benny had his heart pounding, his ears roaring. He didn't like the idea of getting Skinny involved, but if Skinny didn't draw up the list, some stir bug would. And if the newspapers got into the act, which they no doubt would, the public would laugh at their gripes. Hell, they had a right to bitch, the joint really was a human sewer hole. If a guy wasn't cold-blooded when he walked into the place, he damn sure would be by the time he left. At least a square like Skinny could see both sides, speak both languages.

As he turned to leave, he heard someone yell, "Hey, it's comin' over the radio already. Broke right in on the middle of a song. Says a handful of dangerous incorrigibles broke outta Isolation. Says we beat the hell outta twenty-five hostages and we're threatenin' the peaceful cons with knives and clubs."

"Who says?"

"The man on the radio."

"Wha'd he say we were?" Bugsy asked.

"Dangerous incorrigibles."

"What's that?"

"Beats the hell outta me."

"Hey, Freddy, cut me off another little piece."

"Yeah, ya cheap son of a bitch, me too."

Cully was scanning the crowd again. "Hey, Kelly," he called, "have you seen the Indian around?"

"Surefoot?"

"Yeah."

"He's over in Cellhouse Eight playin' chess."

*"Playin' chess?"*

Kelly nodded. "He found some nut over there who claims to be the joint chess champ. The poor sap's probably got his throat cut by now."

# CHAPTER 4

THE word spread through the prison like buckshot:

"We're rioting!"

"What for?"

"Christ knows!"

In the cellhouses, the cons who owned radios disconnected the earphone jacks and turned on the speakers. The outside work crews found cover in the nearest buildings. The men in the guard-abandoned shops bunched up at the windows and watched the walls.

Cully stepped from the side messhall entrance and moved down the ramp to the deserted shopline walk. Every stretch of wall that he could see through the breaks in the buildings was lined with motionless rifle-armed men. It appeared as if every lawman and gun owner in a radius of fifty miles had sped to the scene. There were bareheaded men in civilian clothes, uniformed men in white Stetsons, others in garrison hats with brass insignias, the sun reflecting from the shiny visors. There was only a scattering of prison guards in gray uniforms. Inside the walls the wide-open shop windows were squirming with heads. As Cully started down the walk, cons moved to the doorways. A few stepped out on the lawn between the building and the walk.

"Watch your step, kid," a wizened old con called. "They shot from the walls last time. Killed seven that didn't have no more to do with it than the man in the moon."

Cully had an impulse to wheel and sprint back into the mess-hall. But, as though defying him, his legs kept moving, carrying him closer to the front wall, closer to the guns. Every rifle barrel in sight seemed to be pointed at his bare sweat-blistered chest. They've got orders not to shoot, he kept telling himself, but his already pounding heart pounded faster, and his legs felt mushy-weak as he imagined a volley of rifle lead ripping through the twin bluebirds tattooed on his chest. He moved past the window well where the jug of potato beer had been planted, past the gaping faces in the carpentershop windows, past the waving arms behind the barred windows on his left—Cellhouse Two, where the cooks and messmen slept. He forced his eyes upward. The faces atop the wall appeared grimmer, the rifle bores bigger. He was forty feet away now, oozing sweat, his heart in his throat. The end of the shopline walk was ten feet away. He reached it, turned his cringing back on the rifles, and started down the steps to the printshop in the basement under Cellhouse Two. As he closed the door behind him, his strength came back. He felt a scalp-tingling nudge from the second piece of Benny.

"Didn't they try to stop you?" someone asked.

Cully grinned. "Hell, man, haven't you heard? We're runnin' the joint. We got the deputy warden locked in The Hole."

Four of the five cons assigned to the cubbyhole printshop were standing on a bench, looking out the ground-level window, which faced the front wall. The other, a gangling rack of bones with droopy eyes and close-cropped brown hair, was sprawled on a chair in front of an old weld-patched Linotype machine. In the two years Cully had known Skinny Burns, he had seen the man smile only once—at breakfast the morning Andy Gump had sputtered out his upper plate and stepped on it while scuffling with a con who had reached over the steam table to snatch a second sweet roll. Skinny was smiling now.

"If you're looking for the crusading editor, I just resigned," he said, dragging his long knobby frame from the chair.

"The guys want you to draw up a list of grievances."

Cully watched the smile fade. He should've known. Most lifers—usually once-in-a-lifetime lawbreakers—walked the straight and narrow in prison just as they had outside, especially a squarejohn wife killer like Skinny. The man had built up less than three years on a life jolt, and already he was thinking of what his record would look like fifteen years from now. Still, squarejohn or not, he liked the guy, and if Skinny didn't want to get involved, it was his own business.

He was fumbling for a flippant remark to ease the man's refusal when Skinny said, "I was hoping they'd ask. How soon do they need it?"

"Right now."

In less than ten minutes, the Benny racing through his bloodstream, Cully was back on the shopline. Cons were now moving in all directions. Some had been looting the food supply in the storeroom above the kitchen. Ignoring the rifle-lined walls, they were legging it back to the cellhouses with armloads of canned goods, loaves of bread, and raw meat. Cully recognized a con from Cellhouse Seven. "How'd you get out?" he called.

"They threw in the keys," the con called back. He was dragging a loaded gunnysack across the lawn.

A noisy gang was gathered in front of the milk house at the far end of the shopline. One of the cons, toothless, shirtless, and badly in need of a shave, his hands heaped with eggs, came trotting toward Cully, shouting, "Eggs! Been here six years and never seen one. They must feed 'em to the screws."

Cully nodded. He was moving up the ramp to the side messhall entrance.

Except for a few coffee-drinking huddles, the messhall was deserted. Cully moved under the archway into the rancid-smelling kitchen. The steamy area around a double row of stationary cooking caldrons, sheltered by a paint-blistered metal canopy hanging from the ceiling, was untended. The largest caldron— chest-high and four feet in diameter—was billowing steam, hissing and belching as a spasmodic flow of navy beans cascaded over the brim. Beyond, a steady sizzle and crackle came from the egg-and-meat-covered surface of the giant coal range, surrounded now by cons wielding spatulas, forks, and just about every other type of kitchen utensil shaped to flip a chunk of meat. The white tile floor was grimy, wet, and slippery with grease. As Cully started toward the huddle in front of the pantry, he noticed several Isolation cons at the table in the far corner reserved for kitchen and messhall guards. They were being served by con cooks. He spotted Kelly and turned that way.

Kelly, his jaws working full tilt, was hunched over a porcelain platter, hacking away at a still-sizzling T-bone steak. He glanced up as Cully approached. "C'mon, dig in. You'll never get another chance. This is the kinda meat the bulls eat. We get the gristle and stringy stuff—the scraps those phony convict butchers grind into hamburger meat." He wiped a hairy forearm across his mouth. "First time I ate off a plate in over six years. Food tastes better off a plate. C'mon, dig in."

"I'm loaded on Benny," Cully said. "You want me to kill a million-dollar glow?"

Kelly flapped a hand. "I can get higher on T-bones. You lookin' for Fletcher?"

"Yeah. Where's he at?"

"I left him in Cellhouse Four. He's gettin' a shave and haircut. He's got a meetin' comin' up with the wheels out front as soon as you get him that list."

"I got it in my pocket."

"Better get it to him."

"Did you guys talk to the warden already?"

"The warden's at a convention in Ohio. Becker and some slick-talkin' dude I never saw before is handlin' the show. He calls Fletcher sir."

"Did they let you guys through the front gate?"

"Hell, no. We stood on the sidewalk in front of the Control Room. They were up on the wall."

"How's Red gonna give 'em the list?"

"They'll lower a string like they did with the keys. Better let him know you got it."

Cully found the big redhead primping at the mirror behind the raggy swivel chair which served as the Cellhouse Four barbershop. The freckled skin of his face, bleached white from lack of sun, was as smooth as paper. His hair was cut close to his head. He had on a starched blue-denim shirt and sharply creased dungarees.

Cully unfolded the list of grievances and handed it to him. "This is a rough outline—enough to get the ball rollin'. Skinny said he'll have a five, six page petition in a coupla hours."

As Fletcher read, the expression on his face grew progressively more sullen. By the time he looked up, he was scowling. "Hell, man, he's got the chow and the buckets way down here at the end. Unbalanced diet! Inadequate plumbing in the old cellhouses! Crissake, man, they're feeding us garbage, and those goddamn buckets are enough to gag a maggot. And what about the tear gas? Not a goddamn word! He knows they're gassing in Isolation. And he knows damn well they're not suppos'ta use gas on anyone locked in a cage."

Cully dragged a hand across his face, deliberately, a rush of irritation disrupting his Benny glow. "Look, man, this is gonna be splashed all over the newspapers by tonight. Skinny said our best bet is to play down the livin' conditions and go after the big stuff—on-the-job trainin', another headshrinker, some sociologists, stuff like that. He says if we ever get a trainin' and treatment program in here, the livin' conditions are bound to improve."

"He did, huh? Well, he's not getting gassed every time he opens his mouth, and he's probably got a connection in the butchershop packing him a steak sandwich every night. Anyway, what the hell do I care about on-the-job training? I can't learn a trade in The Hole. And to hell with another headshrinker. All they do is get a guy more time."

A crowd had gathered. Two Isolation cons, one with a meat cleaver shoved in the waistband of his dungarees, had moved beside Fletcher and were peering at the list of grievances in his hand. Both were grimacing, shaking their heads. Cully had an impulse to snatch the list and tear it up. Hell, if he had any sense, he'd be in the paintshop straining off a batch of shellac, getting higher than he already was, instead of wasting his time with these harebrains. Here was Skinny sticking his neck out to help, and the stupid bastards were low-rating the guy. Besides, the big redhead was acting as if the whole show was his. *He* didn't go for on-the-job training. *He* didn't go for another headshrinker. Who the hell did the single-o bastard think he was? Casually, forcing a grin, he reached out and plucked the list of grievances from Fletcher's hand. "Yeah, man, you can do a better job than this. I'll tell Skinny to forget it."

"Hey, wait a minute!" Fletcher snatched back the list. "This'll hav'ta do. I haven't got time to make up another one."

"Okay, use it then. Only I can't see why you're squawkin'. I thought this list was suppos'ta be a stall while you guys tunneled your way—" He broke off as Fletcher frowned and rolled his eyes, turning his back on the onlookers, most of whom were mainliners, not part of the Isolation gang.

"Man, dummy up on that tunnel," he muttered. "I don't trust these mainline cons."

"Aw for crissake, Red, everyone's in on this now. As long as we've gone this far, we might as well try to improve the joint. You think the public cares if the bulls gas a few hell raisers in The Hole? They figure we deserve it. But they might do somethin' about the conditions that affect all seventeen hundred of us. Hell, this goddamn zoo is fifty years behind time."

"So what? I couldn't care less. As soon as I deliver this list, I'm—"

"Hey, Red!" Rick, the Reformatory transfer, the ferret-faced kid with the blue dot tattooed on his cheek, came shoving through the crowd. "Hey, you guys, Bugsy needs help. The guys from the other cellhouses are gangin' up in Isolation. Some of 'em got shivs. If they get at the hostages, we'll get the blame. That's what Bugsy said."

"Aren't the cages padlocked?" Fletcher asked.

"Yeah, but they won't be for long. Some crazy ol' bastard went after a sledge."

"Do they know Bugsy's got the key?"

"He told 'em you had it."

Fletcher grabbed Cully's arm and towed him into the corner. "When it comes to a shiv," he whispered, "Bugsy's gutless. He'll threaten a guy with one, but he'd never use it. And if someone pulls one on him, he'll fold up. He'd give 'em the key in a minute."

"So what am I suppos'ta do?"

"How about moving the hostages to the upstairs storeroom

behind the steward's office? It's easier to keep everyone out up there. I'd do it myself, but I've got to get this list out front."

Cully glanced over the sweaty, tense faces around him, stalling, ignoring Fletcher. Why should he get in any deeper? Now was the time to get lost. Hell, the party could last three, four days, and he might just as well go huckly-buck. Once the bulls got back inside, he wouldn't be seeing daylight again for Christ knows how long. There was plenty of yeast in the butchershop cooler, and the upstairs storeroom was loaded with sugar, prunes, figs, and raisins. Hell, if he started brewing a batch of raisinjack right now, the stuff would be bubbling by midnight. And while he was waiting for the juice to ferment, he could be nipping on the shellac in the paintshop supply locker. He was about to say, "Get someone else," when Fletcher motioned to the con with the meat cleaver and called, "Hey, man, give Cully that battle-ax. He's moving the hostages up to the storeroom."

"Says who?" Cully snapped. "Besides, who needs a weapon? If you don't think I can handle myself with my hands, get somebody else."

"Suit yourself, but the loudmouths around here are going to be loaded with false courage before long. The powerhouse gang is juiced up already. They must've had a batch brewing."

"The paint gang, too," Rick said. "They got into the shellac."

Cully snatched his arm. "How d'you know?"

"I heard 'em talkin'."

"Serves me right!" Cully muttered, and whacked the barber chair.

"It wouldn't hurt to carry this," the con with the cleaver was saying. "Even a nut'll think twice before jumpin' a guy with a meat-ax in his hand."

"Better get going," Fletcher said. "And if Surefoot's over there, don't let him get close to Andy Gump." He turned back to the mirror.

Cully stood there shaking his head. "Man, I'm weak! No wonder I'm in jail. I can get talked into anything."

"C'mon," Rick said, "let's get over there before Bugsy flips out."

Reluctantly, his jaw muscles rippling to the nerve-strumming rampage of the Benny, he followed the swaggering bony-shouldered kid past the shower shed and through the rear door to Isolation. The stench had lost its strength. The buckets had been emptied.

CHAPTER **5**

THERE were at least fifty cons from General Population ganged up in front of the first four cages on the Segregation side of Isolation. Others were leaning over the rail on the second tier, shoving, yelling, stomping the sagging steel walkway. Several more were heckling from the Control Room doorway. Bugsy, Gigolo, and Coolbreeze Clark were elbowing their way back and forth between the crowd and the cage doors.

"Hey, Briston, you got the key?" someone called as Cully approached. "Give us Andy Gump and Peek-a-boo Perkins."

Cully veered toward a radiator against the wall. The man who had called, a middle-aged burglar serving life on the Big Bitch, the state's Habitual Criminal Law, was normally quiet and easygoing. He was gripping a sledgehammer now, his usually pleasant face flushed and wild-eyed. And there were other men Cully knew only by sight, men he had never heard speak, yelling now, their faces contorted.

Wishing he'd told Fletcher to go to hell, he eased into the crowd, his eyes sorting out the loudest agitators. There was Duke Trusdale, a flophouse pimp and goofball junky on the streets, a would-be tough guy in prison. All mouth, no guts. There were five or six from the glamour-boy clique, weight lifters and beboppers, their hair combed in ducktails. They seemed to be doing most of the yelling. No trouble there. The muscles were strictly for show. They'd take it on the heel-and-toe if it came to a fight. The ashpit gang from the powerhouse, dirty and sweaty, some in hip-high rubber boots, would be the hardest to handle—especially Punchy Philips. Sober, Philips was a good-natured clown, but high on raisinjack, as he seemed to be now, he'd attack the warden. He was yelling in at Grossman, waving a foot-long French knife. Gigolo was laughing at him; so was Coolbreeze Clark. But Bugsy's worried eyes kept flitting to the knife. Fletcher had been right, the muscle-bound lame-brain was scared stiff.

"Get Big Red!" he shouted as Cully shoved to the front of the crowd. "Hurry up, man! There's gonna be trouble!" He was gripping a butcher knife, awkwardly, as if his arm were paralyzed. "I don't wanna use this, but these guys are askin' for it."

Ignoring the questions being shouted at him, Cully shouldered his way past the occupied cages, glancing in at the hostages as he passed. Deputy Warden Fisk was standing at the steel-latticed door, looking out at the crowd, seemingly unruffled. Sergeant Gallaway was pacing the floor behind him. Next door, Miles Murry, the psychologist, and Parole Officer Campbell were sitting on the bunk—a straw-mattressed rack of sagging steel suspended by chains from the wall. In the next five-by-seven steel box, as though hypnotized by the glare of a sixty-watt bulb, Hicks, the Isolation guard, and Dirtyneck Dugan, one side of his head shaved and bandaged, stood at rigid attention against the back wall.

As Cully looked into the next cage, a burly Negro in rubber boots whacked the flat of a coal shovel against the door. Grossman, who had been laid out like a corpse on the bunk, sprang to a sitting position, clutched his chest for a moment, then flopped back down, flinging an arm across his face.

Punchy Philips let out a gravelly yell. He lunged past Cully and rattled the cage door, jabbing the blade of the French knife through the food wicket. "Get down on your knees, you dirty ol' bastard! Start sayin' your prayers." Philips was an ex-heavyweight fighter in his late thirties. His punch-flattened face was flushed, and sweat was streaming from his shaved head. "Lookit what he did! He's even a disgrace to that crummy uniform. Lookit! He pissed in his goddamn pants! Here, I'll spot ya this." He threw the knife inside the cage. "C'mon, let's drag the bastard out here and put a diaper on him."

The noisy crowd pressed closer. Grossman was pawing his chest, his head rolling from side to side. The assistant steward, Peek-a-boo Perkins—the nickname alluded to his habit of watching for food-pilfering cooks through the crack in the pantry door—a squat flabby-faced man with a shaggy black mustache and a few oily strands of hair plastered sideways over his otherwise bald head, was standing beside the bunk. He was wearing a rumpled white shirt, a grease-smeared apron, and the expression of a man who had died with a grin on his face.

"Get the belly robber, too!" someone yelled.

The sight of Grossman had been enough to deaden whatever sympathy the sight of the other hostages had aroused. Cully's concern gave way to callousness. Why should he risk a shiv in the back for their safety? Hell, if he were to make a move for the wall while any one of them was on tower duty, he'd get gunned down like a mangy wolf. Besides, he'd be jumping right in the middle. When the party was over, he'd get it from both sides— from the officials for being a ringleader and from the cons, especially the hardnoses, for playing Boy Scout. He was shouldering his way back along the cages, hoping there was still some yeast left in the butchershop cooler, when he was jostled against one of the steel-latticed cage doors and found himself facing a pair of eyes staring out through the inch-square openings. Deputy Warden Fisk was looking at him in a way that made him want to shout, *Crissake, man, what am I suppos'ta do?*

Instead, he turned and yelled, "Dummy up! Dummy up! You guys that aren't in on this, clear out." He looked for help: Bugsy was useless, and if he knew Gigolo and Coolbreeze, they'd like to get at Andy Gump themselves. Knowing how Punchy Philips liked to imagine himself the powerhouse con boss, he lunged, caught Punchy's arm, and shouted in his ear, "Get your crew together, and run these loudmouths back to the cellhouses."

Punchy had been yelling in at Grossman, rattling the door. As he swung around now, the scowl vanished from his cauliflowered face, and an expression of businesslike belligerence came over it. He grabbed the coal shovel from the burly Negro and, holding it sideways across his chest, began shoving into the crowd. "Back to your holes! C'mon, you guys from the powerhouse, gimme a hand. Help me run these punks outta here." He made a bayonetlike thrust at one of the weight lifters. "G'wan, get goin'! You punks that ain't got no business here, get back to the cellhouses."

Driven back by the scramblers in front, the crowd began backpedaling into the gray-bricked dressing-in area in front of the cellblock, then out the door, and into the Control Room. Gigolo and Coolbreeze pounced on the middle-aged con with the sledgehammer and snatched it from him. Bugsy, his voice loud and belligerent again, was threatening with the butcher knife, flaunting his veiny muscles. All he had on was a pair of tight wash-frayed dungarees, the legs ripped off above the knees. The skin of his chest, shoulders, arms, and legs was as defaced as the wall above a urinal in a waterfront dive. A sheen of sweat brightened the obscene conglomeration of hand-needled tattoos—symbols. epigrams, and pornographic sketches, all blue, the ink faded and the lines bleary, like those on a blotter.

Some of the cons in the crowd had never seen Bugsy. Like Fletcher, he had been in the prison five years, transferred from the Reformatory after a riot, and also like Fletcher, he had spent perhaps thirty scattered days since his arrival in General Population. Many cons in the prison had grown up with him in the Training School and Reformatory, others knew him from Isolation, but to those who had never seen him, his appearance was scarier than the butcher knife. Square-jawed and beady-eyed, with a bull neck and a shaggy blond mop, he looked capable of cold-blooded bare-handed murder.

Cully grabbed his arm and swung him around. "Gimme the key. I'm movin' the hostages up to the storeroom."

"I ain't got it. Besides, Big Red give orders not to open the doors."

"Gimme the goddamn key! And put that knife away before you hav'ta use it."

After glancing around, as though to see if anyone had heard, Bugsy reached up and set the butcher knife on the girder ledge under the second-tier walkway. Then, his eyes sliding everywhere at once, he gave Cully the key.

The noise had moved into the Control Room. Discounting Punchy Philips and the juiced-up gang from the powerhouse, the crowd in front of the cages had dwindled to perhaps a dozen. The remaining hecklers—the loudest being Duke Trusdale— had turned on Fisk. As Cully stood there undecided, debating whether to move the hostages two at a time or all at once, he heard Fisk say, "Insulting me isn't getting you anywhere. If you men feel you have reasonable requests—and I believe you have—appoint a spokesman and take your requests—"

"Demands!" Trusdale snapped. "Not requests, big shot— *demands!*"

Shouting, "Dummy up, ya two-bit pimp!" Punchy Philips plunged past Cully and stumbled over a lime-streaked metal bucket getting to Trusdale. "Let the man have his say." He gave Trusdale a shove. "G'wan, get in the wind. Ya ain't got no business here anyway."

Trusdale, who had the reputation of being all mouth, apparently lost his head. He shoved back. "You've got a number just like me, Philips. Do your *own* time."

Cully glimpsed the action from the side: the sudden turtle-like contraction of Punchy's shaved head and a rippling of muscles across his back, accompanied by a sound similar to the smack of a soggy ball colliding with the fat end of a baseball bat. Trusdale's shock-contorted face hung for a moment above Punchy's head; his greasy black hair stood straight up. Then he was on the floor scrambling toward the wall, and Punchy was pleading, "C'mon, fellas, let's break it up. We ain't gainin' nothin' by bustin' each other's jaws."

Apparently the blow hadn't affected Duke Trusdale's hearing. He scrambled to his feet and headed for the gateway in the mesh-steel partition which screened the cellblock from the dressing-in area. The remaining hecklers followed.

"C'mon out and stick together," Cully said as he unlocked the heavy padlocks. "We're takin' you guys up to the steward's office."

Fisk came out first. His white shirt was plastered to his skin; his fat still-boyish face was flushed but otherwise impassive. Sergeant Gallaway, like Fisk, a balding stocky-fat man about forty, followed. His good-humored Irish face, always on the verge of a grin, was pale now; his eyes were dull. He looked sick. Another door opened, and a blond crew-cut head eased out. Murry, the pear-shaped psychologist, confronted by the men he'd been hired to humanize, stood in the doorway leaning out, his lips twitching as though in search of a safe spot to release a smile. Finally, prodded from behind by Parole Officer Campbell, he stepped from the cage.

Punchy barked, "Move! Get out here!" and Isolation Guard Hicks, Dirtyneck Dugan, and Peek-a-boo Perkins came sidling out. Grossman hadn't stirred. He lay on the bunk, clutching his chest, groaning.

Cully poked his head inside the cage and said, "C'mon, Andy, you're holdin' up the parade. Front and center."

"I can't, boy. My heart. In the name of God, take me to the hospital."

"Want us to drag him out?" Punchy asked.

"Naw," Cully said, swinging open the door. "Let him stay here. Surefoot'll be around to handle the hospital cases."

Grossman lifted his head, flinching as his eyes groveled over the bulldog-mean expression on Punchy Philips' face. He opened his mouth as though to make a last-ditch plea for mercy; then, groaning again, he slid from the bunk and joined the huddle of hostages in front of the cages.

The foul-smelling cellhouse was quiet now. Except for Punchy and a few ash haulers from the powerhouse, the cons from General Population had cleared out. Some were watching from the Control Room doorway. A few were standing in the doorway at the rear of the cellhouse, beside the jagged hole in the wall, the hole opening into the shower shed. Crumbled bricks and chunks of concrete were strewed about in the mortar dust back there. Broken glass from several smashed windows littered the floor. Several rusty buckets had been kicked from the upper tiers, splashing lime-chalky water over the walls and radiators. The cellhouse, always despondent to the eyes, now had an aura of utter desolation.

Cully felt momentarily depressed, weary, detached from the

faces and voices around him. Although the Benny was still surging through him, the initial blast had roared itself out. He'd be needing a booster before long. As soon as the hostages were safe in the storeroom, he'd scrounge up another jolt. No more errands. Why should he throw his weight around? If there was any more strong-arming to do, let Fletcher do it. And to hell with a tunnel. He had too much of his sentence behind him to be thinking of escape. Let the stir bugs dig. He'd set up housekeeping in one of the shops and ride it out on Benny and hooch. No one could say he hadn't done *his* share. How many guys would've grabbed Grossman? And the list of grievances— hadn't he got Skinny Burns to draw up the list? Hell, he was neck-deep in trouble right now. And the Indian—a knife-happy psycho waiting to bury a shiv in his back. There was a way to handle that, though. He'd jump the Indian before the Indian jumped him. He'd Sunday-punch the crazy bastard, stomp his hands, smash the bones, put him out of action. He glanced around. Christ, everyone was watching him, waiting for orders, as if he were the warden.

He motioned to Bugsy. "Get Gigolo and Coolbreeze and run that bunch outta the doorway back there. Then clear us a way through the messhall. And watch out for Surefoot." He turned to Rick, who was dogging his heels. "Find Fletcher and tell him to count me out. Once I get these hostages up to the storeroom, I'm done."

"He might not like it."

"*Like it?* Who gives a damn what he likes? Get goin'." He swung around and glared at Grossman, who was still pawing his chest, his head hanging limp. "For crissake, quit snivelin'! Over four years I've watched you crack the whip around here; now all of a sudden you're a sick old man."

"In the name of God, boy, let me go home to my wife."

Punchy lunged at him, his shaved head blood-red, the cords in his neck protruding like cables. "Ya rotten ol' bastard, I oughta strangle ya! I'd be on the streets right now if it wasn't for you." He gave Grossman a shove, then turned apologetically to Cully. "The dog framed me. Two days before I was suppos'ta see the parole board, he starts ridin' me—and when I tell him to lay off, he gets me throwed in The Hole."

Grossman bolted between Fisk and Gallaway as Punchy took a swipe at him.

"Forget it," Cully said.

"I oughta at least slap up on him."

Cully gave him a playful shove. "C'mon, we gotta get these people outta sight." He started to give the hostages a word of assurance; then, noticing the respectful attention they were giving him, he gave them a surly glance instead and said, "You guys haven't got any friends around here, so walk fast and stay in a bunch." He wasn't a good Samaritan, he told himself; he was moving them to protect his own neck.

Punchy and what was left of his crew—a few half-shot ash haulers in hip boots and ragged sweatshirts—brought up the rear as Cully led the hostages through the back door of Isolation and started them toward the messhall door, diagonally across the vacant high-ceilinged area which once housed Cellhouse Three. There were forty or more cons from General Population standing around in groups of three and four. They closed in as the hostages passed.

"Hey, Cully," someone called, "where'd ya bury the other seventeen? Radio says twenty-five hostages."

"Yeah, we're suppos'ta be knee-deep in blood," a raspy voice shouted. "Radio says we're killin' each other."

Cully flapped an arm. "Tell those goofs out front to call the hospital and check with the doctor."

"Radio says the doctor's a hostage, too."

"He is like hell. He's over in the hospital—free to come and go as he wants."

As Cully slowed, the hostages began bunching up behind him. His way was blocked by a crowd forming in front of the messhall door. There wasn't a con from the initial breakout in sight. No one had cleared the way. Bugsy, Gigolo, and Coolbreeze had left him in a lurch. "C'mon, you guys, spread out." He was through. As soon as the hostages reached the storeroom, he was bailing out, like the rest. No one seemed to give a damn, so why in hell should he? "C'mon, you guys, spread out. If you want in on this, sign up with Big Red Fletcher. He's lookin' for help."

Punchy and the ash haulers had formed a cordon around the hostages. The huddle began shuffling forward now, as the crowd drifted apart, clearing a path to the door.

"Get Andy Gump!" someone yelled.

"Let's castrate the ol' bastard," a harsh voice shouted. "Fix him so he can't get his cookies when he gets a guy slammed in The Hole."

"What about Peek-a-boo?"

"Let's make the slob eat some of that garbage he's been feedin' us."

"Check Dirtyneck's collar," someone shouted in falsetto. "If it's greasy, I'm sendin' him home for a clean shirt."

As the crowd guffawed, Cully herded the hostages into the messhall and up the main aisle toward the kitchen archway. The messhall was quiet. Perhaps thirty cons, mostly messmen in dingy T-shirts, were perched on tables, drinking coffee. A few began heckling. The floor at the rear of the gymnasium-size messhall, from the kitchen archway to the double door leading to the shopline, was a mass of smeary footprints. A gabble of voices came from the smoky kitchen beyond.

As Cully entered, the rancid stench of burning grease momentarily took his breath. Smoke seared his eyes. From the throat clearing and coughing going on, it sounded as if a pack of barking dogs were running amok. More than a dozen men, crouched under a swirling canopy of smoke, were still frying meat and eggs on the sizzling grease-streaming range. Someone had opened the spigot on the largest cooking caldron, flooding the concrete-ridged enclosure around the steam caldrons with one hundred gallons of still-bubbling bean soup. The oversplash, perhaps ten gallons of the mushy liquid, formed trampled puddles along the outer ridge. A slushy mass of footprints completely covered the white-tiled floor. The kitchen looked as if a herd of hogs had swarmed through it.

Kelly came shuffling across the room, flat-footed, as though he were walking on ice. "Where ya takin' 'em?" he called. He had shaved, watered down his hair, and put on a mattress-striped shirt. The cheeks of his haggard face were powdery-white and bulging with food. A leaf of lettuce dangled from his overloaded mouth.

"Upstairs," Cully said. "G'wan back there and clear those guys off the steps."

Cons from General Population, their shirts crammed with canned goods, some carrying loaded sacks, were scooting past. They kept their faces averted, as though they did not want to be recognized by the hostages, who had bunched up behind Cully, their backs protected by Punchy and the ash haulers. Grossman, seemingly more concerned now over his exposed position in the huddle than over his heart condition, was slipping and sliding in a smear of bean soup, trying to wedge between Peek-a-boo Perkins and Dirtyneck Dugan.

Kelly hadn't moved. He thumbed the remains of a sandwich into his mouth and began talking around it. "What about the grub? These pack rats are wipin' us out. They're haulin' all the chow to their cells."

"So what?" Cully said. "You're doin' okay."

"Yeah, but what about tomorrow? And what about the fifteen hundred other guys that ain't helpin' themselves. What're *they* gonna eat?"

"The men should be fed," Fisk said. He had moved beside Cully. "Have the cooks and waiters—"

"Shut up!" Kelly cut in. "Keep your nose outta this. We're givin' the orders around here now."

"Have the cooks and waiters set up their regular chow lines," Fisk went on, unruffled. "If you men hope to gain anything from this demonstration, you'll have to start conducting—"

"Hey, Andy!" someone yelled, and Grossman's face swung around just in time to stop the ponderous flight of a waterlogged head of cabbage. He lurched, staggered for a moment, then dropped to his knees on the slippery floor, one hand shielding his face, the other groping for support.

"Knock it off, you guys!" Punchy shouted. He grabbed Grossman's arm and yanked him to his feet. "You're lucky it wasn't a meat cleaver."

Grossman pawed at him. "They'll kill me. Take me out front. In the name of God, I'll see that you get a parole."

*"Parole?"* Punchy held a fist in his face. "Don't talk parole to me. I'll punch your lights out. I'd be on the streets right now if it wasn't for you."

"C'mon," Cully said, "let's get 'em upstairs. Punchy, you go ahead and run the pack rats outta the storeroom. G'wan, Kelly, clear the steps."

As the hostages filed into the steward's office and through the storeroom doorway, Cully noticed the painful expression on Sergeant Gallaway's face. He waited until everyone had entered the storeroom, then caught Gallaway's eye, and motioned him back into the steward's office.

"Nothin' to worry about, Sarge," he said as Gallaway entered the unoccupied office. "You guys are safe up here."

"It's not that, Briston. I've never gone out of my way to bother anyone around here. It's my ulcers. My ulcers are gnawin' a hole in me."

"Want out?" Cully asked. "I can get you as far as the front gate." He could almost feel Gallaway's ulcers stop gnawing. For a moment it looked as if the man were going to say yes; then he shook his head.

"I'll sweat it out with the rest. But thanks anyway, Briston."

"I'll get the doc."

"No, thanks. I'll make out all right."

"How about some milk or some of that chalky stuff they hand out at the hospital?"

"Well, maybe—"

Cully walked to the storeroom doorway and motioned to Punchy. "I'm goin' over to the hospital and pick up some of that chalky stuff for ulcers. Gallaway's ulcers are killin' him. So how about takin' over up here?"

"For how long? I got a full jug planted in the ashpit. I don't wanna get stuck up here. Besides, I'm liable to lose my head and strangle that goddamn Grossman."

Cully glanced toward the outer door and listened for a moment to the squabbling voices coming from the kitchen below.

Someone had to stay with the hostages. He thought of the yeast in the butchershop cooler, of the Benny still in circulation, and decided it was either Punchy or himself, and he had other plans. Knowing of the ex-fighter's weakness for flattery, he said, "We need someone up here who everyone respects. Hell, Champ, you're about the only guy in the joint that can handle the job."

Punchy shook his head, stared at the floor, shrugged, and finally let out a sigh of resignation. "Yeah, I guess you're right. Spread the word—this is outta bounds up here. First guy that gives me a bad time gets bombed." He drove a scarred, knobby-knuckled fist into the palm of his hand.

"I'll spread the word," Cully said and started for the door, feeling as if a load had been lifted from his back.

He was halfway down the stairs when he heard a high-pitched yell and spotted Rick sliding across the kitchen floor. The skinny kid was waving his arms, shouting, "Get the hostages! Big Red wants 'em out front right away."

Choking off an angry retort, Cully continued down the stairs and walked toward two middle-aged cons who were sitting on a pushcart beside the coalroom door. He bummed a cigarette from one, a light from the other, and returned to the foot of the stairs, where Rick was waiting.

"Big Red and I were just on television," Rick said. "They got a camera on the wall. That's why he wants the hostages out there. He's gonna line 'em up on the sidewalk in front of the Control Room to show the public they're still alive."

"Who besides you and Fletcher were out there?"

"Nobody. Just me and Big Red."

"Where are the other guys from Isolation?"

"I don't know. Probably diggin' a tunnel somewhere."

"Man, what a screwed-up affair. Did Fletcher pass on that list of grievances?"

"Sure. It's over the radio and television already."

"What is?"

"The reasons why we're rioting."

"Who's suppos'ta be rioting?"

Rick shrugged. "You and me and Big Red, I guess."

"Now ain't that a goddamn shame! There's seventeen hun-

dred cons in this joint, and you and me and Big Red are rioting. Well, kid, it's just you and Big Red from now on out because I'll be busy brewin' up a batch of raisinjack." Flapping a
hand disgustedly, he walked away. "And tell Big Red to smile
real pretty for the television camera. Maybe he can get the public to install a sink and toilet in his cage."

Rick caught up to him. "I ain't goin' back out there," he
said. "I'll help you make the raisinjack. How much you gonna
make?"

Cully stood there awhile, watching a con at the range flip
pork chops. Then he grinned. "Well, partner," he said, looping
an arm around the skinny kid's neck, "we can't disappoint the
public. We're suppos'ta be rioting. So I guess we'll hav'ta make
enough to turn the whole joint on."

CHAPTER **6**

BY late afternoon all six steam-heated caldrons under the battered metal canopy were brimful and frothing with a yeast-impelled concoction of prunes, raisins, figs, and sugar. The puddle of bean soup, which had coagulated along the concrete ridge, had been hosed down the drain, and now the overflowing foam from the caldrons was being tracked over the slippery tile floor.

A few cons were shuffling back and forth under the canopy, sniffing and peering into the caldrons. Others were gathered around a blaring radio in front of the coalroom. Fletcher, Bugsy, Rick, and Skinny Burns were in the pantry, arguing loud enough to be heard over the noise of the radio. The range was deserted, and no one was sitting at the duty guards' table. Curiosity had dwindled. Most of the sight-seers had returned to the cellhouses to listen to the newscasts. An hour earlier the musky aroma of raisinjack had reached the gun towers, inciting the newscasters to further speculations on the number of dead behind the walls.

"Are you sure?" Cully said to the leathery old con standing beside him, an ex-moonshiner who had been volunteering technical advice all afternoon. "Maybe if I turned up the steam just a notch, the stuff would work faster?"

"Hell's fire, boy! That's the worst thing you could do. Too much heat'll kill it. Keep it like I got it—lukewarm. The way she's workin' now, she'll have a kick to it by mornin'."

Cully could feel the onset of a Benny hangover—a squirmy, irritable feeling. He had started into the sorry-he-had-taken-it, never-again stage. Next, depressed and jittery, he'd be looking for a scapegoat, itching for a fight. "Get away from that goddamn pot! The stuff isn't ready," he called to a con who was dipping a cup into one of the caldrons. Christ, one more piece of cotton would've kept him sailing until the juice was ready to drink. He glanced toward the pantry. Fletcher was still high, so were some of the other cons from Isolation, but no one was putting out a lousy strand. He'd sweat it out, though. He'd be damned if he'd beg.

"Keep an eye on the juice," he said to the old con and started across the slippery floor just as someone shouted, "News! News!"

There was a rush toward the radio in front of the coalroom. Then the kitchen grew still.

". . . nine o'clock this morning," the newscaster was saying. "Since then the riot-torn prison has been run by Alan Fletcher, a twenty-five-year-old armed robber described by prison officials as 'the most dangerous man behind the walls.' "

Cully glimpsed the cocky grin on Fletcher's face as the newscaster went on: "Shortly before noon today, proclaiming himself the representative of seventeen hundred dissatisfied inmates, Fletcher presented the prison officials with a list of demands. To make certain that these demands are given careful consideration, the rioting inmates are holding hostages, twelve prison employees, including the associate warden. It is not certain at this time if all are still alive. In the absence of Warden Sullivan, who is flying back from a convention of penologists in Cleveland, Ohio, the governor has sent the attorney general to look into the touchy situation. For an on-the-spot report, we take you now to Neal Seaburg at the prison."

There was a moment of silence, a whir, a background of murmuring voices, and then a low, tense voice broke in: "Here in the crowded lobby at the front of the prison the tension is mounting with each passing minute. Behind these heavily guarded walls are seventeen hundred convicted felons. Many are believed to be under the influence of a homemade intoxicant, called raisinjack. Others, to use convict terminology, are high on Benny—amphetamine, a stimulant obtained from the cotton cartridge inside certain nasal inhalers. According to

## THE RIOT

Doctor John Saunders, the prison surgeon who was interviewed briefly earlier this afternoon, the drug supply in the hospital has not been threatened. Apparently the riot leaders have tacked a do-not-touch sign on the hospital, as well as on Doctor Saunders, who is permitted to leave and enter the prison unmolested. However, as the doctor stated in the brief interview this afternoon, he has confined his movements to the hospital and knows nothing of what is going on in the rest of the prison —the three recently built cellhouses; the shops; and particularly in the so-called hub of the prison, where most of the activity seems to be centered, a large seventy-year-old building in the center of the prison which houses the Control Room, several upstairs offices, four antiquated cellblocks, and the dining room and kitchen. It was in this building, in the Isolation cellblock adjoining the Control Room, where at nine o'clock this morning a handful of disciplinary cases took command of the prison. And now somewhere in this building there are twelve prison employees being held hostage. At least the prison officials maintain there are twelve. However, Alan Fletcher, the inmate spokesman, an armed robber who looks more like a college athlete, a young man who has spent thirteen of his twenty-five years in reform school and prison, still insists that only eight hostages are being held. Four may be dead. We do not know. No word has come from behind the walls for over three hours now. In Fletcher's last appearance before the television cameras, he stated, in effect, that an inmate representative body of fifty elected delegates was discussing the situation and he would report the outcome as soon as the meeting ended. Meanwhile, all we can do is wait.

"Standing beside me now is Lieutenant William Becker, the last prison employee to withdraw from inside the prison this morning, the man whose courage and quick thinking not only prevented more hostages being taken, but—"

The reporter's voice was smothered by a grumbling uproar in front of the coalroom.

"My *hee*-ro!" someone shouted in falsetto.

"When I saw the prick," someone yelled, "he was headin'

for the front gate like Jesse Owens—leadin' the pack by twenty yards."

"Dummy up!" Cully shouted. "Let's hear what the wino's got to say."

When the uproar quieted, Becker's twangy voice was coming over the radio: ". . . twenty-two years next month. I started workin' here when I was nineteen years old."

"Big deal!" someone shouted. "This is the only place in the world the dumbo can earn a livin'."

"Hold it down!"

". . . know that many men behind these walls are listening to this broadcast," the reporter was saying, "so, with this in mind, you may be reluctant to answer this next question. Having been a part of the prison for twenty-two years, Lieutenant Becker, do you feel that the inmate body as a whole is justified in making the demands it has?"

There was a pause, a double blast of throat clearing, then: "Well, I'll probably get my tail chewed for spoutin' off, but it won't be nothin' new. First off, convicts in no prison at no time got any right to grab hostages. That's kidnappin', and kidnappin's against the law. Second, we're runnin' a penitentiary here, not a trade school. I know there's been lotta talk in the papers lately about treatin' convicts like sick people, but I don't go along with that at all. As for some of the other stuff, I'll admit the plumbin's not quite up to par in the old cellblocks, but there's nothin' wrong with the food and—"

Hoots and boos, loud enough to carry to the walls, cut off the sound of the radio.

Someone shouted, "Let's tear the goddamn joint down!"

"Later! Later!" a high-pitched voice yelled.

And then came the usual chorus of: "Dummy up! Knock it off! Hold it down!"

The grumbling abated. Becker was saying, "No, I don't go along with that either. Fletcher's no mama's boy, but I wouldn't call him the most dangerous man behind the walls. Don't get me wrong, he's a troublemaker all right, but compared to some of the other fellas involved in this—the ringleaders, I mean—

he's almost a gentleman. There's an Indian fella in there—skinny little runt, never has much to say—but believe you me, there's one little fella you better keep both eyes on. And I got an eighteen-inch scar across my belly to prove it."

"The man assaulted you?"

"*Assaulted me?* Come close to cuttin' me in half. Happened seven years ago durin' a shakedown. I walked into the runt's cell to confiscate some contraband—sackful of chess pieces he whittled out of state-owned wood—and the next thing I know he's comin' at me with a shiv—that's a homemade knife. Well, believe you me—"

Cully was moving away from the radio, scanning the hazy kitchen for a dark, bony face. An hour or so earlier, while making a Benny-quest through Cellhouse Eight, he had come across the Indian and a fat baby-faced con playing chess in one of the cells. As he had entered, hoping Surefoot would make the move which would settle matters between them, the Indian had looked up, grinned, and then gone back to studying the chessboard. And when the fat con, beaming like a cradle-restrained baby about to be rescued, had cried, "Ah, another chess player!" Surefoot had scowled and snapped, "Keep your mind on the game! Cully doesn't play chess." That had been more than an hour ago. But Surefoot was nowhere in sight, so apparently the fat con was still sweating it out, one eye on the chessboard and the other on the razor-sharp shiv which had been lying across Surefoot's lap.

As Cully turned back to the radio, Becker was saying, "No, I don't know what Warden Sullivan would do if he was here. But my advice to the cooler heads in there is to get that meetin' over with and turn those hostages loose before there's a lotta unnecessary bloodshed. And believe you me—"

He was cut off by hoots, boos, and shouts:

"Get your goon squad and c'mon in!"

"My *hee*-ro!"

"Wait'll Big Daddy gets back," someone yelled. "He'll have that clown countin' our dirty socks for the next five years."

"Man, Becker's as good as fired," another con shouted. "He booted his job when he abandoned ship this morning."

"That was a strategic withdrawal."

"Yeah, those streaks I saw goin' across the lawn must've been low-flyin' jets."

"Hell, he's civil service," an elderly con said. "Nobody gets fired from civil service."

As Cully started past the pantry door, Skinny Burns reached out and touched his arm. The droopy-eyed editor of the prison paper, true to his word, had composed a six-page petition and for the past hour had been trying to talk Fletcher into carrying it to the front gate. "Can you spare a minute, Brewmaster?" he said. "C'mere and join our representative body of fifty elected delegates."

"Get off the needle," Fletcher snapped. He was sitting on top of a table inside the pantry. Rick and Bugsy were sprawled on a tipped-over pile of cereal sacks—full sacks, the same size and shape as hundred-pound sugar sacks. Holes had been kicked in some of the paper bags and scattered heaps of oatmeal and farina covered the floor. "That character out front puts everything into his own words," Fletcher went on. "All I told him was that about fifty of us guys were talking it over. The only stall I could think of."

Cully had moved beside Skinny Burns in the doorway. Although he still felt responsible for having got Skinny involved, he, too, had refused to carry the petition to the front gate. "Why don't you forget about the petition, Skinny?" he said. "The guys who give a damn about straightenin' this joint out are scared to come outta their cells. The rest of us are either diggin' tunnels or lookin' for kicks. Hell, one way or the other—even if they hav'ta use hand grenades—they're comin' back in here before long. And when that happens, us guys that started this aren't gonna see daylight for two, three years."

Skinny rustled the papers in his hand. "That's the first item in here—no reprisals. Before the hostages are released, the commissioner of corrections has to publicly state that none of the men involved in this will be prosecuted or punished in any way."

Fletcher sneered, wagged his head, made a spitting sound.

"Man, you really are a square. The same commissioner made the same promise to end the riot at the Reformatory five years ago. The next day they shipped fifteen of us here and threw us all in The Hole. Besides, reprisals or not, I'm not ruining my reputation by taking that ass-kissing petition out front. We humbly request this! We humbly request that! I don't humbly request a goddamn thing. All I'm doing is stalling those clowns out there while we dig our way out of here. We'll be gone by tomorrow night."

Despite the depressive Benny letdown, Cully felt like laughing. In his tour of the prison an hour earlier, he had seen the start of tunnels in the basements of the three buildings closest to the walls: the powerhouse, the auditorium, and the ventilator-adjustment room under Cellhouse Six. Although it had seemed as if every suspected stoolie and known rapo in the prison had been wielding either a sledgehammer, pry bar, pickax, or shovel, under the direction of an Isolation con, none of the holes in the three basement walls—at least up until an hour ago—had penetrated the concrete deeper than six inches. As far as Cully was concerned, the tunnel projects were a joke. Unless a noisy air hammer was used—which would wise up the guards on the walls, if they weren't already wised up—the shanghaied stoolies and rapos would still be chipping away at concrete tomorrow at this time. "You better come down off that Benny, Red," he said. "There's not a chance in hell of tunnelin' out by tomorrow night."

"We'll make it. We'll work those rapos around the clock. Once we hit soft dirt, we're gone."

Shaking his head, his homely face twisted in disgust, Skinny moved inside the pantry and sat down on a torn sack of oatmeal. "If the people in front knew how poorly organized things were in here, they'd walk in and take over. Here you have a perfect opportunity to improve the conditions in this prison, to let the people in the state know how behind times—"

"Aw, for crissake, get off that crap!" Bugsy said. "If you wanna improve the joint, take that ass-kissin' petition out there yourself. Huh, Red? And don't give us that crap about not wantin' to get your picture taken. If you're so worried about your relatives and their friends seein' your mug on television, put somethin' over your face. Huh, Red?"

"Why don't *you* take it out there, Bugsy?" Cully said. "You'd look good on TV. Hell, with all those sexy muscles, I bet a thousand broads would be buggin' the warden to get on your correspondence list."

"I don't take too good a picture."

"Put somethin' over your face. Just show your muscles."

"Aw, go to hell!"

Fletcher guffawed. "How about you, Cully? Why don't you take it out?"

"My agent doesn't want me makin' any public appearances without his okay. Besides, I'm through. I figure I've done my share. I'm already screwed up bad enough to blow my good time—and maybe a little extra—without showin' myself on TV. Anyway, I'm with Skinny. Hell, I've got a mother and two married sisters back in Milwaukee. If my kisser got splashed over nationwide TV, they'd have heart attacks."

"Look, Fletcher," Skinny said, "why don't we do it this way? I'll take this petition up to Fisk, and you take him out front and let him deliver it. If you hope to stall the people out front, you've got to make them believe this is an organized demonstration. Especially in an hour or so when the warden gets back. He's not stupid. Right now sixteen hundred of the seventeen hundred cons in here are in their cells listening to radio reports. They don't want anything to do with you guys."

*"Who don't?"* Bugsy came scrabbling over the cereal sacks. "Show us the guys and we'll lump up their heads. Huh, Red?"

"And another thing," Skinny went on, ignoring him, "some inmates are eating and some aren't. You should gather up the food in the cellhouses and bring it back to the kitchen. Start running chow lines. With a little organization—"

"Let 'em eat in the cellhouses," Cully cut in. "I've got eight hundred gallons of raisinjack brewin' in those pots. There's no room to cook food."

"You ought to dump it," Skinny said.

"*Dump it?* Man, go take a vote. I'll bet nine-tenths of the cons in here would rather get drunk than fed."

"Christ, Cully, have you tried to imagine what this place would be like with four, five hundred drunks roaming around?"

"No one knows. It never happened before. But we'll know by tomorrow night."

Skinny turned away, his droopy eyes pleading. "How about it, Fletcher? This won't cast any reflections on your reputation. I'll take the petition up to Fisk, and you take him out front and let him deliver it. All you're doing is escorting him—and stalling for time."

"Not Fisk. He's liable to order the guards to rush us."

"How about Murry?"

"Y'mean the headshrinker?"

Skinny nodded. "He hasn't been around long enough to get used to the smell of the buckets, much less the tear gas they've been using in Isolation. Also, he strikes me as the sort of guy who'd get carried away. You know, really play the role, the convict's pal. Without him knowing it, he'd be organizing the inmates in the cellhouses, and you guys would have all the time you need."

"Sounds phony to me," Bugsy said. "Huh, Red?"

Fletcher was squinting at Skinny. "I don't dig you, Burns. What can you gain? Man, you're a lifer, you hav'ta do eighteen years before you're even *eligible* for parole."

"I can gain plenty. If the legislature in this state ever modernizes the penal system, the mandatory minimum would be lowered, maybe to ten years, maybe even to seven. And believe me, Red, I want out. I don't like it here."

"There's a lotta tunnel digging going on. Grab a shovel."

"Not me. I want out the front gate."

"No guts," Bugsy said. "If I was a lifer, I'd make a run for the wall every time they opened my cage."

"You are a lifer. You're doing it on the installment plan," Skinny said, and turned back to Fletcher. "Let's go up to the storeroom, and I'll give this petition to Murry. I'll tell him to have whoever's in charge out front study it overnight, and we'll meet with reporters tomorrow. Inside the walls. No cameras. Okay?"

"Good deal," Cully said. "Make it in the afternoon; we'll serve refreshments. The juice'll be ready by then."

"You ought to dump the stuff," Skinny said.

Cully grinned. "Why, hell, I couldn't do that. The juiceheads are countin' on me. Besides, I need somethin' to knock a Benny hangover—like a coupla stinkin' strands of cotton. But I guess nobody's puttin' out any." After glancing pointedly at Fletcher, whose eyes displayed a telltale Benny glaze, he turned and walked toward the frothing caldrons.

He was skimming the mushrooming foam from the caldrons, his ears tuned to a steady stream of advice from the old ex-moonshiner, when he heard someone yell, "Don't trust those guys, Fatty. They'll make a girl outta you."

Flanked by Skinny and Fletcher, Murry, the pear-shaped psychologist, was crossing the slippery kitchen floor, half skating, half trotting to keep up with his long-legged escorts. He was gesturing with both hands, his mouth going a mile a minute, his head swinging from side to side.

Skinny had the guy pegged right, Cully thought, and went back to skimming foam. He looked up when a gruff familiar voice, close to his ear, said, "Where they takin' the head-shrinker?"

Kelly's haggard face was hanging over the caldron. His straight black hair was mussed and sprinkled with sand. One of his jutting cheekbones was scratched and dirt-smeared.

"What happened to you?" Cully asked.

Kelly flicked his eyes toward the old ex-moonshiner, then motioned Cully farther under the canopy, in the drainage area between the two rows of stationary caldrons, and whispered, "Remember that tunnel that caved in behind the auditorium coupla years ago? Well, I did some crawlin' around under the stage and found the entrance. It was never completely filled in."

"So?"

"So we dig through the loose fill, and we're on our way. Won't take more than six hours to reach the wall. We'll come up right under the gun walk dressed in guard uniforms. Be a cinch at night."

"Who besides you and me know about it?"

"Just the two guys diggin' over there right now. Both good-heads, I've known 'em for years."

"What about the guys workin' on the other tunnel in the auditorium? The one under the dressin' room."

"They're still tryin' to get through the concrete. They don't know about the one under the stage."

Cully squatted on his heels, shaking his head. "Christ, I don't know, Kelly. I've already done over four years on a lousy beer-joint burglary. I'd hate to parlay the ten I got into a twenty."

"What'n the hell's the difference, kid? Twenty, fifty, five hundred, it's all the same. You're an ex-con when you leave here."

"Yeah, I know, but—"

"You won't last any longer on parole or discharge than you will on escape. Those bloodsuckers out there'll keep houndin' you the rest of your life. Believe me, kid, you better grab whatever freedom you can while the grabbin' is good—even if it's only for a day or two."

"I was kinda figurin' on keepin' my nose clean when I get out. You know, gettin' a job and settlin' down somewhere."

"You're dreamin', kid. Forget it. You're screwed with a record. If you couldn't get along out there before, how'n the hell d'you expect to make it with an ex-con label on your back? Believe me, kid, you can't. I've tried."

Cully looked away. "Why don't you invite someone else?"

"Don't trust anyone else. Tell one of these loudmouths in here your business, and the whole joint knows it."

"Well, you don't hav'ta worry about me."

"If I thought I did, I wouldn't be talkin' to you." Kelly shrugged and started between two bubbling caldrons. "I'll remember this smelly slop when I'm drinkin' that good free-world booze tomorrow night."

Cully, still squatting on his haunches, stared for a few moments at the rivulets of foamy liquid creeping toward the drain; then, abruptly, he sprang up. "Wait a minute," he called to Kelly, who was moving under the kitchen archway. "Don't count me out yet. I'll let you know later."

CHAPTER **7**

CULLY had passed the early evening watching the foam-capped caldrons from the comfort of the warden's custom-made easy chair. Rick had dragged the chair into the kitchen from the carpentershop, where, according to the worried carpentershop con boss, the warden's wife had sent it to be reupholstered. From where it sat now, wedged between the cup sink and a metal table equipped with stationary can openers, Cully could see all the main gathering spots in the kitchen and still enjoy the privacy of a secluded corner.

After mulling over the tunnel offer for almost two hours now, he was still undecided. There was more to it than just crawling from a hole and wiring up a car. It was over a hundred miles to the nearest city of any size, over three hundred miles to the Coast, with nothing but one-street hickvilles along the way. There was nowhere to get lost, and the whole route could be easily roadblocked. He damn sure wanted out of the human zoo, but how long would the vacation last? An hour? Three days? A week? He could never go back to Milwaukee; they'd be looking for him there. If he could make it to the Coast, though, to Carol's one-room pad, or Jean's, or Ginger's, he'd at least get laid. It was almost worth the gamble. Hell, it was almost worth the gamble just to watch a woman walk or plant his elbows on a bar again. Christ, he was twenty-seven now, and he stood a damn good chance of getting tried for inciting a riot. Three, four, maybe even five more monotonous years ahead. Time would wrinkle his face and turn his hair gray before he walked out the front gate. And then how long would his freedom last? Like Kelly had said, a man ought to grab it while the grabbing was good. He wiped the sweat from his chest. He'd have to make up his mind before long.

"Hey, Jitterbug, pour a little more sugar in that end pot," he called to Rick who was skimming foam from the caldrons. The old ex-moonshiner had left in a huff after Rick had whacked him with a stirring paddle for getting too bossy.

Skinny Burns was carrying two cups of coffee into the pantry to Fletcher and Murry, who had just returned from their third trip out front. The psychologist had put on a suit coat, and from a distance it looked as if he had either shaved or scrubbed his face. He seemed to be enjoying himself. The last newscast had carried a tape recording of his voice, in which, among other things, he had said, "Though I do not approve of their method, I do sympathize with the demonstrators in so far as the progressive action asked for in the petition I have just handed to Warden Sullivan is sorely needed."

His statement had drawn a thunderous, floor-banging, window-smashing ovation from the cellhouses. Cons had come flocking to the kitchen, as though to pledge their support to what now appeared to be an officially sanctioned riot, but the sight of six chest-high caldrons of frothing raisinjack and a swaggering display of belligerence by Bugsy and several cutlery-armed Isolation cons had sent all but a few back to the cellhouses. Still, Skinny had accomplished his first objective. There was to be a meeting with the press inside the walls tomorrow afternoon; this meant that the tunnel diggers had gained at least eighteen hours.

Cully was watching a con at the range. The fires had gone out in all but one of the six fireboxes, and the con was scavenging the greasy scrap-littered surface of the range, picking up charred bits of meat and gristle, stuffing his mouth, licking his fingers, snatching for more. Cully had passed the man at least a thousand times in the past four years, had walked beside him in the yard line many times; but never once had he heard the man speak, and never once had he heard anyone speak to the man. He had a pasty face with dark sunken eyes and a heavy-lipped mouth, always moist and hanging half open, exposing two jagged rows of big tobacco-stained teeth. There were more than a hundred zombis just like him behind the walls, and some were roaming the kitchen now, sniffing for food like stray dogs. There were still some canned goods in the storeroom upstairs, and Cully had an impulse to go up there and bring down a few cases of something. He'd feed the poor bastards. Then he decided against it. The zombis were too used to being kicked around. They'd probably figure he was trying to poison them.

"Here's another one that's gonna get his skull cracked!" someone shouted, and Cully glanced toward the long table in the corner, normally the table where the duty cooks and mess-hall guards ate. It was heaped high now with stacks of thick Manila folders, records from the Control Room filing cabinets, a skeleton history of every man behind the walls. Fortunately, at least for the men who had wangled lighter sentences than their crime partners by turning state's evidence on the sly, the base files were kept in a vault under the Administration Building.

For the past hour a dozen or so self-appointed judges had been digging through the records in search of victims: stoolies, bootlickers, undercover homos, and even sex offenders who'd been passing themselves off as thieves. Papers were strewed over the floor. The censored folders were being tossed on the range, where two cons were feeding them to the fire in the still-active firebox. Although the Control Room files contained only a skeleton history of the man, plus disciplinary reports and personal letters written to the officials—called snitch-kites by the cons—the judges had already weeded out more than forty victims. There was to be a mass head-whipping session as soon as all the folders had been examined.

"Here's another snitch-kite from Duke Trusdale," someone called. "Snitchin' off the guys in the next cell for havin' their radio on speaker."

"Throw it in the evidence pile."

"Yeah, I never did trust that loudmouth pimp."

"Hey, get a load of this one!" a guttural voice shouted. "Two goddamn pages! It's from that new queen in the library—that horse-faced blond. The fruiter says—"

"Throw it in the pile. We'll go over it later."

"Damn right!" the guttural voice went on. "Those freaks might swish around here like broads, but they're convicts just like we are. She gets the same as the rest."

"Yeah, there's one in there from Gravel Gertie, too."

"Tough titty! We'll bust her in the mouth—put her outta business."

Cully's folder had already been tossed in the fire. Having nothing to hide, he had spread his record over the table: twenty-six disciplinary reports—mostly for insolence, consumption of raisinjack, and fighting—and three scribbled half-page letters to the former deputy warden: one, dated last year, asking to have his yard privileges restored so that he could fight on the Fourth of July boxing card; one demanding that the state reimburse him for the tube of toothpaste a guard had stepped on while searching his cell; and one asking to be assigned to the roof-tarring crew. In all three he had been careful not to use the word "please."

Feeling the confidence and self-satisfaction which comes from having the respect of the ingroup, his sweaty face took on a cocky grin now as he rose from the warden's easy chair. "Hey, Jitterbug," he called to Rick, "keep the peons off my throne. I'll be back in a little while."

Quiet and nearly deserted now, the huge messhall was gathering shadows in the fast-fading rays of the sun. The rows of sagging tabletops were spotted with coffee puddles and littered with scattered stacks of stainless-steel cups. A few zombis were shuffling along the aisles, as though waiting for the dinner gong to sound.

Cully stepped from the messhall into the dreary high-ceilinged hall which once housed Cellhouse Three. At the far end was the shower shed and the rear door to Isolation. Directly across from Isolation, at the rear door to Cellhouse Four, three cons were dismantling a welding rig. One was coiling the burner hose, while the other two were lifting one of the shoulder-high yellow tanks from the cart, which apparently was too wide to pass through the doorway.

Cully stood there awhile looking across the hall, beyond a

partition of widely spaced bars behind which was Cellhouse Two, the cooks' and messmen's quarters. It was identical to Isolation—a pile of steel near collapse and five tiers of primitive-looking cages with narrow walkways passing in front of the steel-latticed doors. Cellhouse Four and Cellhouse Five, also identical, were part of the same building. They were located in the southwest section, separated from the kitchen and messhall by a courtyard, while Isolation and Cellhouse Two, on opposite sides at the front of the building, were separated by the Control Room and the offices above. This building had originally been the entire prison, a fortresslike structure with two inner courtyards: one, the courtyard behind the Control Room, was now used as an exercise yard for segregated prisoners; the other, between the messhall and cellhouses four and five, enclosed an open sewer half the size of a backyard swimming pool, called the Wishing Well, where the sanitation buckets used in the four old cellblocks were emptied twice a day.

Cully moved closer to the barred partition. Cooks and messmen in white pants and T-shirts were leaning over the tier railings.

"What's happenin', Cully?" a greasy-haired Negro called.

"If you've been listenin' to the radio, you know more than I do."

"When we gonna feed the guys?"

"There's nothin' in the kitchen. The pack rats took it all to their cells."

"How about the beans and oatmeal? We could cook 'em up some of that."

"Man, are you tryin' to start a riot? You know damn well these guys in here don't go for beans and oatmeal. Besides, some nut's got all the steam pots filled with raisinjack."

The Negro laughed. "Is the nut's initials C as in Cully and B as in Briston?"

Flapping an arm, Cully started toward the rear door to Cellhouse Four, where a noisy huddle had formed around the welding rig.

"Pick it up and carry it," a fat Mexican was saying. He was glaring into the pale face of a man in his early forties, a quiet friendless con, who Cully knew was serving time for incest. The Mexican had a hammer in his hand.

"I'm ruptured," the man said. He was standing beside one of the yellow tanks which had been removed from the rig. "I can't lift it. It's too heavy."

The Mexican raised the hammer. "Pick it up, you low-down bastard! That rupture didn't bother you when you were humpin' your daughter."

The man just stared at him.

"Pick it up!" the Mexican repeated. "You think I won't use this?"

The man nodded. "Go ahead," he whispered hoarsely. "I'd be better off dead."

Cully's face was inches from the upraised hammer. No one was moving. It was so quiet that he could hear the two men breathing. He knew the Mexican, knew him well enough to know that he would hit the man with the hammer, not in anger, not even because he wanted to, simply because he had said he would, had said it in front of onlookers. Unless someone offered a face-saving way out, he was certain the Mexican would use the hammer. For a vivid second he visualized the blow: a sickening smack, a choked-off cry, blood spurting from the friendless con's head. "Cool it, Poncho," he said. "What good is it gonna do? If the guy can't lift the goddamn tank, he can't lift it."

"That's not the point. He's a rapo."

"So are about three hundred other guys in here. You gonna knock 'em all in the head with a hammer?"

"If I had my way, I would."

"Aw, for crissake, forget it." Stepping past the Mexican, he squatted in front of the closest tank and wrapped his arms around it. As he started up, he felt a familiar Benny blackout coming on and braced himself to keep from pitching forward. When the dizziness passed, he rose slowly, balancing the heavy tank on one shoulder. "Where to, Poncho?"

Grinning, obviously relieved, the Mexican tossed the hammer on the floor and began wheeling the dismantled welding rig away from the doorway. "We need it under Cellhouse Six. The wall down there is reinforced with steel bars."

"What about the cops on the wall?"

"What about 'em?"

"You'll tip 'em off. They'll see us carryin' this acetylene tank and put two and two together."

"Naw. They'll think we're cuttin' off the cell doors."

"I wouldn't bet on it," Cully said, but the heavy tank was bruising his bare shoulder, so, rather than stand there talking, he started into Cellhouse Four, past the barber chair and along the line-forming area at the front of the cellblock. "Kick open that door," he called to a con perched on the abandoned cellhouse sergeant's desk.

As he stepped outside, into the barred L-shaped enclosure, similar to a cattle-loading pen, which led to Cellhouse Six forty yards away, he spotted Bugsy, Gigolo, and Coolbreeze Clark coming across the hospital lawn. The barred gate to the pen, usually locked, was open. He wrestled the heavy tank to the sidewalk and waited at the gate, massaging his shoulder.

Sweat was streaming from his face and rolling in crooked rivulets down his neck and over the tattooed bluebirds on his chest. Although the sun had sunk behind the wall, the air was still as sultry as it had been all day. Above the section of wall that he could see at the front of the prison, silhouetted against a graying sky, was an almost solid line of heads, shoulders, and rifle barrels. Thirty yards to his left, along the stretch of west wall visible between the hospital and Cellhouse Six, the motionless rifle-armed men were an arm's length apart. Directly below the gun walk on which they were standing, flush against the outer wall and fifty yards farther south, somewhere behind the auditorium, was the spot Kelly was aiming his tunnel. With darkness for cover, Cully decided, and the wall guards looking inside the prison, there was a good chance of slipping away.

"Did'cha hear the latest?" Bugsy called as he neared the gate. "The *broads* are raisin' hell now. They want the same things we do."

"Where'd you hear that rumor?"

"It's no rumor," Gigolo said. "It came over the radio."

The Women's Quarters, an old brick building with barred

windows housing between thirty-five and forty female prisoners, was located beyond the west wall, almost in line with the auditorium inside the men's prison.

"What next?" Cully said. "Man, this is turnin' into a three-ring circus."

"I'm all for it," Bugsy said. "We're gonna get Big Red to go out front and demand that the warden let some of the broads in here to talk things over. Or else let some of us go over there."

"Man, you're stir-crazier than I thought you were. Besides, most of those broads over there look like ex-pugs."

"How d'you know what they look like?"

"The first summer I was here I saw 'em every Sunday. They use'ta come to the ball games and sit in the upper bleachers, where the outsiders sit. It looked like Dogpatch on Sadie Hawkins Day."

"Yeah, but that was four years ago."

"It's still the same—always will be. Sexy-lookin' broads don't get sent to prison. Somebody always gets 'em off the hook."

The door to Cellhouse Four swung open, and two cons came out carrying the second yellow tank stretcher-fashion. The fat Mexican was behind them, the greasy oxygen and acetylene hoses coiled around his neck and shoulders, the cutting tip shoved in the waistband of his dungarees, like a pistol.

"Hey, Poncho," Cully called, "remember when the Women's Quarters use'ta come to the ball games?"

"Sure. Why?"

"Wha'd the broads look like?"

The Mexican grimaced. "Man, you look better. The ones I saw would scare a hungry dog off a meat wagon." Still grimacing, he hurried to catch up to the tank bearers.

"They're built like women," Gigolo said. "That's all that counts with me. Hell, man, I'm doin' life. As far as pussy goes, I'm wiped out. I'm twenty-three years old, and I've had it. I don't get no more. Man, I'd lay any one of those bags over there right in front of the TV cameras."

"Same here," Bugsy said. "I ain't fussy. I been locked up a long time."

Cully gave him a sneering look. "Don't get your hopes up, man. You'd even have a rough time makin' out over there. Those gals might not be as desperate as you think."

"I'd beat your time, wise guy."

"There's a foxy little spook over there that I'd sure like to get my hands on," Gigolo said. "How about it, Breeze? Remember that cute little one we saw in the dentist's chair?"

"She was fine all right," Coolbreeze said, and Cully wondered, as he often had over the past three years, if Coolbreeze Clark had disowned his race. His skin was darker and his facial features were more Negroid than most Negroes in the prison; yet he himself referred to other Negroes as spooks and niggers, and never, at least in the three years Cully had been aware of him, had he seen Coolbreeze associate with other Negroes. He spoke to them and joked with them, but at the weekly movie, in the messhall, and on the yard he was always with Gigolo and, before Gigolo, with another tall good-looking blond-haired kid, who looked just like Gigolo.

"Where're you guys headed?" Cully asked.

"Back to the kitchen," Bugsy said. "We're gonna see Big Red about goin' out front and gettin' those broads in here. And if your friend Skinny Burns butts in, I'm bustin' him in the mouth."

"Why? What've you got against Skinny Burns?"

"He's a phony—always usin' big words, like he thinks he's better than the rest of us. And callin' us inmates, like this was a nut house. I'm a convict, not an inmate."

"Aw, for crissake, quit whinin'. If it wasn't for Skinny comin' up with that petition, we'd all be back in The Hole sniffin' tear gas right now. We could've never stalled 'em without it. Especially with them thinkin' we already killed four hostages."

"They don't think that anymore," Gigolo said. "Accordin' to the last news, the four bulls that were missin' called in from home to say they quit. I guess they kept runnin' when they hit the front gate."

Cully had turned his attention to the lawn between Cellhouse Six and the hospital, where three shirtless cons in paint-spotted dungarees, apparently high on shellac, were heckling the state troopers on the wall.

"Y'guys should get the Medal of Honor for this," one was shouting. "You're riskin' your lives up there."

"Hey, flatfoot," another called, "you with the whiskey nose. Ya wanna make a little drinkin' money? Drop us down a jug, and I'll toss ya up a hand-tooled leather purse worth fifty bucks."

A few of the wall guards in civilian clothes began talking among themselves, but the state troopers stood there motionless, silent, staring down at the cons.

Cully noticed that not one of the wall guards was looking behind or below. Every eye along the stretch of wall between the cellhouse and hospital was trained on the hecklers. He'd have to tell Kelly. If they could rig up some kind of distraction—a fire or even an explosion—and have someone set it off about the time they were crawling from the hole under the gun walk, getting away would be a cinch. He glimpsed Gigolo and Coolbreeze moving away and caught Bugsy's arm before he could follow. "Hold it, man. Give me a hand with this tank."

"Where ya takin' it?"

"Under Cellhouse Six. They hav'ta cut some steel bars in the basement wall."

"Are they still diggin' down there?"

"Yeah. Why?"

"The guys hung it up in the powerhouse and auditorium."

"Where in the auditorium?"

"Under the dressin' room."

"How come?"

"Can't get nobody to dig. The goddamn baby rapers keep sneakin' back to the cellhouses."

"Well, they're still diggin' under Six, so give me a hand."

Beyond a steel-barred vestibule inside the cellhouse entrance, several cons were gathered around the cellhouse sergeant's desk. Setting down his end of the tank, Cully called, "C'mon, coupla you guys do somethin' for your country. Take this down to Poncho."

He walked through the gateway in the partition on the entrance side of the cellblock and started past the cells, along a flagstone gallery perhaps fifteen feet wide and one hundred yards long, enclosed on one side by four tiers of large concrete-walled cells, and on the other by a glazed-brick wall lined with huge windows—hundreds of twelve-by-eighteen-inch, steel-framed panes of glass, which started near the floor and ended near the ceiling fifty feet up. Many of the windowpanes had been smashed. Broken glass and yellow bars of state-issued soap littered the floor. Radios were on speakers all over the cellblock, but only a few cons were moving along the tiers.

As Cully passed the four-man cells, he sensed the wariness around him: closed doors, blankets hanging over the bars on some, anxious faces peering from the dimness beyond; they were mostly older men, white-collar thieves, the forgers and embezzlers who normally had the run of the place. Some were pacing the floor; others were sitting or lying on the double-decked bunks against the walls. He passed a cell with a pad-locked chain wrapped around the sliding door. Christ, he thought, most of the cons were scared stiff.

"What's going on out there, Cully?" A man with wavy gray hair and a prominent nose was standing behind a cell door, gripping the bars. He was showing a mouthful of gold inlays. Two other middle-aged men were sitting on a lower bunk be-hind him. All three were known bootlickers, which presumably made them stoolies or at least potential stoolies.

Cully stopped and grinned at the man. Having sat next to him in the messhall a few times, he knew him well enough to nod to when they passed. "C'mon out and take a look," he said. "You never saw anything like it. Blood all over the place."

The gold inlays vanished behind a squeamish grimace. "It's not that bad, is it?"

"Damn sure is. And it's gettin' worse. You've never written a snitch-kite, have you?"

The man's florid face lost some of its color. "*Snitch-kite?* Certainly not! Why?"

The gold inlays flickered for a moment, but vanished again when Cully said, "There's a buncha crazy bastards over in the kitchen goin' through our Control Room jackets, lookin' for snitch-kites."

"Good God!" the man croaked. "How long do you think this will last?"

"No tellin'. Maybe a week."

Shaking his head as though dazed, the man shuffled away from the bars, and one of his cell partners came to the door. "When are we going to eat?" he asked.

"Beats the hell outta me. All the chow is in the cellhouses."

"We haven't got any."

"Then you guys better get a club and go out and get some," Cully said, and continued along the gallery.

He rounded the rear of the cellblock and started down the gallery on the opposite side. Although the cellhouses were not racially segregated, most of the Negroes—outnumbered ten to one in the prison—celled in the section he was now passing. The tiers were deserted. Most of the cells had four occupants, and the doors were closed. Even the radios were barely audible.

He glimpsed a familiar face and stopped in front of the cell. Railhead Simpson, a slow-moving heavyweight whom he had decisioned twice and knocked out once in the main event on the last three holiday boxing shows, was pacing the floor. The other three Negroes in the cell were sitting on one of the lower bunks.

"What's happenin' out there, man?" Railhead asked.

"Why don't you come out and see for yourself?"

"Too many rednecks lookin' for trouble."

"Don't believe that crap you hear on the radio."

"I got eyes, man. I see 'em walkin' past here—all loaded down with weapons. They're lookin' for trouble all right."

"Not with you guys. Why should they be lookin' for trouble with you guys?"

Railhead grinned. "It's the skin, man. They don't like the color." He glanced at one of his cell partners. "Ask Charlie there. Coupla them boys that broke outta The Hole this mornin' stopped here awhile ago to tell him about it. They mad 'cause he got a white gal comin' to visit him."

"I been in two before," Charlie said. "Only this one gonna be worse. If them studs that broke outta The Hole get high on raisinjack, they gonna be lookin' for blood. And if it's like them other two I was in, we the ones they gonna come lookin' for."

The bull-shouldered Negro sitting next to Charlie snorted and said, "We ready for 'em, though."

Cully shrugged and walked away. What could he say? If a rumble started, the poor bastards wouldn't have a chance.

CHAPTER 8

DUSK was settling over the faceless forms on the wall as Cully crossed the lawn toward the one-story brick building behind Cellhouse Six. Both doors at the front of the seldom-used auditorium in the southwest corner of the prison were wide open. As he started down the sloping aisle, the silhouette of seat backs merged with the darkness, and all he could see was the hazy gray outline of the movie screen at the rear of the stage. At first he could hear nothing; then there was a thud, a scraping sound, and a whispery exchange of voices.

"Hey, Kelly," he hissed, and tapped on the stage floor. "How do I get under here?" It was silent again.

He was groping his way along the foot of the stage when a beam of light swung up from the floor and blinded him.

"It's Briston," someone said.

"Who?"

"Cully Briston."

"He's okay."

The light went out, and a hand caught his ankle. "Get down on your belly and slide underneath."

He found the opening and wiggled under, dragging his bare chest over the grit on the floor. For a moment he was blinded again; then the flashlight beam darted away from his face and began sweeping over the rubble in front of him: chunks of concrete, jagged boards, heaps of rocky dirt. He started to his feet, banged his head on the stage floor, and went sprawling over a pile of dirt.

"Stay down, man! You'll crack your skull."

"*Now* you tell me."

Moving on his hands and knees, he picked his way over the rubble toward a pool of light twenty feet away.

Kelly, his face and torso a sweaty smear of dirt, was hunched on his knees near a rough-hewn, shoulder-wide hole in the concrete floor, working in the feeble glow of a flashlight secured to a two-by-four beam under the stage floor. He was pulling on a rope attached to something inside the hole, straining and grunting as he rocked back and forth. Cully crawled to his side and helped him pull.

"Easy now," Kelly said as a bulging gunnysack slid from the hole, followed by a grinning mask of sweat-furrowed dirt.

"Man, this air smells good!" the mask said.

"Two more trips, and we'll trade again," Kelly said, and unfastened the rope from the sack.

Two dirt-caked forms crawled under the light, seized the sack, and dragged it into the darkness. The man in the hole reached out, grabbed an empty gunnysack and the end of the rope, and disappeared.

"When he gets back, I'll go in and dig awhile," Cully said. "I'll sweat this Benny out."

"You're too big. You'd suffocate in there."

"I'm willin' to give it a try."

"Hell, kid, we got it knocked. Can't be more than six, eight feet from the wall right now."

"Wow! You guys are really makin' time."

"Yeah, thanks to the bulls who were suppos'ta fill in this tunnel. All the lazy bastards did was tear down some of the shorin' and dump a wheelbarrow full of concrete down the hole in the floor."

"What about behind the buildin' where it caved in?"

"Loose stuff. We hauled it right out."

"Are you shorin' it up as you go along?"

"Naw. Why waste time? At the rate we're goin' we'll be ready to make our move by midnight."

"How many?"

"Four—five, countin' you. Are you in?"

Cully grinned. "How can a guy turn it down? What if those

nuts with the big bombs blow up all the booze and women in the world before the parole board turns me loose?"

"You're in then?"

"Why not? If I make it to the Coast, I figure my credit is still good in a few gin mills, and some of the gals I knew must still be givin' it away. I need some fresh memories to live on. One way or the other, I'll be racked up in The Hole sniffin' tear gas for the next two, three years."

"You don't plan on bein' gone very long."

"Not with my luck."

"You're welcome to throw in with the four of us, kid. I've still got a few connections out there. We'll have plenty hardware as soon as we hit the Coast."

"No guns for me."

"You can drive. We'll hoist a few supermarkets and head for Canada."

"Not me. You might think I'm gutless, but I've had it. There's a chance I'll flatten out this ten I got, and I might even pick up another five; but I'm not goin' the pistol route. I doubt if I could hold court in the street, and I know damn well I could never pull a life jolt. Man, if I thought I was gonna wind up dressin' out in the carpentershop in one of these places, I'd hang myself right now. No, Kelly, if I crawl out this hole, it's strictly for entertainment—the kind you can't get in here."

After several seconds of silence Kelly said, "Suit yourself, kid. You'll hav'ta learn the hard way. Once you get a number on your back in this country, you're wiped out. Those bloodhounds out there—" The rope in his hand gave a jerk, and he began pulling, rocking back and forth, his haggard face clenched and streaked with rivulets of sweat.

Again, unrecognizable in the eerie glow of the flashlight secured to the stage floor, the sweaty dirt-smeared face followed a loaded gunnysack from the hole. "I'd sure hate to do this for a living," the panting con said, as the two dirt-caked forms crawled under the light, snatched the load, and dragged it into the darkness. The man in the hole grabbed an empty sack and the end of the rope and disappeared.

Wiping a hairy forearm across his face, Kelly sat back on his heels. "What's goin' on out there? Fletcher still runnin' the show?"

"Yeah, him and the headshrinker. The headshrinker got into the act."

"How'd that happen?"

"Remember when you saw him leavin' the kitchen? Well, he was goin' out front. Skinny Burns drew up a petition, and Fletcher wouldn't take it out there. So Skinny saddled up the headshrinker."

"Whose side is he on?"

"The headshrinker?"

"Yeah."

"Ours, man. He's more on our side than we are. I guess you'd hav'ta call him the ringleader. Been out front three, four times already. Acts like he's really gettin' his kicks. Got on the radio and said he agrees with what we're askin' for."

"What're we askin' for?"

"Everything. You know, like teachin' guys a trade and stuff like that."

"Is the whole joint behind him?"

"I guess so. Only thing is, there's no organization. There's suppos'ta be some kinda meetin' with the press tomorrow afternoon, but the guys with brains enough to talk to the reporters are afraid to leave their cells. You should see it out there. Nine-tenths of the guys are in their cells listenin' to their radios. The stoolies and baby rapers are scared stiff, and the fruiters are havin' a field day. And the jerk on the radio out front keeps sayin', 'seventeen hundred rioting inmates.' Hell, there's only four guys in the act—three cons and the headshrinker. Punchy Philips is up in the storeroom guardin' the hostages, Skinny Burns is writin' the script, and Fletcher is escortin' the headshrinker back and forth. That's it."

"Funny the headshrinker doesn't wise 'em up out front."

"Probably doesn't know what's goin' on. He sees a few juice-heads prowlin' the kitchen and a few psychos from Isolation standin' around with butcher knives and meat cleavers, so he figures it's the same all over the joint. Man, they're better organized in the Women's Quarters. The broads sent a petition out front, too."

Kelly grinned, his dirty face strangely youthful in the hazy light. "If we dig straight ahead for another fifty feet or so, we'd come out in their basement. We could turn this into a real wingding."

"Bugsy and Gigolo are workin' on that now."

"Not a tunnel?"

"Naw, they're goin' first class. They're gonna demand a legitimate get-together."

"Not a chance. The churchgoers outside would scream bloody murder. Wait'll Sullivan gets back, he'll—"

"He's already back. The gasbag got on the radio awhile ago and said 'this uncalled-for demonstration could set the state's penal program back fifty years.' "

"What program? Why, hell, if he had his way, we'd still be rowin' ships. I've been—"

"Dummy up!" one of the dirt haulers whispered, as he crawled into the light. "Someone's in the auditorium."

The barely audible scuff of a single pair of feet moved along the floor in front of the stage, climbed several creaky steps, and made a circle above their heads. Then the footsteps returned to the auditorium floor and began shuffling along the edge of the stage. Something, perhaps a hand, was being dragged along the wallboards at though searching for an opening.

"See who it is," Kelly whispered.

One of the dirt haulers was at the opening. He clicked on his flashlight and swung the beam through the hole. "Who you looking for?"

"Get that light out of my eyes!"

Cully recognized the voice—Joe Surefoot's. He began crawling toward the opening, groping for a rock. He'd get it over with. He'd coax the Indian under the stage and settle it right here. Right under the stage. He'd be damned if he'd wiggle out on his belly and catch a shiv in the back. "Who you lookin' for, Joe?" he called.

"Who's that?"

"Cully Briston."

"What're you doing under there?"

"C'mon under and see."

Kelly was dragging a sackful of dirt from the tunnel entrance. The panting, sweat-drenched digger followed the sack out, and Kelly clicked off the flashlight hanging over his head. The only light—a yellowish mist—came from the flashlight one of the dirt haulers had trained on the pigeonhole opening under the stage. In a moment Surefoot's bony wedge-shaped face appeared, his chin inches from the floor, his glittery black eyes flicking from side to side.

"Lookin' for me, Joe?" Cully said and crawled closer to the opening, a rock under his hand.

The Indian was squinting at him. "Why would I be looking for you?"

"Who you lookin' for?"

"That fat character you saw me playing chess with. He got away on me."

"He's not under here. Try the kitchen."

"I just came from the kitchen. A few over there are going to get it, too. They're suck-holing around the hostages, treating 'em like kings. They never treated us that way."

"Who's doin' the suck-holin'?"

"Red Fletcher for one. He's sitting in the pantry laughing and joking with one of 'em. And that loudmouth bull lover upstairs—the one they call Punchy. He won't let anyone in the storeroom. He's going to get it, too." The Indian's glittery eyes were flitting in all directions. His coarse black hair hung Hitler-fashion over his forehead. "I'll do anything I want to those hostages." His voice had risen steadily. "And if any con tries to stop me, I'll kill him." He was almost screaming.

Kelly came crawling into the light. "Goddammit, Joe," he hissed, "not so loud! We've got somethin' goin' here, don't rank it."

For several seconds the Indian glared at him; then his eyes began roving over the rubble-strewn floor. He slid a bony arm through the opening and propped his chin on his forearm.

"We've known each other a long time, Joe," Kelly went on,

"and I know you got more reason to hate bulls than anyone in this joint, but for crissake, calm down. Don't do anything to make those state troopers rush in here—at least not tonight."

Joe's eyes darted to Cully, then quickly away. "How about me?" he asked. "Am I in, too?"

The two dirt haulers and the sinewy con who'd been digging in the tunnel were squatted behind a heap of rubble. Two of them turned now and crawled into the darkness. The other set the flashlight he was holding on a chunk of concrete and followed. In a moment the flashlight above the tunnel entrance clicked on.

"I'll put it to you straight, Joe," Kelly said. "There's only five of us that know about this. You make six. If you want in, okay. But if we make it out the other side, you're on your own."

"You guys don't want me along?"

"Can't risk it, Joe. You're too hotheaded. You've been in The Hole too long."

"Good! Good!" His voice was a girlish squeal. "You think I can't make it on my own? I'll make it all right! But first I've got some business to settle." He jerked his arm from under his chin, bumping his head on the splintered board above the opening. The beam of the flashlight was flush on his face. He was glaring at Cully. "I don't forget! That goes for you!" He was screaming again.

Cully had an impulse to lunge at the wild-eyed face. He tightened his grip on the rock. The Indian was helpless, his head thrust through the pigeonhole opening like a head on a guillotine block. Then the impulse passed. "Are you threatenin' me, you scrawny bastard? If you are, get under here. C'mon, I'll spot you that shiv. You must be packin' one." He flung aside the rock and began crawling away from the opening. "C'mon, I'll let you get inside. We'll settle it."

For what seemed a minute the Indian just stared at him; then, grinning, he turned to Kelly. "I'll be back as soon as I find my chess partner. We've got a game to finish." His head disappeared, and the scuff of hurried footsteps faded into silence.

"D'you think he'll spread the word?" Cully said.

"About what?"

"The tunnel."

"Hell, no. Who would he tell? He hates everyone."

"Well, if I go out this tunnel, he's not goin' out behind me. I'll go first, and you cover my back. Okay?"

Kelly nodded. "I get along with the nut pretty good. I knew him when he was still half human—before the bulls beat his head soft. And I mean *soft*. Two weeks after he cut Becker, they dragged him into The Hole in a straitjacket. That was seven years ago. His hair was stiff with blood, and his face was so kicked out of shape I didn't even recognize him. I guess they really gave it to him in that padded cell under the hospital— every day for two weeks."

"I oughta bust his hands. If he can't grip a shiv he's harmless."

Kelly shrugged. He was sitting on his heels, his chin on his knees, his wiry arms embracing his legs. The flashlight had tumbled from its perch, facedown. The only light under the stage came from the glow of the flashlight above the tunnel entrance, where a hunchbacked form was pulling on the rope, rocking back and forth.

"Better get out there and see what's goin' on," Kelly said. "Keep us posted. And watch out for Joe."

# CHAPTER 9

CULLY stepped from the auditorium and stood there gaping. The walls were lined with lights. Portable searchlights, like giant yellow eyes, were glaring at him through the breaks in the buildings, over the cannery roof, along the wall to his right. A yellowish mist hung over the prison. Beyond the mist the sky was black. Above and to his right, indistinguishable behind a searchlight, one of the wall guards was laughing. There wasn't a human form in sight.

As he started down the auditorium steps, he heard the muffled sputtering of an air hammer. It seemed to be coming from under Cellhouse Six. He started that way, intending to warn the diggers, then swerved and cut across the lawn behind Cellhouse Five. Why bother? If the wall guards hadn't already heard the hammer, they never would.

As he neared the open windows at the rear of the kitchen, he caught a powerful whiff of raisinjack. The yeasty, musty odor was gushing from the building. A crackling of voices came from inside, accompanied by a radio blaring out rock 'n' roll music. He glanced up at the lighted windows in the steward's office and imagined the worried hostages in the storeroom beyond. For a moment he considered going up and telling Punchy that Surefoot was on the prowl.

He kept walking, listless, his muscles sagging under the weary aftereffects of the Benny. The air was still as muggy as it had been all day. He was sweating.

"Hey, Cully, when's the juice gonna be ready?"

Five or six cons were standing in the beam of a searchlight near the end of the shopline walk, in front of the milk house door.

"Be ready for breakfast," Cully called and kept walking, past the cannery, past the line of searchlights on the wall behind it. Then turning his back on the lights and facing another row of yellow eyes, he moved toward the front of the prison, along the asphalt road which ran past the powerhouse. He thought of going inside and searching the ashpit for the jug of raisinjack Punchy had stashed, then decided that some juicehead from the ashpit gang would have found it by now.

He quickened his pace. The lawn alongside Cellhouse Seven, half the size of a football field, was crowded with cons. T-shirted forms were moving about in the yellowish mist. Others were standing around the water tower in the center of the lawn. A searchlight on the front wall of the prison was slanted skyward, aimed at the red-beaconed reservoir more than a hundred and fifty feet from the ground. Two men, stripped to the waist and wearing what appeared to be top hats, were leaning over the catwalk which circled the giant steel tank. They were shouting down at the wall guards.

Cully stopped beside a dumpy buck-toothed con, called Dingy. "What're they doin' up there?" he asked, peering up through the mist. "Are they loaded? Where'd they get those hats?"

"I dunno."

"What?"

"I said I dunno."

"What's everyone doin' out here?"

"I dunno," Dingy repeated, and let out a whinnylike laugh.

A young con in a silky red-and-white-striped sport coat swaggered past.

"Where'd you get the coat?" Cully asked.

"Man, I'm Uncle Sam."

Cully grabbed him by the shoulder. "Where'd you get the coat?"

"From the tailorshop. We broke into the storeroom where they keep the con show costumes."

"What're those guys doin' up on the water tank?"

"Kicks, man. Kicks."

Squinting upward, Cully moved closer to the reservoir. Even from the ground the towering height had a queasy effect on his equilibrium. He seemed to be tilting backward. One of the cons on the catwalk was balancing himself on the middle rung of the railing. He was yelling down at the wall guards, waving his hat like a broncobuster. The other had started up a narrow ladder toward the red beacon atop the tank. Cully dragged his eyes away. The sight unnerved him.

Gaping cons were crowded in front of the doorway to Cellhouse Seven. Others were strung out along the School Building, a two-story brick building attached to the front of the cellhouse. Cully spotted an Isolation con on the sidewalk fronting the school office and started toward him. The con was facing the prison's front wall, thirty feet from the shadowy forms behind the searchlights.

"Call the police!" he was shouting in falsetto. "Get those roughnecks down from up there."

Cully caught his arm. "What's goin' on?"

"Not a damn thing."

"Anything happenin' over in Eight?"

"The queens are having a ball. And there was a cutting awhile ago. Surefoot cut some fat dude over a chess game."

"Bad?"

"Naw. Just once across the arm."

"Where's he at now?"

"Who?"

"The guy that got cut."

"Beats me. I guess he shoved off while Surefoot was picking up the chess pieces."

"How about Surefoot? Have you seen him?"

"He might be over in Eight again. I saw him heading that way a few minutes ago."

Cellhouse Eight, like cellhouses six and seven, housed four tiers of four-man cells; it was located diagonally across the prison from the auditorium, separated from Cellhouse Seven by a strip of lawn. The door was open. As soon as Cully stepped into the barred vestibule, he became conscious of the activity along the tiers. Compared to the wary silence he had found across the prison in Cellhouse Six, Cellhouse Eight was jumping.

Almost all the cells on the entrance side of the cellblock were occupied by the laundry crew, mostly younger cons, first-termers and Reformatory transfers. Cellhouse Eight was also the prison's tenderloin. Scattered throughout the cellblock were the prison socialites; the bookies, the Benny pushers, the beboppers, and the weight lifters along with their muscle-admiring satellites—the feminine-acting homosexuals, called queens, always referred to in the feminine gender. The other homosexuals behind the walls, mostly prison-made degenerates, were referred to as punks, freaks, or kid fruits, depending on age, appearance, and *modus operandi*. There were perhaps fifteen queens in the prison, and now, as Cully started across the entrance area in front of the cellblock, he counted seven of them scattered among the hip-swinging, finger-snapping group ringed around a portable radio on the cellhouse sergeant's desk. A few were wearing gaudy head scarves, and all seven had made up their faces with homemade lip rouge and eye shadow. One of the queens, a young smooth-skinned effeminate blond called Tina, was dressed in the feathery bra and frilly briefs of a French cancan girl, the costume she had worn in last year's con show. She was alone in the center of the group, going through the bump-and-grind routine of a burlesque stripper.

Sensually aroused by the feminine gyrations, Cully paused as he passed behind the group and stood there watching the graceful movements of Tina's slender soft-muscled body, wondering if the rounded hips and chorus-girl legs were the result of the female hormone pills a guard had been bringing in to her. He was edging closer when he glimpsed the mouthy queen called Ginger swishing his way. Not wanting to be embarrassed by her antics, he made a beeline for the gateway on the far side of the entrance area and started down the flagstone gallery which ran the length of the cellblock.

Radios were blaring from the cells above him: jazz; rock 'n' roll; the Dodger-Giant baseball game. Shirtless cons, some in jockey shorts, were moving along the tiers. A gangling towhead was hanging over the fourth-tier walkway, handing half a loaf of bread to a man on the tier below him. Smoke was drifting across the gallery ceiling.

"The meat ain't done yet," the towhead shouted over the roar of the crowd at Candlestick Park, where Willie Mays had just hit a double.

Twice, on glimpsing a dark high-cheeked face, Cully stopped and peered into an unlighted cell, only to find that the face belonged to someone else, not Surefoot. He had definitely made up his mind about the tunnel—he was going. Also, since talking to the Isolation con in front of the school office, he had made up his mind about Surefoot. He was going to break the Indian's hands.

He was passing a cell with blue gauzy material draped over the bars and a dim reddish glow showing through when a soft voice called, "Hi, Cully. Come in and take a look at my sexy little pad."

He spread the curtain and looked inside. Two shadowy forms, one sprawled and the other curled up, were cuddled, shoulder to shoulder, on one of the lower bunks, their heads against the wall. The reddish glow which illuminated their faces came from a handmade bed lamp covered with red crepe paper. One was Duke Trusdale; the other a queen called Jackie. Trusdale, his greasy black hair dangling in coils over his forehead, was wearing sunglasses. One side of his face was swollen. Jackie was flaunting a foot-long cigarette holder.

"Well, how do you like it?" she asked.

Doilies snatched from the prison officials' laundry hung everywhere—from the wall shelves, the footstools, the headboards on the bunks, the square of cardboard covering the toilet. Even the trash box had a doily draped over the side of it. Embroidered pillowcases and crocheted bedspreads covered the upper and lower bunks on both sides of the cell. A strip of rug, identical to one Cully had seen in front of the altar in the chapel, ran from the doorway to the sink at the rear of the cell. On the floor between the two lower bunks a record player sat on a doily-draped box. Tony Bennett, barely audible, was singing "I Left My Heart in San Francisco."

"Christ," Cully said, "if Andy Gump could see all the contraband in this cell, he'd drop dead on the spot."

"Oh, I don't know, honey," Jackie drawled. "I think the old bastard is a little gay himself. He's constantly hanging around one of the shower rooms. Or haven't you noticed?" She uncurled and flounced from the bunk, like a self-conscious woman, only more so, one hand waving the oversize cigarette holder, the other tugging at her skintight dungarees.

As far as the officials were concerned, Jackie was the most troublesome queen in the prison. In the past three years at least a dozen cons had landed in the hospital or The Hole as a result of fighting over her. In the dim reddish glow of the bed lamp she looked like an attractive young female. She had on a woman's white blouse and wore an ebony-choker around her neck. A peak of black hair showed from under the white silk scarf she had fashioned like a turban around her head and ears. She wore none of the homemade makeup the other queens had on; but her eyebrows were plucked and heavily penciled, and a nostril-quivering aroma of perfume rose up as she fluttered her arrowy hands. She slid an arm around Cully's bare waist. "Come in and sit down."

As usual, he flushed with embarrassment. Although his ego was flattered whenever one of the queens made a play for him, he felt awkward and tongue-tied around them. "Naw," he said, and twisted free of her arm. "I've got to get back to the messhall." He glanced to the side to see if Trusdale was smirking over his clownish performance and was relieved to find the usually sneering ex-pimp slouched on the edge of the bunk, head bowed, cracking his knuckles.

"He's licking his wounds," Jackie said teasingly. "Just look what that mean Punchy Philips did to his face."

"Shut up, bitch!" Trusdale snapped. "The half-wit copped a Sunday on me. You saw him, Cully."

"It didn't look like a Sunday to me."

Jackie laughed and swished to the rear of the cell.

"Christ, man, I was pinned in by the crowd," Trusdale said, his lopsided face twitching, his eyes hidden behind the sunglasses. "Besides, the whole powerhouse crew was backin' him up. Believe me, man, when I catch that punchdrunk bastard alone, he's had it."

"He's alone right now. He's over in the kitchen with the hostages."

Trusdale crunched his knuckles, one at a time, first on one hand, then the other. "It'll wait. What's goin' on over there?"

"Over where?"

"The kitchen. I hear some of these bad-talkin' punks around here are goin' through our Control Room jackets."

Cully nodded. "They're lookin' for snitch-kites."

Trusdale's laugh sounded as if someone had him by the throat. His knuckles were snapping and crackling like dried twigs. His face twitched and then went limp. "I hear they found one on me?"

"Yeah, I heard the same thing."

"It's a frame, man! Someone must've planted it."

Cully shrugged. "Why don't you go over there and straighten things out?"

"I've been thinkin' about it. What do they plan on doin'?"

"Holdin' court, I guess—with a club."

"Not in here!" Jackie struck a dramatic pose, one hand on a jutting hip, the other aiming the cigarette holder at the door. "You're not hiding out in here."

"Shut up, bitch!"

"Like hell I will! You're not putting the heat on me. They're not wrecking my pad. My reputation—"

Cully was walking away, moving along in the shadow cast by the concrete walkway on the tier above him. The crowd at Candlestick Park was roaring again. "Turn down those goddamn radios!" someone yelled, and a yellow blur streaked across the gallery and shattered a wire-meshed pane in one of the floor-to-ceiling windows. A bulldog-faced con standing near the window picked up the bar of state-issued soap and hurled it back in the direction it had come from. "Get wise, you punks!" he shouted.

Cully rounded the rear of the cellblock and started down the other side. The flagstone floor, usually spotlessly shiny, was littered with trash and broken glass. He noticed a dried blood splotch, then another, and began tracking a string of blooddrops through the litter. Halfway down the gallery the splotches swerved into a cell and joined a smear of bloody footprints. A chessboard, with several pieces standing erect, sat on a footstool between the two lower bunks. The rest of the chess pieces were strewn over the floor. There was no one in the cell.

After scanning the cells on the three upper tiers and the cluster of leering faces in front of the cellhouse sergeant's desk, where Tina, slick with sweat, was still performing, Cully went to Cellhouse Seven and made a round of the tiers. He was on the stairway, a few steps from the third-tier landing, returning to the main floor, when he glanced over the railing and caught a glimpse of Surefoot hurrying out of the cellhouse.

He galloped down the stairs, reached the caged-in vestibule, and swung into it just as a troop of noisy cons barged through the door, blocking his way. By the time he shouldered his way outside, the Indian was nowhere in sight. The crowd on the lawn around the water tower had scattered and dwindled. The two top-hatted figures were climbing down the narrow ladder, still fifty feet or so from the ground, barely discernible in the yellowish mist.

"They're hot enough to shoot," someone shouted.

"What happened?" Cully asked a passing con.

"Didn't'cha see? The searchlight was right on 'em."

"I wasn't out here."

"Those nuts up there pissed in a plastic bag or somethin' and slung it at the cops on the wall."

"Wha'd the cops do?"

"Fired a coupla flares at 'em."

Sidestepping a huddle of loud-talking cons, Cully moved to the sidewalk which ran parallel to the front wall, from Cellhouse Eight at one end of the prison to the hospital at the other. The searchlights were glaring down on him now, spreading a bleary haze over the twenty feet of lawn between the sidewalk and the wall. Atop the wall, beyond the haze, he could make out the guards, shadowy and vague in the outer darkness. He crossed the dead-end delivery-truck road and lengthened his stride as he started toward the Control Room, past the plumbing shop, past the shopline entrance, past Cellhouse Two. Under the stationary floodlights jutting from the roof of the Administration Building the wall guards were clearly visible. On the gun walk below the lights state police officials and important-looking civilians were packed three-deep. A searchlight, more powerful than the others, was trained inside the prison, illuminating the walk leading from the Control Room to the heavy steel door below the crowded gun walk.

Cully stopped twenty feet from the door. He could see through the uncovered peephole into the Administration Building lobby, where heads were bobbing in and out of view. He thought of the on-the-spot radio reporter, who was broadcasting from out there, and decided that if the man kept repeating "seventeen hundred rioting inmates" long enough, the sixteen hundred radio listeners in the cellblocks just might take the hint.

It was quiet. Discounting the shadowy traffic between cellhouses seven and eight more than a hundred yards to his right, there wasn't a con in sight. To his left, thirty yards or so, the floodlight above the hospital entrance cast a silvery mist over the flowerbed beside the stairs. The barred gate below the floodlight was shut. He turned and looked up at the crowded gun walk. The police officials and civilians were looking down at him. One of the civilians blinked a flashlight. "Have you a message?" he called.

Cully thought of the tunnel under the auditorium, of the two hours needed to complete the digging. When the time came to crawl out, it would be a lot safer if the officials were at the front of the prison. "Yeah," he said. "The leaders want to release the hostages as soon as possible. They're meetin' in the messhall right now. If they work out somethin' will there be somebody out here to deal with in two, three hours?"

"Tell them yes," an authoritative voice called. "We'll arrange for a meeting with the liaison, Mr. Murry, and three inmates in the lobby of the Administration Building around midnight —or any time after midnight."

Grinning, Cully turned into the Control Room. The room was dimly lighted by a bare bulb dangling on a cord from the ceiling in the screened-in area. The filing cabinets had been

shoved away from the walls, some tipped over, some still standing upright, their empty drawers hanging open. The room had
been thoroughly ransacked. Even the tiny cardboard name tabs
had been removed from the cellhouse count boards. There
wasn't a scrap of paper in sight, other than the *Playboy* magazine in the hands of an Isolation con sitting behind the opening
in the screened-in area.

The con, a flat-nosed hulk with kinky red hair, was sprawled
in Sergeant Gallaway's swivel chair, his legs on the table. There
was no one else in the room.

"Has Surefoot been through here?" Cully asked.

The con grunted, shook his head, squirmed in the chair.
"How could you go for some of this?" he said and held up the
magazine, letting the centerfold drop open. A statuesque nude
was standing in front of a mirror fondling her breasts, her buttocks to the camera.

"I'll take a barroom chippy any day," Cully said. "Those
babes who like to show off their asses in magazines are too hung
up on themselves. Hell, a guy might muss their hair or drool on
'em."

The redhead kept looking at the picture, his thick lips hanging open. "I ain't been laid for six years," he said. "It ain't human."

"There's plenty action over in Cellhouse Eight."

The redhead gave him a dirty look. "I ain't that bad off. Anyhow, I'm a delegate."

"A what?"

"A delegate."

"A delegate for what?"

"For when we meet with the delegates from the Women's
Quarters. Bugsy's workin' on it now."

Cully laughed. "If you wait for that to happen, you won't get
laid for another six years." Flapping a hand, he turned through
the doorway into the Isolation cellblock and started toward the
kitchen.

The smell met him at the messhall entrance. By the time he
reached the kitchen, the musty yeasty odor was suffocating. No

one seemed to mind. The cons under the canopy were strolling past the bubbling caldrons like window-shoppers. The gang around the table in the far corner, where the self-appointed judges were still rummaging through the Manila folders in search of snitch-kites, had grown larger and louder. As he started past the caldrons, he glanced toward the wall clock behind the range. It was ten forty-five.

Rick was stretched out in the warden's easy chair, between the cup sink and the metal can-opening table. Bugsy, Gigolo, and Coolbreeze Clark were perched along the edge of the table. Gigolo motioned and called, "C'mere, Cully. They're gonna dump your juice."

Rick started up from the easy chair. "D'you want your seat?"

"Naw, sit still," Cully said and turned to Gigolo. "Who's gonna dump my juice?"

"Fletcher and the headshrinker."

"It's not Big Red's idea," Bugsy said. "It's that skinny bastard, Burns. He thinks he's a wheel or somethin' because he's the editor of that crummy paper."

"What's the deal?" Cully asked.

Gigolo's handsome face twisted into a sneer. He flicked his eyes across the kitchen, at the pantry door. "It's Fletcher all right. He sold out on us."

"Not Big Red," Bugsy mumbled. "It's that skinny bastard."

"It is like hell!" Gigolo jerked a soggy T-shirt from his hip pocket and wiped his sweaty chest. But for a barely visible patch of golden-blond hair, his chest was boyishly smooth. Tattooed over one nipple was the word SWEET, and over the other, SOUR. Tattooed around his neck was a blue leader line, and printed above it, CUT ON DOTTED LINE. He slung the T-shirt over his shoulder. "Fletcher's makin' goddamn sure he's got someone goin' for him when this is over."

"Like who?" Cully asked.

"Like that lard-ass headshrinker. That's who's runnin' everything now. Fletcher's nothin' but his errand boy."

"Red's playin' it cool," Bugsy said. "Huh, Breeze?"

The muscular Negro shrugged. "I'm not sayin' he is, and I'm

not sayin' he ain't. Only thing I know is, he won't even try to fix up a meetin' for us with the gals from the Women's Quarters."

"Man, that ain't his fault. It's like the headshrinker says; the public won't stand for it."

"What does the public care?" Gigolo snapped, glaring. "Ain't nothin' over there but a buncha whores."

"It ain't the public so much, it's the preachers and church people."

"Screw the preachers! Besides, they don't hav'ta know. If we show those phony bastards out front we mean business, they'll find a way to fix us up with some pussy. Might even send in some call girls. Like I said, I'll personally cut Andy Gump's throat and drag his dead ass out to the front gate. I'll put it to 'em straight—either they send in some broads, or the other seven get the same."

Cully caught himself staring. The big good-looking kid actually meant it. He'd kill the eight hostages for an hour with a woman, any woman. And he had nothing to lose. He was doing life. He'd be better off hanged, and he knew it.

"And that ain't all," Gigolo was saying. "What about the stoolies?" He sprang from the table, jabbing a thumb in the direction of the noisy gang around the table in the corner. "Those guys back there got the goods on at least twenty out-and-out stoolies and over fifty undercover ass kissers, and what does Fletcher say? 'Cool it! Wait till tomorrow.' "

"So we wait till tomorrow," Bugsy said. "We'll still have those snitch-kites. Don't worry, the stoolies'll get it."

Flicking a hand, Gigolo turned to Cully. "What about your juice? Are you gonna let 'em dump it?"

Cully glanced at the frothing caldrons, regretfully, angry with himself for having concocted the smelly mess. His mind was on the tunnel. Why in hell should he care if Fletcher dumped the juice? But it wasn't the juice, and he knew it. In more than four years he had never let a convict tell him what to do, and he wasn't about to start. Still, a rumble with Fletcher could gum up the works. Then, too, he wasn't sure he could lick the big redhead. He glanced at the clock behind the range: a few minutes to eleven. Another hour. "I can't drink all eight hundred gallons myself," he said. "But I'll protect my share. That big pot on the end is mine."

"Fletcher says he's dumpin' it all," Gigolo said.

"And I said that big pot on the end is *mine*. Nobody's dumpin' it."

"I'm with you, man," Gigolo said, and started across the grimy kitchen floor. "C'mon, let's settle it."

Fletcher had been standing in the pantry doorway. Now, followed by Skinny Burns and Murry, the psychologist, he moved a few steps into the noisy kitchen. "Where've you been?" he said, grinning as Cully approached.

Provoked by the grin, Cully brushed past Gigolo and said, "If you're plannin' on dumpin' the juice, keep your hands off that big pot on the end. It's mine."

"What about the other five?"

"They don't belong to me."

Fletcher's grin widened. "Swell, man! Swell! We were going to empty three, but seeing that only one belongs to you, we'll empty five."

Cully flushed. He might've known the big redhead would pull something like this. The cocky bastard sure knew how to play it cool. Feeling like a fool, he started to say, "You handle the business out front; I'll handle those pots," but Skinny Burns, his long droopy-eyed face even sadder-looking than usual, laid a hand on his shoulder and said, "Why don't you get rid of it all, buddy? If this turns into a drunken brawl—"

"Yes, let's be sensible about this," Murry cut in. "We need the pots for cooking."

Cully swung around. "*We?* How'd you get in the gang, fat ass?"

"Cool it, man!" Fletcher said, stepping in front of the psychologist. His even white teeth were still set in a grin, but not his eyes. "He's with us all the way. If it wasn't for him—" His voice was cut off by shouts from the crowd around the radio in front of the coalroom:

"News! News! Dummy up! News!"

There was a rush toward the radio. As Cully started that way, someone caught his arm. It was Rick.

"What about the raisinjack?"

"Dump it."

"All of it?"

"Yeah, all of it."

He began wedging through the crowd. To hell with the juice. He wouldn't be around to drink it anyway.

". . . a matter of hours," the voice on the radio was saying. "For further developments, we take you to Neal Seaburg at the riot-torn prison."

There was a whir, a sharply cutoff gabble of voices, and then: "According to Warden Sullivan, the information was brought to the front of the prison by an inmate messenger only minutes ago. After asking if an official with the power to negotiate was on the scene, the messenger stated that the riot leaders were meeting in the prison messhall and were hopeful of ending the rebellion and releasing the hostages within a few hours. This came as a complete surprise. Earlier, the twenty-five-year-old inmate spokesman, Alan Fletcher, and Miles Murry, a psychologist at the prison who is being held hostage, had requested a meeting with the press inside the prison tomorrow afternoon. In view of this latest development, Warden Sullivan has arranged to meet at midnight with three inmate leaders and psychologist Murry here in the Administration Building lobby in the front of the prison."

Grinning, Cully wedged farther into the crowd. Fletcher and Murry were standing in front of the radio, gaping at each other. Suddenly Fletcher wheeled and began shouldering his way through the crowd. Still gaping, Murry followed.

As Cully turned his attention back to the radio, the grin on his face shrank into his whiskers.

". . . sound of air hammers in the southwest corner of the prison where inmates are believed to be tunneling under the wall," the voice on the radio was saying. "The entire area surrounding the outside of the prison has been lighted with portable floodlights, and heavily armed state troopers are—"

Cully was shoving through the crowd, shouting and waving at Rick across the room. The spigots on two caldrons were already gushing raisinjack. Rick was reaching for the third.

"Off! Turn 'em off!" Cully shouted, and nearly lost his footing on the slushy floor as he vaulted over a stationary table and made a grab for the spigot on one of the gushing caldrons.

"Now what?" Rick asked when the flow had been stopped. "I thought you said dump it?"

"Don't let it bug you. I just found out I'm not goin' anywhere," Cully said, and glanced at the wall clock. It was one minute to eleven. "You and Gigolo guard the juice. And send word up to Punchy to watch out for Surefoot. I'll be back."

He started to the auditorium to warn Kelly.

# CHAPTER 10

TOO Benny-logged to sleep, just listless enough to doze, Cully had passed the night and early morning in and out of the warden's easy chair, trading off with Rick and Gigolo, two guarding the raisinjack, while the other sprawled in the easy chair. Coolbreeze Clark, apparently having missed out on the Benny score, had slept on the floor under the cup sink, on a greasy mattress dragged in from one of the cellhouses. He was still lying there, snoring.

Except for Coolbreeze and the radio, the kitchen was quiet. Sight-seers, like morning-after viewers of a tornado, were strolling through, a few hungry zombis were prowling for food, and several cons were still hunched over the paper-strewn table in the corner. But gradually during the night, as the novelty of a guardless prison faded, the crowd had drifted back to the cellhouses. Even the yammering of the deserted radio in front of the coalroom, as though it were aware of having no listeners, had dropped to a drone. The only evidence of "seventeen hundred rioting inmates"—an occasional squabble of voices—came from the pantry.

Shortly after midnight, perhaps encouraged by a newscast announcing Warden Sullivan's promise of amnesty to the ringleaders if the rebellion ended without further violence, the inmate chairman of the institution's chapter of Alcoholics Anonymous and two other socially active cons, sneeringly called joint politicians by the antisocial majority, had joined Fletcher, Skinny Burns, and Murry, the psychologist, in the pantry.

The discussion had been going on for nearly eight hours now.

Several times during the night Fletcher had escorted the psychologist from the kitchen, presumedly to the front gate. On their return each time the cons in the kitchen had crowded in front of the pantry door, and Fletcher had made an announcement: "We're demanding that the state legislature investigate the joint." And once: "We just demanded a permanent inmate council." And after the last trip: "There's going to be a meeting with the press in the offices above the Control Room at four o'clock this afternoon." And when the Isolation cons, more interested in immediate entertainment, had asked, "What about that meetin' with the broads in the Women's Quarters?" or, "When do we tamp-up on the stoolies?" Fletcher had brushed them off with a "Cool it, man," and returned to the conference in the pantry.

Several times during the night the pantry clique had huddled in the doorway and stared threateningly out at the frothing caldrons. Cully had returned their stares, and now, as the morning sun began rising over the shoeshop roof and glaring into the kitchen through the dusty windows, the smelly concoction in the six caldrons was still bubbling, unmolested.

"Get up and move around, Jitterbug," Cully called to Rick, who was laid out like a corpse in the warden's easy chair. "You've gotta walk it off."

The skinny ferret-faced kid was experiencing his first Benny hangover. His complexion, naturally pallid, had turned a dirty gray. His lips were the same shade of blue as the tattooed dot on his cheek. "Yeah, okay," he mumbled, but not a muscle in his body rippled and his bloodshot eyes stared straight ahead.

"C'mon, you'll get sicker just sittin' there." Cully grabbed his wrist and pulled him from the chair. "Move around. Walk it off. I'm goin' up to the storeroom. If Fletcher tries to dump the juice, give me a yell."

On his last visit to the storeroom, a few hours earlier, Andy Gump had put on another show, squirming on one of the mattresses Punchy Philips had laid out for the hostages, grimacing, and clutching his chest. "That's about his fiftieth heart attack," Punchy had said. "He gets one every time someone comes in here."

Obviously embarrassed, Deputy Warden Fisk had stopped pacing the floor to watch the performance. "Why don't you men release Mr. Grossman?" he had said. "As unpopular as he is with the inmates, he's only making your job of protecting us more difficult."

And Grossman had stopped performing long enough to glare at Fisk and say, "You're the one who should be sufferin'. You're the one who caused all this."

As Cully passed the coalroom now, he noticed a bloody handprint on the doorjamb and another on the wall inside. He stopped and looked into the high-ceilinged windowless room. There was no one inside. A sixty-watt light bulb hung on a long sooty cord from the ceiling. Makeshift seats, mostly orange crates, cluttered the floor. The range tender's chair—a grimy pillow-padded wooden armchair—was in front of a rickety table against the rear wall. The tabletop was a dripping mess: coffee puddles; soggy cigarette butts; sloppy stacks of metal cups. The wall above the table was covered with crudely defiled photos from girly magazines—the scanty costumes shaded out, breasts and pubic hair penciled in. The top board on the coalbin to the left of the door had been ripped from its casing, scattering coal over the floor in front of the doorway.

As Cully glanced at the splintered board, he glimpsed a movement at the rear of the coalbin. Squinting into the blackness, perhaps fifteen feet from the edge of the bin, he made out what appeared to be the head and shoulders of a hunched motionless form. "What'n the hell you doin' back there?" he asked.

There was no reply. The obscure form remained motionless. Thinking he might be having a Benny hallucination, he picked up a chunk of coal and tossed it to the rear of the bin. The form moved, gasped, and mumbled something.

He backed away. Then, imagining Surefoot crouched in the darkness with a shiv, he snatched up another chunk of coal. "C'mon out, you sneaky son of a bitch!" He made as if to throw.

"Don't. I'm hurt." It wasn't Surefoot's voice.

The form was crawling over the coal into the light, bulky shoulders, a fat soot-smeared pain-twisted face.

"Holy Christ!" Cully said. "What happened to you?"

The man reached the edge of the bin and sagged against the wall. His T-shirt was splotched with blood. A filthy blood-soaked rag was knotted around the biceps of one arm. Rivulets of dried blood, mingled with dirt and coal soot, had run in crooked streaks the length of his arm, over the back of his hand, and had clotted in ugly crusts between the fingers. Sweat, like a mass of tiny blisters, covered his soot-smeared face, and his eyes had a faraway look, like the eyes of a groggy fighter. "Have you seen him?" he asked, and Cully recognized the man. He was Surefoot's chess partner.

"C'mon." He slipped a hand under the man's unimpaired arm and tried to help him from the coalbin. "C'mon, I'll take you to the hospital." His fingers sank into the fat, soft as mush and feverishly hot.

"No!" The man's eyes had come alive. He was trying to crawl back into the darkness. "Leave me alone. Let me stay here until it's over. He'll find me in the hospital."

Cully released the mushy arm, angry for a moment, disgusted by the sight. The gutless tub of lard was twice the size of the scrawny Indian and so goddamn gutless that he'd rather croak in a coalbin than help himself. "I'll get you a butcher knife," he said. "If he comes after you again, bury it in his neck."

The fat con had risen to a sitting position, legs sprawled, his back against the bin wall. He just stared at his blood-crusted hand, shaking his head.

The radio on the orange crate outside the door was humming and whining, hung on two stations, a hillbilly singer and a coffee commercial. The voices in the pantry were squabbling again. And Cully was wondering if he could deliberately stick a knife in a man. He never had. He doubted if he could. Not deliberately, not in cold blood. He'd have to be out of his mind, crazy mad, wild drunk. So would most of the other cons in the prison. Quite a few carried shivs, and quite a few talked graveyard talk, but how many meant it? Unless they were scared or unless they had let their mouths get them into a jam they couldn't wiggle out of, how many cons in the place could deliberately stab a man? Maybe twenty. Maybe less. All psychos. Still, the tub of lard should at least have guts enough to defend himself.

He'd sit right there and let the Indian cut him again. Christ, even a churchgoing old lady had more guts than that. "You better go to the hospital," he said. "You got a fever. That arm is infected."

"When it's over. I'll go when it's over."

"When what's over?"

"The riot."

"Hell, man, that might be a week from now. You'll lose that arm. You're liable to be dead by then."

The fat con's eyes had come alive again. Grimacing, he scoonched closer to the edge of the bin. "I've got a new transoceanic portable. And money. My wife sends me money every month." Groaning, using his opposite hand, he lifted his blood-streaked arm and laid it across his lap. "Tell him to leave me alone. He'll listen to you. All you'd have to do is tell him. Just tell him to leave me alone. I'll give you everything I've got—everything I'll ever get." The con was crying.

Cully turned away, embarrassed. He moved farther into the room and sat down on a wooden box. The radio outside was still humming and whining. Two cons passed the door. Both nodded and grinned when they saw him. He turned his back on them, rudely, so that they wouldn't come in.

Keeping his eyes away from the coalbin, he tried to imagine himself inside the fat con's skin. What would the past four years have been like if he hadn't learned to use his fists in the Navy? Christ, compared to the average con in the place, he was living a life of ease. "There's not many good-heads like Cully Briston in here." How many times had he heard it? He could use his fists, and he wouldn't back down from a fight; that made him a good-head. Hell, he could be the phoniest bastard in the joint, and most of them would still be calling him a good-head—to his face. The loudmouths steered clear of him, and the hustlers were always cutting him in on their scores—raisinjack, Benny, special-made food. Even most of the guards gave him an easy way to go. The goddamn monotony was bad enough, but what if he had to creep around with his eyes on the ground, afraid to open his mouth? Not just once in a while, but day in and day

out, year after year. Christ! What if he had to bow down to every
loudmouth in the joint? And the poor slob in the coalbin wasn't
the only one. The place was full of guys just like him, just as
chickenhearted, just as helpless. Stooges for the loudmouths.
Kicked around and robbed by the vultures. If they took their
troubles to The Man, they were stoolies, and then even their
fellow stooges would go out of the way to make life more miserable for them. If they asked The Man for protection, they
got it—Segregation, the same as The Hole. Christ, what a snake
pit!

He glanced toward the coalbin. The con was still crying.
How the poor slob had ever got reckless enough to break a law
outside was beyond him. "Why'd he cut you?" he asked with
forced gruffness.

The con struggled to control his quivering lips. "I don't know.
He's insane."

"Should've never told him you were a chess player."

The con nodded. "When he'd win, he'd accuse me of throwing the game. When I'd win, he'd accuse me of cheating. Finally, I told him I couldn't concentrate anymore—and he
stabbed me."

Cully got up. "C'mon, get outta that coalbin. I'll walk you to
the hospital."

"Will you tell him?"

"Yeah, yeah, I'll tell him. He won't bother you anymore."

They left the kitchen through the back door and started
down the shopline walk. The fiery glare of the sun reflected
from the kitchen windows, but the walk and the deep-green
lawn on either side were in the shade of the building which
housed the shops.

Revived, perhaps by the lazy scene—a motionless sky and a
quiet, almost deserted shopline—the fat con waddled along beside Cully, swinging his good arm, beaming, sighing over and
over, "I'll never forget this. Honest to God, I'll never forget
this." His eyes were bleary and red-rimmed, his chinless round-
cheeked face a sweaty smear of coal soot. Blood was seeping
under the filthy rag knotted around his arm. In daylight he

looked even bloodier and grimier than he had sitting in the coal-bin. Four cons, perched on the railing of the messhall ramp, stopped talking and watched them pass.

"What happened to him?" one called.

"He spent the night in the Women's Quarters," Cully said and nudged the fat con on.

At the shopline entrance, where the shopline walk met the main sidewalk which ran parallel to the front wall, the lazy scene ended. Bundle-ladened cons, like passing caravans of gypsies, were moving in both directions. Some were carrying their personal belongings east, toward cellhouses seven and eight. Others were moving west, past the Control Room, and turning onto the walk which led to Cellhouse Six. The sweaty-shirted troopers on the wall, protected from the blazing sun by jungle helmets and goggle-size sunglasses, were watching in silence.

A shirtless flabby-chested con, his flushed face streaming sweat, was pushing a loaded wheelbarrow past the shopline walk. Atop a swaying heap of cardboard boxes sat a two-gallon pickle jar filled with water, ferns, pebbles, and a school of frantically swimming goldfish.

"Where's everybody goin', Bernie?" Cully asked.

"We're tradin' cells. I'm movin' in with my crime partner. Been tryin' to make the move for years."

"You'll be movin' back in a few days."

The con, straining to balance the swaying pickle jar, glanced hastily over his shoulder and said, "Everybody's movin'. It'll take 'em a year to untangle this mess."

The passing cons were gawking over and under their burdens at the soot-smeared blood-splotched fat con who had a death grip on Cully's arm. Noticing this, Cully steered him across the sidewalk and started along the lawn. After a few steps, he stopped, did a double take, then walked on, grinning.

In front of the Control Room, halfway down the walk leading to the heavy peepholed door which opened into the Administration Building lobby, sat a man in a baggy tan suit and a stiff felt hat. He was sitting on a cardboard box. His arms were folded across his chest, and he was talking to the troopers on the wall above the door. "I'm a citizen just like you guys," he was saying. "I finished my sentence at eight o'clock this mornin'."

Cully stopped beside him. "Won't they let you out, Smitty?"

The man looked up, imploringly, an expression of anguish on his face. The suit he wore fit and looked like a burlap sack. The cheap gray hat sat squarely on his ears. "The bastards won't even answer me. Six years and eight months I wait for this day and here I sit." He spat on the walk, glared up at the troopers, and spat again.

"Where'd you get those sharp threads you got on?"

"From the clothin' room. This is my dress-out suit. I got fitted for it three days ago." He snatched off the hat and flung it on the walk. "Jesus H. Christ! Wouldn't't'cha know somethin' like this had'a happen?" He sprang up, cupping his hands around his mouth. "You blockheads up there better listen to me! I'm bein' held illegal! Tell that birdbrain warden out there to get on the goddamn stick. Smith—nineteen-eight-forty-six. I'm an hour overdue right now."

A crowd had gathered in front of the Control Room.

"Let him out, you duty-happy idiots!" someone shouted.

"Tell 'em you wanna see a lawyer, Smitty."

"He's bein' held illegal!"

As Cully and the fat con started across the lawn toward the hospital, Smith shouted, "My constitutional rights are bein' violated! So tell 'em to get off their dead asses out there!" He was still shouting when Cully moved up the steps to the hospital entrance.

He reached through the barred gate and knocked on the wooden door. Apparently someone had seen them coming. The door was swung open before he had stopped knocking.

The young doctor, minus his glasses, his lean face slightly drawn, stood behind the barred gate. His white smock was starched and spotless. He glanced from the bloody rag on the fat con's arm to Cully. "An accident, I suppose?"

Cully nodded.

The doctor unlocked the gate and stepped aside as the fat

con entered. When Cully made no move to follow, he shut the gate and locked it. "I received a call from the hospital in town this morning. Captain Malaski is coming along fine."

Cully grinned. "I'll tell the boys. They'll be sorry to hear it."

"Is Mr. Gallaway still having pain?"

"I haven't asked him."

They stood there awhile, awkwardly; the doctor tapping the heavy key on the bars, Cully avoiding his eyes. The fat con had gone into the sick-call room to the left of the door. In front of the Control Room thirty yards away, Smith was still demanding his rights. Finally, Cully said, "Who besides you opens this gate?"

"No one. Why do you ask?"

"How long do you plan on bein' here?"

"As long as I'm needed."

Cully moved closer to the gate. "Look, Doc, if a skinny Indian tries to—"

"He's already been here—several times."

"Wha'd he want?"

"He's looking for a friend of his."

"He hasn't got a friend."

"I believe he's looking for the man in there." He glanced toward the sick-call room. "Is he?"

Cully shrugged. "Just don't let him in. He's nothin' but trouble."

The doctor started to close the door, then opened it again. "How are the hostages?"

"Okay—so far."

"I don't understand you men. What can you gain by holding hostages that you can't gain without them?"

"C'mon, Doc, you're not that square. You know damn well the bulls would've crashed in here by now if we didn't have hostages. Besides, we're gonna trade 'em for girls."

"*For girls?*"

"Yeah, that's the latest rumor. Five for each hostage. We're gonna ask for female volunteers from eighteen to sixty-eight. The fellas figure there oughta be enough female publicity hounds in the country to—" The door banged shut in his face.

The hecklers blocking the sidewalk in front of the Control Room had picked up their bundles and boxes and moved on. A straggling string of bedrolls was bobbing down the walk again. Several noisy cons were guiding a flatbed cannery cart, heaped head-high with bedding, boxes, books, and magazines, up the shaded walk alongside Isolation, past the shattered paint-blackened windows, toward the barred enclosure leading to Cellhouse Six. Smith was still sitting on his rope-bound cardboard box twenty feet from the door to freedom, arms folded, legs crossed, his crumpled gray hat squarely on his head. "You're lookin' at an honorably discharged war veteran," he shouted up to the troopers on the wall as Cully turned into the Control Room.

The floor had been swept, and the metal filing cabinets in the screened-in area had been set upright and lined along the wall. Devoid of the memos, records, and Manila folders usually scattered about, the room looked neat but desolate. A few cons were roaming the thoroughly looted offices beyond the second entrance. Behind the table at the opening in the screened-in area, Bugsy Matthews was slouched in Sergeant Gallaway's swivel chair. He was squeezing a pimple on his chest. His thick, crudely tattooed legs, bare from the middle of his thighs to the tops of his cutdown brogues, were propped on the table, crossed at the ankles.

"Close the door," he said, frowning belligerently. "I don't want them mainline creeps snoopin' around in here."

Cully kicked the door shut. "Who the hell are you? You wearin' a badge now?"

"I'm on duty." He flicked his eyes at the telephone on the table beside his elbow. "Big Red don't want nobody but me touchin' that phone."

Cully leaned through the opening, his elbows on the ledge. "Is there someone on the switchboard out front?"

"I wouldn't be sittin' here if there wasn't." He twisted on his hip as Cully reached for the phone. "Whad'da ya doin'? Big Red don't want nobody but me callin' out front."

"Calm down, Dumbo, this is business," Cully said, and dialed the O.

In a moment a man's voice said, "Switchboard."

"This is riot leader Matthews speakin'," Cully said gruffly, and slapped Bugsy's hand away from the cutoff button. "Get the TV cameras ready. I'm comin' out in the nude."

Laughing, he dropped the phone and ducked under the opening as Bugsy made a frantic grab for the cord. Then, wagging his head and singsonging, "Big Red don't want nobody but me touchin' that phone," he walked mincingly into Isolation and started toward the kitchen.

He was crossing the high-ceilinged hall which once housed Cellhouse Three when he noticed the brisk two-way traffic in the messhall doorway. Cons were scooting in and out, carrying jugs, buckets, cans, and jars.

He darted across the hall and intercepted a dumpy head-shaved con, who was legging it toward Cellhouse Four with a brimful scrub bucket and a gleeful grin. "Who said you could take that juice?" he asked, and the man, no longer grinning, stopped in his tracks, slopping raisinjack over his feet.

"Why jump me, Cully? I ain't the only one. Everybody's dippin' in."

"Man, the stuff isn't ready yet."

"The hell it ain't!" a passing con said. "I drank two cupfuls five minutes ago, and I can feel it already." He let out a howl.

Cully broke into a trot. He reached the messhall doorway, sidestepped a bucket-carrying con, and sprinted up the aisle.

# CHAPTER 11

FROM the hivelike activity around the steam caldrons, it appeared as if every raisinjack drinker in the prison had got the word. At least fifty cons were milling about under the metal canopy, drinking, yelling, dipping into the caldrons with jars, cans, stainless-steel coffee cups. A few were sitting on the floor, straining the soupy concoction through dish towels and handkerchiefs, but most were drinking right from the caldrons. The noise was deafening, and the musky odor stirred up by the commotion was overpowering.

Cully was stunned by the sight. He hadn't thought this far ahead. A few laughs, a fistfight or two, but with every loudmouth in the joint tanked to the gills, anything could happen. There were weapons all over the place. Some of the Isolation cons were still carrying knives and meat cleavers. Christ, what a madhouse! He imagined himself shouting, "All right, you guys, knock it off! Get back to the cellhouses," and then imagined the reaction. They'd horselaugh him out of the kitchen. He'd be called every kind of phony bastard in the book, including a stool pigeon. He wouldn't mind a fight so much, but when it came to cutting off their juice, they'd gang him. Hell, it'd be like snatching bones from a kennel full of starving dogs. Grinning, feigning indifference, he moved under the archway and leaned against the wall.

Fletcher, Skinny Burns, and a tall hook-nosed con called Preacher were standing near the pantry. Preacher was the chairman of the prison's Alcoholics Anonymous group. On more than one occasion he had taken a beating, and once a lead pipe over the head, in an attempt to break up a raisinjack party involving A.A. members. The nostrils of his big hooked nose were flaring now, and his mouth was as tight as a seam. So was Skinny's. Fletcher, although wearing his habitual cocky grin, was watching the activity around the caldrons with obvious impatience.

Cully caught sight of Rick and Gigolo and started toward them.

"Stuff ain't bad, Cully," someone called.

"Yeah, man!" another shouted. "Ya oughta go in the brewery business when ya get out."

Rick had a halfful gallon can in his hands. Gigolo was drinking from a mason jar. "How come you guys let 'em go hucklybuck?" Cully asked. "If you couldn't keep 'em away, you should've made 'em line up and rationed it out."

Gigolo dragged a forearm across his mouth, grinning. "Are you kiddin', man? I'll tell you what—you get 'em in line and start rationin' it out, and me and Rick'll watch how you do it."

"Couldn't stop 'em," Rick said. "We told 'em twenty times you didn't want nobody dippin' in. That big bastard over there told us to tell you to go to hell. Said the stuff you made it from belonged to the state."

Cully glanced toward the con Rick had indicated, a big rawboned Swede who worked in the powerhouse. At least half the powerhouse gang was standing nearby. He knew Rick and Gigolo were waiting for him to collar the big Swede who was drinking from a coffee pitcher several feet away, but he couldn't force himself to do it. He turned away. "The juice isn't ready to drink," he said weakly.

Rick held out his can. "Here, try it. Don't taste too good, but it's got a pretty good kick."

"How would you know?" Cully snapped and brushed the can aside, angry with himself, certain that Rick and Gigolo were inwardly smirking at him. He had an impulse to shove his way through the commotion in the drainage area between the caldrons and open the spigots, but again he imagined the reaction. Christ, he should've never made the juice. "What about the hostages?" he asked.

CHAPTER **12**

BY noon two caldrons were empty, and the lushes who hadn't been scared off by the violent atmosphere of the kitchen were dipping into the remaining four. From the canopy above the scummy caldrons hung a sign reading, A.A. MEMBERS HANDS OFF, put there by Preacher, who, after having lost three fistfights and a ladle-swinging match, was now in a corner of the scullery nursing a lacerated face and a two-gallon pickle jar full of raisinjack. Red Fletcher and Murry, the psychologist, were still out front. According to the last newscast, they were meeting with the warden and the commissioner of corrections in the warden's office.

"God, what a mess!" Skinny Burns said for at least the fiftieth time since the free-for-all had begun. He was perched on the metal utility table, looking down at Cully who was spread out in the warden's easy chair. "Dump the stuff, Cully. For crissake, dump it. We meet with the press in less than four hours."

"Have somebody put up another sign," Cully drawled, his eyes floating over the cursing crowd around the caldrons. "Have it say 'closed till five P.M. Anyone caught dippin' will lose his library privileges.'" He belched. "And sign it Carl L. Briston, Esquire, Actin' Warden." He belched again.

"It isn't funny, Cully."

"Aw, for crissake, Skinny, quit worryin'. So we murder each other. Man on the radio says it costs the taxpayers fourteen hundred bucks a year to keep a guy in here. Hell, that's more than four times as much as I stole. Just think, if we wipe out half the population, we'll be savin' those poor workin' stiffs out there over a million—" He broke off. Fletcher and Murry were coming through the archway.

"Now don't start calling him a policeman again," Skinny said. "Fletcher's handling this right. If he quits, there's nobody to take his place."

Murry had turned toward the pantry. Fletcher was coming in their direction.

"I didn't call him a policeman, I called him a cop," Cully said, and began to get up from the chair, aware of his weary drunk-clumsy limbs, wishing them stronger, more agile. He wasn't about to back down. Still, he had no intention of starting an argument either. Of one thing he was certain now, Fletcher had backed off an hour ago because he had been called a cop, not because he had lacked the nerve to open the spigots on the caldrons. The big redhead wasn't afraid to fight. He was just too much of a hoodlum to play the part of a cop.

"Well, Briston, I'm taking off my badge and giving it to you," Fletcher said, grinning that cocky grin of his. "You filled the loudmouths with false guts, so I figure it's up to you to dummy 'em up."

"Say wha'cha mean."

"I just came from the warden's office. If they find one stiff in here when this is over, every one of us from Isolation is going to be tried for murder—and you grabbed Andy Gump. Remember?"

"So?"

"So they're whipping heads in Cellhouse Eight."

"Whose heads? Stoolies?"

"What's the difference? In case you don't know it, those squares ouside figure killing a stoolie is just like killing a human being."

The crowd around the caldrons had grown quiet. A half circle of sweaty bleary-eyed faces was closing in. Sobered, his groggy senses coming to life, Cully sorted out the faces: seven or eight Isolation cons, not counting Fletcher, the rest from General Population. "G'wan back to the cellhouses," he said. "And stay outta that goddamn juice till we get this straightened out."

It was silent for a moment; then someone said, "How about pullin' your own time, Briston?" The sneering drawl came from a tall con with a blunt pockmarked face. His oily black hair, carefully mussed on top, was combed into a sleek duck-tail in back. He was dipping a two-gallon jar into a caldron ten feet away.

Scattering the crowd, Cully covered the distance in two strides and a lunge. He grabbed, whirled, and shoved. The jar, halfful of raisinjack, went flying over a scramble of shying heads and crashed in a sprawling downpour against the tile wall beside the archway. The con staggered back, caught his balance, and stood there glaring. He cocked a fist as Cully came toward him.

"Swing," Cully said. "Go ahead, man, swing."

The con circled, still glaring. "You're not messin' with no punk, Briston. I'm warnin'—"

The last word was whooshed out as Cully, feinting a left, rolled out of a crouch and jackknifed the con with a round-house right, driving it wrist-deep an inch above the belt. The con dropped to his knees, retching and hugging his stomach as raisinjack gushed from his mouth.

Nauseated by the sight, a sour taste in his throat, Cully turned away, colliding with Coolbreeze Clark.

"Ya sure sobered that stud up," Coolbreeze said, and Cully was struck by the thought that, discounting Coolbreeze, he hadn't seen a colored con all day.

The crowd was drifting into the messhall. Beyond the cal-drons, except for the chunky psychologist standing in the pantry doorway, the filthy kitchen was deserted. Still gagging, his pockmarked face the color of a fish's belly, the con got up and shuffled toward the messhall. Bugsy, who was standing under the archway, apparently having just arrived, gave the con a shove as he passed.

"Let's get over to Cellhouse Eight," Fletcher said, his voice flat, his face stripped of its habitual smirk. "I don't like being a cop anymore than you guys do"—he glanced at Cully—"but these loudmouths around here aren't going to get their kicks at my expense. They had a pretty good idea who the stoolies and ass kissers were before they went through the records. Why wait for a riot? They should've been taking care of business all along—at their own risk."

"That's right," Bugsy said. "They're doin' it now because they know we'll ride the beef. Huh, Red?"

Fletcher turned his back on him. "Murry says we should lock the stoolies in Isolation and keep everyone away from 'em until this is over. He says—" Grumbling drowned him out.

Besides himself and Skinny Burns, Cully counted nine Isolation cons and six mainliners. Like himself, the mainliners were in-and-outers, called hardnoses by the guards, men who spent as much time in Isolation as they did in General Population.

"Screw Murry," one drawled. "Who the hell is he?"

"Yeah, let's concentrate on gettin' laid," Gigolo said drunkenly. "What about that meetin' with the Women's Quarters?"

"I'm with you, man."

"Me, too."

"Yeah," someone said, "tell that fat-ass headshrinker to lock the stoolies up himself."

Fletcher was leaning against an empty caldron, the smirk back on his face. He waited until Bugsy, shouting, "Dummy up! Dummy up! Big Red's givin' it to you straight," had moved away from in front of him, then said, "In case you clowns don't know it, some guys in here are still doing time for a riot killing in nineteen thirty-eight." He glanced over his shoulder at Murry, who was still standing in the pantry doorway. "Say what you want about him, but he's talking it up for us out there. Believe me, he's getting right up in the warden's face."

"I'm with Red," someone said.

"Same here."

"Take a vote," Gigolo muttered. "I say we oughta concentrate on gettin' laid."

"Aw, for crissake, let's get organized," Cully said. "Go ahead, Red."

"Well, first we've got to corral the stoolies. Then we've got to get the groceries back and start running chow lines."

"So what are we waitin' for?" Cully grabbed a stirring paddle and handed it to Rick. "You'll need an equalizer, Jitter-bug."

"Okay," Fletcher said, "three of you guys stay here. See that no one bothers Murry and be ready to give Punchy a hand if anyone tries to get at the hostages upstairs. And keep the lushes out. Don't let 'em pack the raisinjack back to the cell-houses." He looked toward three Isolation cons leaning against the cup sink. "You guys stay here. The rest of us'll take a hike over to Cellhouse Eight."

Fourteen of them left the kitchen through the rear-side door, rounded the milk house, and hurried down the asphalt delivery-truck road, past the powerhouse, then veering across the sun-swept lawn alongside Cellhouse Seven, through the patch of shade cast by the towering water tank.

Cons from General Population were strung out in groups along the way: sprawled on the lawn, bunched up on the walk, leaning against the school building. The reaction at seeing four-teen well-known hardnoses bearing down on them was spon-taneous: one in the group would glance to the side, do a double take, then alert the others. Faces would swing around, hang for a moment, and then the group would either drift apart or play dead. A few of the onlookers, groggy-eyed and grinning drunkenly, tagged along, shouting questions:

"Where ya guys goin'?"

"Who's gonna get it?"

"Ya need a good man?"

"Blow!" Fletcher said. "We got all the help we need."

As they moved along the walk in front of the school office, less than thirty feet from the front wall, the troopers trained their rifles on them. "Don't even look up at the clowns," Fletcher said as they approached the door to Cellhouse Eight.

The tiers on the entrance side of the cellblock were deserted. Most of the sliding cell doors were shut. As they moved past the sergeant's desk, toward the gateway in the ceiling-high par-tition of bars at the far side of the cellblock, a harsh rumble of voices and laughter rose up. Halfway up the gallery a crowd was milling about. Cons were leaning over the tiers. Fletcher and Cully broke into a trot.

The shuffling, neck-craning crowd had formed a wide half circle around what appeared to be the aftermath of a brawl. A middle-aged con was spread-eagled on the flagstone floor, a shiny red lump protruding like an egg from his forehead, blood leaking from his nose. Duke Trusdale, his oily black hair hanging in coils, was down on all fours, panting, spitting out blood. Another con was sitting hunched over, his head between his knees. Four others were standing rigid against the wall. One was chewing paper and being fed more by a rangy young con in a torn T-shirt and a blood-spattered football helmet. Shouting, "Open up!" the young con slapped the chewing con's face and crammed more paper into his mouth.

Cully began skirting the crowd. Most of the jeering was coming from inside the half circle, where a dozen or more cons in football helmets were ganged around the victims. One wore a catcher's chest protector. A few were carrying baseball bats. All were known loudmouths, and all appeared to be high.

As Cully shouldered his way past the onlookers, he glimpsed Surefoot's dark bony-cheeked face through a break in the crowd, and their eyes met for a moment. Then a con grabbed Cully's arm and shouted, "They're makin' him eat a three-page letter he wrote to the warden," and when he looked back through the break, the Indian was gone.

Fletcher had already bulled his way through the crowd. Lunging now, he snatched a baseball bat from one of the cons and sent him reeling into the onlookers. "If there's any head whipping to be done around here, we'll do it," he shouted, and heaved the bat over the heads of the backpedaling crowd.

Bugsy, Gigolo, Rick, and the others were forming a ring around the cons in football helmets. Three of them had been involved in the Isolation breakout the morning before. The rest were from General Population.

"Lay off!" Bugsy yelled as Duke Trusdale, crawling stealthily toward the onlookers, was slammed flat on his back by a rib-cracking kick from the con wearing the catcher's chest protector.

"Get screwed!" the con shrieked, and began kicking insanely at Trusdale, who was writhing on the floor, his knees drawn up to his chin, both hands protecting his crotch. "No convict tells me what to do!" He was aiming a kick at Trusdale's unprotected head when Cully grabbed him from behind and slung him to the floor.

As the con scrabbled out of reach, Cully glanced about. The crowd had scattered. Cons were scurrying along the tiers, some were ducking into cells. Everyone around him was shouting, cursing, shoving. Fletcher and the rangy young con, who'd been feeding paper to the con against the wall, were standing beside him, yelling at each other.

"Did'cha read the letter?" the young con was shouting. "The suck-holding fink was asking the warden for permission to buy flowers for that lousy shoeshop screw who died last year."

Fletcher gave him a shove. "Get going! We'll take care of him."

Cully watched as the con shoved back. Fletcher threw a punch, missed, swung, and missed again. Finally, after getting butted in the chest several times, he managed to jerk the heavy plastic helmet from the con's head, clamp on a headlock, and whirl him off his feet. The con scrambled up, snatched his helmet, and took off in a rubbery-legged trot for the rear of the cellhouse.

Cully turned away, surprised by what he'd seen. The big redhead was slow and clumsy. He'd be a pushover in a fight.

All but three of the helmeted cons had fled and regrouped near the end of the gallery. Two were being driven that way by Rick, who was swinging the oar-size stirring paddle at their legs. The third, the one wearing the catcher's chest protector, was on his back with Bugsy kneeling astride his chest. Bugsy had his fingers hooked through the earholes in the helmet and was banging the con's head on the flagstone floor. The plastic hitting the stone gave off a crack as sharp as a rifle shot. The con was clawing frantically at Bugsy's hands.

"Hey, ya muscle-bound idiot!" a drunken voice called from the tiers. "Quit wreckin' the goddamn athletic equipment."

Bugsy jumped up. "Who's the wise guy?" he shouted, glaring along the tiers as Cully hoisted the groggy con in the chest protector to his feet and pushed him toward the rear of the cellhouse, where the other cons wearing the foothall helmets were just rounding the cellblock, disappearing from sight.

Fletcher had lined the victims along the wall: Duke Trusdale, the middle-aged con with the lump on his forehead, and five others. Now, looking up at the cons leaning over the tier railings, he cupped his hands around his mouth and shouted, "We're locking these guys up for their own protection. There's a list out, so you finks and ass kissers who think you might be on it better get down here while the offer is good. We're not coming back."

Shouting broke out on the tiers:

"You heard the man, Johnson. Get your ass down there."

"That means you, Madison."

"You must be on that list, Binger. Get movin'."

"Who's got the list?" a husky con wearing a baseball cap called from the third tier. "Read off the names."

"Let's get with it!" someone shouted. "Drag that fat stoolie from the tailorship out here."

"There he is!" a high-pitched voice yelled. "Grab the bastard!"

There was a scuffle on the second tier. What looked like a football pileup quickly untangled and a fat bald con was boosted over the railing, squealing, his stubby legs thrashing the air. He clung for a moment, eight feet from the gallery floor; then someone pried his fingers from the rail, and he landed with a thud on his rump.

Others were drifting from the tiers, straggling along the gallery, sidling up to the hangdog group forming along the wall.

"Honest to Christ, Cully, it's a bum beef," Duke Trusdale blubbered through swollen, still-bleeding lips. "You've known me a long time, man. You know damn well I'm as solid as they come."

An Isolation con standing near Trusdale gave him a shove. "G'wan, ya loudmouth fink, tell your story walkin'."

Trusdale waited until the con had turned his back, then edged closer to Cully and muttered, "Every one of these punks are gonna get it. I been around too long to take this kinda crap."

"Why tell me, man? If you don't want protection, cut out. There's a baseball bat on the floor down there."

Trusdale hitched at his dungarees and glanced belligerently at the bat, as though struggling to control his anger. Then, noticing that the group along the wall had started toward the front of the cellhouse, he darted around Cully, wedged himself between the two oldest cons in the group, and shuffled along between them.

Twenty-two cons were escorted from Cellhouse Eight, seventeen more were picked up in Cellhouse Seven, and another dozen or so joined the chain-gang-like procession as it moved along the front sidewalk, past the downpointed rifles on the wall.

"Somebody catch the next newscast and see what they got to say about this," Fletcher said as the line started through the Control Room and into Isolation.

Tiers three, four, and five on the Segregation side were used, one man to a cage. Fletcher was at the fifth-tier lever box, swinging the heavy steel bar which ran along the top of the doors into place, and Cully was clamping on the last fist-size padlock when a panting con came stomping up the worn steel steps, shouting, "Hey, Red, get over to Cellhouse Six right now! They're raisin' hell with the spooks."

"Who is?"

"That same bunch—them crazy bastards in the football hats."

"Man, don't panic," Fletcher said. "The colored studs can take care of themselves."

"Maybe so, but they ain't got nothin' to fight with. And them crazy bastards got backin' now. There's thirty-five, forty of 'em over there—all drunk. They're talkin' about castratin' Charlie Wells 'cause he's got a white broad comin' to see him."

Fletcher shoved the con aside and leaned over the railing. On the lime-splashed glass-strewn floor five tiers below, the cons who had escorted the procession were scattering—some toward the Control Room, others toward the door at the rear of the cellhouse. "Hold it!" Fletcher yelled. "More trouble."

Cully was galloping down the loosely-bolted stairs, remembering his conversation with Railhead Simpson the day before. He reached the main floor and was caught up in the jabbering crowd gathering in front of the cellblock.

"What's the score, Cully?"

"They're over in Six now."

"The same bunch?"

"Yeah, only more of 'em." He started toward the rear door. "Get our guys together in the hall back there."

He sprinted to the rear door, then diagonally across the hall-like vacancy to the inside messhall entrance. A few cons were sitting on one of the battered steam tables. Others were perched on the shabby wooden tables farther back. "C'mon, you guys, we need some help," he called, then crossed the hall to Cell-house Two and called to the cooks and messmen moving along the tiers. Then, sprinting diagonally across the hall again, he shouted through the fan-shaped wicket into Cellhouse Four.

In less than two minutes the hall was rumbling. At least a hundred cons were swarming around Fletcher.

"What's happenin', Red?" someone shouted.

"There's trouble in Six. The loudmouths are talking about castrating one of the colored studs."

There was silence, then grumbling, louder and louder:

"So who gives a damn?"

"Yeah, let 'em do it."

"Count me out," said a short muscular con with a scarred flat-nosed face. "I'm prejudice'."

Cons were walking away, still grumbling: "Oughta get 'em all."

"It'd serve 'em right," someone said. "They're always talkin' about their 'white hoes' like every white whore on the streets is hustlin' for a shine."

"Don't put 'em all down, man. They don't all talk that jive."

"Don't hand me that crap! These jailhouse spooks are all the same—big-time pimps!"

"That's right," the short muscular con said. "To hear 'em talk, they all got a Cadillac and a coupla big-titted blondes waitin' for 'em out there."

"You're prejudice', man," the con beside him said.

"Y'goddamn right I'm prejudice'. Wanna make somethin' of it?"

"Cool it!" Fletcher shouted. "We're doing this to save our own hides. I just talked to the warden—if the bulls find anyone totaled-out when they get back in here, us guys that started this are getting charged with murder."

Cully glanced about. Except for Coolbreeze Clark, who was standing beside him, there had been perhaps ten Negro cooks and messmen in the crowd. All but three were heading back to Cellhouse Two. Calculating that close to five minutes had passed since the con had brought the word, he stepped in front of Fletcher and shouted, "You guys that don't want in on this, shove off. The rest, c'mon."

At least sixty cons trooped into Cellhouse Four, out the side door, and through the barred enclosure leading to Cellhouse Six.

As Cully swung open the door and started through the cage-like vestibule, he slowed for a moment, struck by the silence; then the shouts and shuffling feet of the cons behind him came rushing into the building. "Murder charge or not, I'm done after this," he said to Fletcher as they trotted past the sergeant's desk and turned through the gateway in the barred ceiling-high partition on the far side of the cellhouse.

A hundred yards away, at the rear of the trash-littered gallery, a jam-packed crowd was gathered. Faces were swinging their way. As they neared, someone yelled, "It's Fletcher!" and a string of bobbing football helmets began rounding the rear of the cellblock.

"Back up!" Cully shouted. "They're goin' around the other side. We'll cut 'em off at the door."

The cons in back, apparently reluctant to lead the charge, kept pushing forward, blocking the gallery.

"Skip it," Fletcher said. "Let's straighten this out first."

The Negroes, about fifteen of them, armed with nail-barbed chair legs, woodcarving chisels, leather-tooling mallets, and twisted lengths of angle iron, evidently wrenched from their bunks, were bunched in the corner of the gallery. Judging from the scowls on their sweaty faces, they seemed more than willing to make a fight of it.

Railhead Simpson, a thick-shouldered two-hundred-pounder, his shaved elongated head slick with sweat, was whacking an angle iron against his thigh. "Let 'em come, Cully," he said. "They don't scare us none. We ain't gonna start it, though. Hear?"

The bystanders grew quiet. Between twenty and twenty-five white cons were still confronting the Negroes. Most were armed: shivs, kitchen utensils, a few baseball bats, a length of lead pipe, a rusty claw hammer. All were young, and most appeared drunk: flushed faces; bloodshot eyes; sagging mouths. A few began sidling around the rear of the cellblock. Only one seemed eager to carry on—a heavyset, pimply-faced Reformatory transfer whom Cully knew slightly, a tough-talking bebopper who had picked up a cheap reputation shortly after his arrival the previous year by stabbing an aggressive middle-aged homosexual. He was standing closest to the Negroes, sneering, gripping a meat cleaver. As the cons behind Cully and Fletcher began backing away, he swung around and shouted, "Who you guys with, us or the shines?"

"You got the meat-ax, baby," Railhead said. "What more help ya need? C'mon, let's me and you get on it."

Cully glimpsed the closed doors on the cells above him, the Negroes watching from the inner shadows. He heard the grumbling behind him and sensed the bystanders' resentment of Railhead's boldness. Stepping to the side, he caught the pimply-faced bebopper's eye and said, "Go ahead, man. Me and Big Red'll see that nobody jumps in." He flung out his arms. "Get back, you guys. Give 'em room."

The sneer on the bebopper's pimply face went limp. He stood there awhile, looking around, twitching a grin. "Why me? I didn't start this rumble. The bastards who started it cut out." The cons around him were easing into the crowd. After several seconds he was standing alone. "I'm not chicken, but —well, hell, man, I haven't got anything against these colored fellas." He was talking to no one in particular. His eyes kept sliding to the meat cleaver hanging from his hand. Finally, blurting "The hell with it," he dropped the cleaver on the floor and backed into the crowd.

Fletcher laughed, shattering the tension, and someone called, "What happened up there?" followed by a round of shouting:

"He settled out of court."

"How chickenshit can ya get?"

"Let's go back and catch the news."

The cons in the rear were moving away. As the crowd in front began breaking up, a light-complexioned Negro with grease-plastered hair stepped from a cell on the second tier, leaned over the rail, and shouted, "This our end! Keep them young studs away from back here, or there be trouble."

Those who heard turned, stopped, and stood there glaring up, muttering.

The muttering spread and grew louder, and the crowd began forming again. Cully glimpsed the scowling faces, the curse-twisted mouths, the Negroes rehuddling in the corner. He was groping for something to say, a witty remark, a tension breaker, when Railhead Simpson came stomping across no-man's-land, aiming his jaw at the con on the tier, shouting, "Shut yer face, girl! Get! Hear?" He reared back, acting as if he were about to throw the boomerang-shaped length of angle iron in his hand, and the con on the tier darted into a cell and rammed the sliding door shut. In a moment the cons were laughing, and the crowd began breaking up, moving on again.

"Let's shove," Fletcher said, catching Cully's eye. "There's nobody looking after the stoolies."

Cully nodded. "C'mon, Railhead, I'll buy you a drink—and if you promise to quit botherin' the white folks, I'll even let you win our next fight."

Railhead was grinning, shuffling toward a cell that looked as if a wrecking ball had demolished the interior. "No thanks, man, I'm stayin' right in my house till this is over."

By the time Cully reached the front of the cellblock, most of the cons from the other cellhouses had left the building.

About fifteen Isolation cons and seven or eight mainliners were gathered around Fletcher, who was standing on the cellhouse sergeant's desk.

"We meet with the press in a few hours," he was saying. "I want the groceries back in the kitchen by then. We've got to start running chow lines." He glanced at Gigolo and Coolbreeze. "Make a round of the tiers in here and spread the word."

"How about that meetin' with the Women's Quarters?" Gigolo said. "Let's take care of the important stuff first—like gettin' laid."

"Later, man. After we meet with the press." He turned to Skinny Burns. "Murry says we should line up some guys with a little meat on their heads to do the talking. You line 'em up, okay?"

"How about Collins?" someone said. "He's got a high I.Q."

"Big deal!" a sneering voice drawled. "With that and ten cents he can get a cup of coffee when he gets out."

Fletcher glanced at Cully. "We've got to keep the fanatics away from the reporters. Where's Kelly?"

"Damned if I know." He hadn't seen Kelly since early morning. At that time the haggard Irishman was still raving about his useless tunnel, threatening to strangle the cons who had alerted the wall guards by using an air hammer. "He's probably sleepin'."

"Good! Let him sleep," Fletcher said, and vaulted from the desk. "Who wants to baby-sit? Coupla you guys hustle over to The Hole and look after the stoolies. The rest of us'll run down those punks and make 'em take the football helmets and baseball bats back where they belong."

Cully had moved to the cellhouse door. As he shouldered it open, a gust of heat rushed past him, arousing the raisinjack, filling him for a moment with a calm, to-hell-with-everything feeling. The fiery sun was pouring through the barred enclosure which caged in the walk, spreading a zebralike pattern over the concrete. The lawn on either side of the enclosure was beginning to show the strain of two waterless days. The air was heavy, motionless. There wasn't a con in sight, only a fat bandaged arm waving from the bars on a second-story hospital window. Cully waved back. Then the peaceful moment ended.

As the gang from inside crowded out on the walk, the side door to Cellhouse Four banged open, and first one shirtless con plunged out, then another. The troopers on the front wall were moving along the gun walk.

"What's going on?" Fletcher yelled.

One of the cons stopped, turned, cupped his hands around his mouth, and shouted, "They're headin' for The Hole. They got gas. They're gonna burn the stoolies!"

"*Holy Christ!*" Fletcher cried and swung around, not the faintest trace of cockiness on his face. "We'll try to cut 'em off on the shopline. Some of you guys go around back with Cully. The rest come with me." He started through the barred enclosure, sprinting past Cellhouse Four, toward the front of the prison.

Cully and six others left the enclosure through the back gate. The troopers on the wall beyond the auditorium readied their rifles as the group rounded the corner of Cellhouse Five and raced along the walk between the cannery and the rear of the block-square building which had once housed the entire prison. The smell of raisinjack, billowing like smoke from the rear kitchen windows, hung as dense as a cloud in the motionless air between the two buildings. The shopline walk was blocked, so was the lawn on either side. A silent gaping crowd, five deep and shoulder to shoulder from the milkhouse to the rear kitchen door, was facing the front of the prison.

As Cully elbowed his way through, his reading connection, a bespectacled mousy-looking check forger, who worked in the library and supplied him with sexy, under-the-shelf novels, called battery chargers, caught him by the arm and cried, "They've got gas in those cans! They're going to cremate the boys in Isolation."

Ahead, halfway down the shopline, there were about ten of them, the sun reflecting from their white plastic helmets. They were carrying bright-red ten-gallon fuel cans, two men to a can, moving along in spurts, gesturing toward the crowded gun walk atop the wall at the front of the prison, where armed troopers and a few men in civilian clothes were watching their approach.

Cully, followed by over half the onlookers, had started down the shopline and was running past the seesawing heads in the wide-open laundry windows when from ahead there came a shout and a swinging around of faces. The can-carrying gang broke into a stumbling trot. The scramble of bobbing helmets and lurching fuel cans was nearing the main sidewalk at the front of the prison when, like a lunging dog on a leash, the commotion came to an abrupt halt. The cans were abandoned, and the white helmets scattered. Fletcher and his group were swinging into the shopline entrance.

He was through; after this was settled, he was going to find a peaceful spot and get drunk, Cully told himself, as he singled out a fleeing helmet. It belonged to the con wearing the catcher's chest protector. He was sprinting along the lawn, the loose-fitting helmet bouncing on the bridge of his nose, a drunken grin on his face. Cully tackled him knee-high. He heard a whoosh, glimpsed the helmet skidding across the walk, and felt his shoulder dig into the con's groin as they landed with a jolt on the ground.

The con groped for a headlock, grabbed for hair; then, croaking, "I give! I give!" he twisted around, hunched up on his knees, and covered his head with his hands, his face to the ground, like an ostrich.

Cully scrambled to his feet and was aiming a size-eleven brogue at the con's jutting rump when he heard someone gasp, "Here! Over here! Give me a hand!"

Skinny Burns, his eyes bulging from a blood-red face, his bony fingers tearing at the arm around his neck, was sprawled on his belly on the ground, the anchor in a three-man bind. A con in a football helmet had a stranglehold on Skinny, and an Isolation con had a stranglehold on the con in the football helmet. Skinny's mouth was still moving, but no sound was coming out.

Cully piled on. He dug through the squirming, grunting heap, found a wrist, and pried the arm from Skinny's neck.

Skinny crawled free as the other two cons rolled across the lawn and into a window well.

"Get the hell outta here," Cully shouted over the scuffle and yammer around him as he boosted Skinny to his feet. "G'wan, get lost."

White plastic football helmets were careering over the lawn, kicked about by trampling feet, as the cons who'd been wearing them scurried like trapped mice to evade the fists and grabbing hands coming at them from every direction. Bugsy, wild-eyed, sweat streaming down his face and corded neck, his heavily veined muscles glistening in the sun, was racing from one huddle of pommelers to another, waiting for an opening, throwing a punch, then darting away. Cully watched now as Bugsy found an unprotected back and landed a vicious kidney punch. The young con dropped as if his legs had been slashed away from under him. Fletcher had a con on the ground, kneeling astride his chest, shouting in his face. A blond crew-cut twenty-year-old was sidling toward the carpentershop door, limping, a hand over his mouth, blood leaking through the fingers, running over his chin, dripping on his chest. The gun walk on the visible portion of the wall in front was jammed with spectators. Two beefy-faced men in short-sleeved white shirts were watching the melee through binoculars, the sun glinting from the lenses.

Standing there, disgusted and feeling guilty, trying to convince himself that the yelling, cursing rumble going on around him would've happened anyway, that someone else would've brewed the juice, Cully made up his mind. He shoved his way through the bystanders and up the crowded ramp to the outside messhall door.

The air inside was stagnant. The putrid stench was sickening—a mingling of garbage, rancid grease, and raisinjack. There was no one in sight. Except for the yammering on the shopline, coming through the half-open windows, the kitchen was quiet.

Cully picked up a five-gallon pot from the pot-storage table alongside the scullery and started toward the steam caldrons. He was almost there when he stopped, stood for a moment, then returned to the table and exchanged the five-gallon pot for a ten-gallon pot. He filled it with raisinjack and shoved it under the pot-storage table, building a camouflage of empty pots around it. Then he walked under the canopy, inside the concrete ridge surrounding the drainage area, and opened the spigots on the three still-frothing caldrons.

He was slouched against a caldron, his chin propped on his folded arms, his eyes on the raisinjack gushing down the drain, when he glimpsed a movement. Murry was moving away from a window in the corner, coming toward him. The window faced the shopline. Apparently the psychologist had been watching the brawl outside.

"Better late than never," Murry said.

Cully ignored him. He kept his eyes on the swirling, gurgling drain. The shouting outside had faded. Two cons started under the archway, paused for a moment, then turned back into the messhall.

Murry moved closer to the caldron and stood there awhile fingering a button on his sport jacket. Finally, he cleared his throat and said, "I'd like to thank you for rescuing us from that mob yesterday."

Without lifting his chin from his arms, Cully said, "Don't thank me, man. If there wasn't a hangin' law in this state, you guys would've been up for grabs."

After a pause, Murry said, "Nevertheless, I'd like to thank you." And after a longer pause, he asked, "How much time are you serving?"

"Ten years. For a two-bit beer joint burglary."

"Are you a repeater?"

"First time."

"You won't serve much time," Murry said over the swoosh and gurgle of gushing raisinjack. "You'll be paroled after serving two years—maybe less."

"You really think so?" Cully gave him a sidelong stare. The man looked like an overgrown mama's boy. Probably been going to school all his life. He'd read all the books on the subject, and now, after sitting on his big can in a cubbyhole office above the Control Room for a month, he was an expert, an old hand at the game. He had the system down pat. "Look, man, I've been in this zoo over four years already, and after gettin' roped in on this screwball deal, I'll probably be here four more. And don't hand me that song and dance about keepin' my nose clean. I can't." He caught a movement at the corner of the coalroom: a black-haired head, quickly withdrawn, a shadow darting away. He moved around the caldron to get a better look, but Murry was standing in his way, talking.

"As long as the violence is kept under control," he was saying, "the men involved in this demonstration won't be punished. I'm sure of it."

"Big break! If I got turned loose today, I'd still figure I got a royal screwin'." He heard a gravelly voice and glanced over his shoulder.

Punchy Philips, his cauliflower face set in a drunken grin, was coming under the archway.

"Who's upstairs with the hostages?" Cully asked and crossed the drainage area, sloshing through the flowing raisinjack.

The grin on Punchy's face twisted into a frown. "Don't start givin' orders, kiddo. I'm not gettin' paid to—"

There was a thud overhead, a trampling of feet. Cully heard a hoarse cry, then another. He lurched on the slippery floor, caught his balance, then broke for the rear of the kitchen.

CHAPTER **13**

CULLY paused for a moment in the storeroom doorway. Behind him, Punchy was stomping across the steward's office, panting, cursing. Farther on, Murry was still clumping up the stairs, calling, "Reason with them! Try to reason with them!"

For the moment he stood there, it was as if the motionless figures in the room beyond were posing in front of a camera. Sergeant Grossman was on his hands and knees, as though trying to crawl through the wall, his mouth sagging to one side, his face the color of a dingy bed sheet. Deputy Warden Fisk and Sergeant Gallaway were standing straddle-legged on each side of him, shielding him. Both were clutching a cot-size mattress, chest-high, ready to lunge. The faces of Parole Officer Campbell, Dirtyneck Dugan, and Hicks, the Isolation guard, hung like waxwork over Peek-a-boo Perkins, who was sprawled on a scattered heap of cardboard cases, gaping, his doughy face oozing sweat, his bloodshot eyes fixed with unblinking intensity on the sinewy bony-faced Indian crouched to the right of the door, the ten-inch blade of a wickedly honed boning knife jutting from his fist.

"Drop it!" Cully shouted just as Punchy rammed him from behind, and the faces in the room began jumping about, changing expressions, making sounds. He snatched up a quart can of tomatoes and acted as if he were about to throw it. "Drop it, Joe! You can't get us all."

The Indian was bouncing on his toes, still in a crouch, his raving eyes leaping from Cully, to Grossman, to the door, back to Grossman. "He's the one I want. He's got it coming. He used a hose on me once." The Indian's voice was a singsong shrill. "I was handcuffed to the bars. He beat me with a hose."

"I was followin' orders, boy," Grossman croaked. "In the name of God, I was followin' orders!" He let out a hoarse scream and flung himself facedown behind Fisk's legs as the Indian lunged and made a swipe with the knife, nearly slashing Fisk's thrust-out mattress in half.

Punchy shouted, "Grab the crazy bastard!" and hurled a quart can across the room, just missing Surefoot's head as the Indian darted back, crouched, his eyes jumping about again.

Cully had moved closer. He was less than ten feet from Surefoot now, still holding the can as if he were about to throw it. Cagelike shadows, cast by the sun pouring in through the barred windows, slanted across the littered storeroom floor and up the cracked walls. He glimpsed the deputy warden inching through the cage of shadows, holding the slashed mattress like a shield, the cotton stuffing bulging out. He glimpsed Punchy picking up a can, glimpsed the keen-edged boning knife in Surefoot's hand, and suddenly his limbs felt weak, clumsy. He remembered a knifing he'd seen in the yard the summer before and caught a fleeting mental picture of a con lying on the concrete basketball court, his stomach laid open, the muscles slashed from side to side, hardly any blood, just laid open like a slab of meat and the guts showing. He forced his eyes away from the wicked-looking knife.

"Try to reason with him, Briston," Murry called. He was in the steward's office, a few feet beyond the storeroom door, stretching his neck like a woodpecker.

"C'mon, Joe, for crissake, forget it," Cully said. "You're not the only one in on this."

"Mind your own business! You're all bull lovers! Suck-holes! Bigmouths!" He was screaming. "You punched me once, Briston. You'll never do it again!" He sprang through the shadow-barred sunlight.

Cully threw the can. It nicked the Indian's shoulder and crashed against the wall. He leaped to the side, saw the length of razor-sharp steel go skimming past his chest and whirled just as a quart can of tomatoes caromed off the Indian's back.

"Got him!" Punchy yelled as Surefoot's head snapped back. His skinny arms flew up. The knife went skidding across the floor. The Indian was still reeling, groping, trying to focus his eyes, when Cully clubbed him along the jaw. Surefoot spun, hung for a moment, and Cully clubbed him again, harder. The Indian pitched headlong to the floor and sprawled facedown in the sunlight, under the slanting shadows cast by the bars.

Grossman was the first to break the silence. "I can't stand any more," he croaked. "In the name of God, take me to the front gate."

No one so much as glanced at him.

Cully was staring down at Surefoot's small bony hands lying limp on the floor beside his head. The Indian stirred, moaned, flexed his legs. The fingers on his right hand curled, uncurled, curled again, and Cully slid his foot closer, trying to muster up the willpower to lift his leg, to stamp down, to smash and grind his heel into the knife-hungry hand. He turned away, disgusted, calling himself a sucker, a gutless square.

"Let's tie the nut up," Punchy said. "Coupla you guys gimme your belts, and I'll show ya how I ustta hog-tie them supermarket managers."

By the time Punchy had Surefoot's ankles bound and his wrists lashed to the small of his back, the Indian was fully conscious. One side of his forehead was skinned and flecked with blood, and the edge of the tomato can had left a purplish welt below one shoulder blade.

He lay there quiet and motionless. He was stretched flat on his chest and stomach, his face propped upright on his chin, his black hate-glazed eyes stalking the movements around him.

"Now what?" Punchy said, lumbering to his feet. "We gonna let him lay here till it's over?"

Cully glanced at Surefoot, then looked at Fisk. "You got any ideas?"

The deputy warden was sitting slumped over on a case of canned goods, sweat dripping from his chin, his soiled white shirt plastered to his back. "Why d'you suppose this man has been kept in Isolation for the past seven years? If I thought there was a chance of him getting along in General Population, don't you suppose I would've released him?"

"In other words you figure we should throw him back in The Hole where he belongs?"

"Not where he *belongs*, I didn't say that. No one belongs in a smelly steel box without ventilation or plumbing."

"Oh, yeah? I bet it really spoils your day when you hav'ta put some poor guy in there," Cully said and instantly regretted having said it. In the month since Fisk had taken over behind the walls, the number of disciplinary cases sent to Isolation had been cut at least in half.

Fisk was smiling. "You're in the same position now as I was, Briston. You have a man here who is disrupting the orderly running of whatever it is you men are running. You don't seem to have much choice—or at least we don't have much choice in a case like this. We can either release the man with a reprimand or isolate him." He glanced down at the hateful eyes glaring up at him. "I doubt if a reprimand would have much effect in this particular case, and it would seem to me that even a smelly steel box would be more comfortable than lying trussed up on the floor."

"He should be isolated and kept under guard," Murry said with authoritative finality. He had moved into the sun-streaked storeroom and was leaning against a stanchion, frowning, one foot cocked behind the other. Unlike the other seven hostages, whose bloodshot eyes showed the effects of sleeplessness and anxiety, Murry gave the appearance of a man who had enjoyed a restful night's sleep.

Cully gave him a surly look. Perhaps it was the mama's boy face or the schoolteacher's voice or maybe the take-charge attitude, but whatever it was, the man irritated him. "Did you work in some other prison before you came here?" he asked.

"No," Murry said. "Why?"

"How old are you?"

"How old am I?"

"Yeah."

"I don't understand. What diff— I'm twenty-nine."

"Where'd you work before you came here?"

Murry kept glancing at Fisk, smiling, as though wanting the deputy warden to know that he wasn't taking the questioning seriously. "I was with the state welfare department."

"Doin' what?"

"Counseling."

"Convicts?"

"No. As a matter of fact, I was counseling unwed mothers."

"Well, we don't have that problem in here, so why don't you forget about counselin' and get ready for your next television appearance." He turned away. "C'mon, Punchy, grab an end. We'll take ol' Joe back home."

"Before you go—" Fisk said, and waited until Cully was looking his way before flicking his eyes at Grossman, who was stretched out on his back, gasping, clenching and unclenching his hands. "Why don't you release him?"

Cully walked to where Grossman was lying on a lumpy cotsize mattress and looked down at the man. A strip of sunlight slanted across his face, highlighting a patch of grizzly whiskers, his veiny nose, one red-rimmed eye, his withered mouth. He looked strange, pathetic. The habitually harsh expression of his face had shrunken into a prunelike network of furrows.

"Please, boy," he whispered hoarsely. "In the name of God, turn me loose."

Sergeant Gallaway was sitting on a case a few feet away, his elbows on his knees, his head in his hands, staring at the floor. Across the room, the soiled bandage on his partially shaved head hanging raggedly over one ear, Dirtyneck Dugan was pacing back and forth. Surefoot hadn't moved. He lay flat on his chest, his chin on the floor, his piercing black eyes fixed on the boning knife under a radiator ten feet away.

Grossman groaned, rolled on his side, clutched Cully's ankle. "Please, boy! I'll put in a good word for you. I'll see that—"

"Aw, for crissake, quit whinin'." He jerked his leg away, disgusted by the feel of the liver-splotched hand. "Why you? Why the hell should *you* get turned loose? You don't hear Gallaway whinin' about his ulcers. And what about Dugan? He's got a gash in his head. Never even asked for an aspirin. Give me one reason why you should get turned loose and not the others.

Name one con in here you ever treated like a human bein'. Name just one, and I'll get him up here. If he puts in a good word for you, I'll personally take you to the front gate."

Grossman groaned, went limp, dragged a hand over his face. "My heart, boy. My heart can't take much more."

"You'll hav'ta come up with somethin' better than that."

"I'm an old man."

"How old?"

"Almost fifty-six, boy."

"Hell, you're still a kid. You'll be makin' life miserable for guys in here for another twenty years. That's if you're lucky enough to be alive when the troopers get in here." He remembered a rumor he'd often heard, the rumor that Grossman was the state's hangman, substantiated by a con from the front accounting office, who claimed that Grossman always received a four-hundred-dollar check for special duty at the end of each year. There had been only two hangings in the past four years, both baby rapers, and he would've put the rope around their necks himself; but the thought of Grossman's doing it made the act sadistic. "How long have you been knockin' down that extra four hundred a year?" he asked, and from the sudden expression of panic on the man's face he knew the rumor was a fact.

"It's part of my job. Somebody has to do it. Somebody has to punish them."

"And what about you? You're a sadistic old creep. You've been gettin' your kicks in here for over thirty years. What if there's no God? Who's gonna punish you? Not the law." He glanced to the side, grinning. Fisk met the grin with a cold stare, shrinking it. The other hostages, including Murry, were examining their hands, the floor, the cracks in the walls. A shout drifted in from outside. He could hear voices in the kitchen below. He turned back to Grossman. "No, you old bastard, if you're ever gonna pay for all the misery you've handed out, we're the ones who'll hav'ta see that you do. And we'll probably never get another chance."

"That's right," Punchy said. "I'd be out on parole right now if it wasn't for him."

Grossman moaned, clutched his forehead, and Fisk said, "Why don't you give him a break?"

Cully turned, grinning again. "You know, this is the first time in my life I've ever been The Man. It's always been the other way around. Hell, you guys get to play God every day. I'll probably never get another chance. Anyway, I'll hav'ta give it some deep thought—at least for a coupla days. You know, like the judges and parole board members do. Why, hell, you can't expect—"

There was a rush of voices, the scuff of feet, and Fletcher, followed by several Isolation cons, came clumping into the storeroom.

He moved beside Murry. "What's going on?" He glanced at Surefoot, who had squirmed to his knees, his eyes glaring at the boning knife under the radiator, his fingers clawing at the belt which bound his hands behind his back.

"He tried to get us hung," Cully said.

"Whose side are you on?" Surefoot yelled, and began crawling on his knees toward Fletcher. "Get these belts off me. Grossman's got it coming. Everybody's always talking how they'd kill him if they had the chance. Now Briston's protecting him. He's going to get it, too!" He lurched, lost his balance, and fell on his side. "Get these belts off me! Grossman's got it coming! I've got a right to cut his throat!" He was screaming.

Fletcher had been edging away from the Indian, glancing about, from Fisk, to Murry, to Cully. "Why'd you tie him up?"

"We're takin' him to The Hole."

"Christ, man, we can't turn on our own kind."

"*Our own kind?* He might be your kind, but he's not my kind. The guy's a psycho."

"He's still a solid con. He's not a stoolie."

"Go ahead, untie him. If you do, I'll stomp his hands to a pulp right here. The bug's not plantin' a blade in my back."

"Look, man—" Fletcher drawled.

The familiar smirk was forming on his face when Murry said, "He's right, Alan. The man should be isolated."

Fletcher flushed, obviously embarrassed by the psychologist's first-name familiarity. He got the flush under control and began frowning and biting his lips, thoughtfully, pretentiously, as though wanting the onlookers to know that the decision was still his to approve or veto. Finally, he said, "Don't put him on the same side as the stoolies. And see that he gets smokes and magazines—and a chess set if he wants one."

He was handing Cully the padlock key when Surefoot, snarling like a snapping dog, made an openmouthed lunge at Cully's leg. The Indian had snagged a wad of raisinjack-soaked dungaree and was snapping at flesh when Cully caught his throat and pressed his head to the floor. "I'm warnin' you, Joe! Try to bite me again and I'll punch your teeth out." He released his grip. The Indian just glared at him.

Punchy grabbed the belt binding Surefoot's ankles, and Cully dug his hands under his armpits. As they started from the storeroom, Cully heard a guttural sigh and glimpsed a fluttering hand. Grossman, still sprawled on his back, was making the sign of the cross.

Downstairs, there was a huddle of shirtless cons in front of the coalroom. The radio was on full blast. ". . . intoxicated and wearing football helmets," the familiar voice of the on-the-spot reporter was saying. "The fighting was observed from the walls. According to eyewitnesses, several men were carried from the scene. Whether unconscious or dead, we do not know. As yet no word has come from inside. However, from the sudden quietness behind the walls, it appears that the leaders of the rebellion are back in control. Shortly now, elected representatives of the inmate body will meet with members of the press inside the prison, at which time—"

"Gangway!" Punchy shouted, and the cons in front of the radio looked around, just stood there gawking for several seconds, then spread, and formed a line. No one spoke as Surefoot was carried past.

Although the smell of raisinjack still saturated the sultry air, the stench of rancid grease and garbage had faded to an occasional whiff. Cooks and messmen in white pants and T-shirts were bustling about. A few were hosing down the area around the steam caldrons. Canned goods, cardboard boxes, and food-filled pillowcases were heaped along the wall. Cons from General Population were coming through the archway, carrying more.

Boosting Surefoot higher, his hands wedged under the Indian's sweaty armpits, Cully skate-walked over the slippery floor, aware of a sudden slowing of motion, swinging faces, craning necks. He imagined himself being thought of as a self-appointed cop, and not wanting to be questioned, he kept his eyes on the back of Punchy's head. What could he say? They'd never understand that *somebody* had to do it. *Somebody* had to be a cop. Christ, how did he ever get himself in this deep? As he passed the pot-storage table, he noticed that the pots hadn't been moved. His ten-gallon stash was still there.

They were carrying Surefoot past the steam table at the front of the messhall when Kelly came through the door. He stopped, stared for a moment, then backed out the door, and fell in beside Cully as they started diagonally across the hall-like vacancy toward the rear door to Isolation.

"Puttin' him in The Hole?" he asked.

Cully nodded.

"Kinda chickenshit, ain't it?"

"Not as chickenshit as bustin' his hands."

"Doesn't seem right to me. You're playin' it *their* way. You know, lockin' a guy up."

"Got any suggestions?"

"Why don't you untie his legs? Let him walk."

"Would you walk to The Hole for another con?"

As they neared the door to Isolation, Kelly stepped aside, then caught up to Cully inside. "All that diggin' and crawlin' last night damn near killed me. Every bone and muscle in my body aches. If it wasn't for that meetin' with the press, I'd check into the hospital and lay in a tub of hot water till this is over."

Cully tightened his grip. His shoulders burned, and his arms were going numb. "Skinny Burns is roundin' up some guys to do the talkin'," he said, remembering that Fletcher had hoped to keep Kelly away from the reporters.

"Not for me, kid. I'll do my own talkin'. And I got plenty to say."

They were moving along the littered floor on the Segregation side. Overhead, from the three top tiers occupied by the cons who had been locked up for protection, an undertone of voices accompanied the scuff of their feet. They rounded the front of the cellblock, maneuvered through the narrow gateway in the heavy mesh-wire partition on the Isolation side, and set Surefoot on the floor in front of the third cage. He rolled on his side, glaring.

Sunlight, pouring through the jagged holes in the paint-blackened windowpanes, splashed against the cage doors, and cast an unfamiliar brightness over the sagging pile of steel. Chunks of glass, puddles of limewater, trampled buckets and black padlocks littered the floor.

All the padlocks were snapped shut and battered as though by a sledgehammer. Cully picked one up and inserted the flat square-toothed key Fletcher had given him. The padlock opened. He found an untrampled bucket which still contained an inch or two of lime solution, clapped on a rust-corroded lid, and set it inside the cage. Then he helped Punchy remove the belts from Surefoot's wrists and ankles.

Surefoot was stepping into the cage, seemingly resigned, when he whirled. Cully ducked the bony fist, but not the spray of saliva. Wiping a forearm over his face, he kicked the cage door shut and clamped on the padlock. The Indian was raving.

"You should've killed me! I'll get you now if it's the last thing I do. You and Andy Gump. You're both as good as dead!" He pressed his face against the steel-latticed door and spat again.

"Should've never locked him up," Kelly said as they moved into the dressing-in area in front of the cellblock. "Should've tried to talk to him."

"How'n the hell ya gonna talk to a stir bug like that?" Punchy said. "Listen to him. He's a ravin' lunatic."

Cully flapped a hand. "He's gone, man. They'll probably transfer him to the state hospital when this is over." He glanced at Kelly. "You wouldn't be thinkin' of bustin' him outta that cage?"

"What makes you say that?"

"Oh, I don't know. You've known him a long time and—

Hell, you were gonna cut him in on the tunnel last night, weren't you?"

"Why not? Why should I care who he kills out there? I'm not a citizen. Don't even belong to the human race anymore. Been in and out of this snake pit for twenty-two years. Came through that front gate when I was twenty years old." His haggard face, normally sallow, was angry-red and streaming sweat. He swung an arm in the direction of the Isolation cages. "The way I look at it, the state made that Indian like he is. If the people out there don't give a damn about how their jailhouse is run, they deserve to get their throats cut. Joe came in here ten years ago —a nineteen-year-old kid with a five-year rap for stealin' a car. He got fifteen more for cuttin' Becker—plus he got his brains beat soft. Since then he's spent seven years in a stinkin' cage, treated worse than a mangy dog. And you know what? He'll spend ten more years in a stinkin' cage. Then he'll get committed to the state hospital—a worse snake pit—and he'll spend the rest of his life in and out of a straitjacket. I feel sorry for the kid. So why shouldn't I cut him in on a tunnel?"

"Forget it," Cully said and looped an arm around his neck. "You're just a bitter ol' bastard. And doin' all that diggin' last night didn't help none."

Kelly grinned. "Hey, I forgot to tell you, kid. I donated the tunnel to Gigolo and Bugsy Matthews. There's about ten of 'em over there now, burrowin' for the Women's Quarters. When I left 'em awhile ago, they were diggin' like crazy men—less than forty feet from a buildin' full of females." He winked and dug an elbow into Cully's ribs. "Might even go for a little myself. How about you, kid?"

CHAPTER **14**

BY four o'clock in the afternoon the mercury in the big thermometer outside the Control Room had crept five points past the one hundred mark. Under the unyielding glare of a cloudless sky, the troopers lolled along the gun walks, limp and listless, looking down on a prison described by the on-the-spot radio reporter as a "slumbering volcano."

Smoke curled from the towering powerhouse chimney, spread and hung for a while, then drifted away in wisps. The aroma of fresh bread had overpowered the smell of raisinjack on the shopline, and messmen were hurrying from the kitchen, to the milk house, to the butchershop in the basement below the laundry. An hour earlier, on the strength of a rumor carried from cellhouse to cellhouse, more than six hundred cons had ventured from their cells and straggled to the messhall, where they were given a boloney sandwich, a cup of coffee, and the promise of a meal later in the day. The cooks, bakers, and firemen had gone back to work.

In the thirty-one hours since Sergeant Grossman had negligently unlocked the door to Isolation, the arrangement of the population had been turned topsy-turvy. More than half the seventeen hundred cons behind the walls had packed their belongings and moved at least once. Some had exchanged cells several times. Except for Joe Surefoot, a permanent Isolation case, and Duke Trusdale, a frequent loser in Disciplinary Court, as detested by the guards as he was by his fellow convicts, the other sixty-five cons now locked in The Hole were of the type called model inmates by the officials, the men who were given the most trusted job assignments—clerks, runners, cellhouse orderlies. Now, under convict rule, they weren't even being fed. Their cells and personal property had been confiscated by the cons who had broken out of Isolation the morning before, most of whom had never been in General Population long enough to accumulate personal property.

The loudmouths were sleeping it off. After the brawl on the shopline, four had been carried to the hospital. There was still some raisinjack drinking going on, but the drunks who had been farsighted enough to hoard a few jugs were also cagey enough to stay out of sight. Not so the queens. The queens were going huckly-buck. A dumpy hairy-chested queen, called Mama Bear, had moved into Cellhouse Five, the prison's skid row, and had already earned herself a new nickname: Iron Jaws. A few stir bugs were still strolling about in top hats, tails, and striped sport coats—costumes used in the annual con show—and Smith, 19846, was still sitting on his rope-bound cardboard box twenty feet from the Administration Building door, demanding to see a lawyer; but otherwise the prison was outwardly quiet.

In the northwest corner, inside the windowless auditorium, Gigolo and his handpicked crew of hardnoses were digging toward the Women's Quarters. Inside the cellhouses, hundreds of radios were picking up the four o'clock newscast. And at the front of the prison, in the largest office above the Control Room, the meeting with the press was about to get under way.

There were at least thirty men in the room: three newsmen, Deputy Warden Fisk, psychologist Murry, and the rest convicts. Most of the cons were crammed shoulder to shoulder along the walls—some standing; some squatting; others sitting on chairs, benches, filing-cabinet drawers, overturned wastepaper baskets. The reporters had been seated in leather-cushioned swivel chairs behind two desks, which had been shoved together in the center of the room to form a conference table. Fisk and Murry were sitting at each end. Fletcher, Skinny Burns, and a tall, beady-eyed con in his early thirties, called Walkie-Talkie, the prison's most virulent social critic, were standing in front of the table. The air was smothered under a suffocating canopy of cigarette smoke, and what little there was left to breathe reeked of sweat and the putrid odor of sour raisinjack.

"Hold it down, you guys," Fletcher shouted over the jabbering along the walls. "How'n the hell d'you expect 'em to print our gripes if they can't hear 'em?"

Cully was sitting next to Kelly on a bench beside the door. He had promised to keep an eye on the high-strung Irishman, who had already developed a murderous aversion to one of the reporters, a swarthy, once-muscular man around forty who introduced himself as Sam Lagato. He was from one of the national syndicates. Grinning and winking, he had swaggered into the room saying, "I would've brought in some broads, but I couldn't get enough to go around." He needed a shave and wore a rumpled white shirt, rolled up to the elbows and unbuttoned at the chest. His thick body was as hairy as a gorilla's, and his teeth were laden with gold. The hair on his head was thin, pitch black, and kinky.

The other reporters, both neatly dressed in sport shirts, one representing a wire service and the other picked by his competitors to represent the independent newspapers in the state, were quiet and obviously uncomfortable. According to the newsmen, the warden had limited the number of reporters to three. "He thinks you boys may be wanting more hostages," Lagato had said with a wink and scoffing laugh.

The room was still noisy. Walkie-Talkie and Skinny Burns were talking to the wire-service reporter. Fletcher was talking to Lagato.

"Lookit the phony bastard!" Kelly said, digging an elbow into Cully's ribs.

Lagato was sprawled in his chair, face tilted upward, hands clasped behind his head. His wrists were hairy and abnormally thick. A wristwatch was buried under the hair. He laughed now, flashing a mouthful of gold bridgework, as the jabbering subsided and Walkie-Talkie's high-pitched voice rose up like a siren. He was waving a sheaf of paper.

"Here's the proof!" Walkie-Talkie cried. "These are receipts from the butchershop, signed by the steward. Read 'em, and you'll see that we get the bones and scraps, and the screws get the choice cuts." He slapped a receipt on the table. "Take this one for instance. June sixteenth—forty pounds of T-bone steaks for the officer's dining room, one hundred and eighty pounds of utility meat for the mainline. We're the mainline. D'you know what utility meat is? Bones and scraps. The scraps make stew, and the bones make the juice they mix with flour and call gravy. That's the way we get our meat."

Lagato reached for the receipts. "What's your name, Slim?"

Kelly was off the bench before Cully could grab him. "Don't be askin' names, Mac. Makes no goddamn difference who says what. Just stick to facts."

The wire-service man and the thin middle-aged reporter who was representing the independents glanced at the grumbling cons along the walls as though they were wishing they had never entered the prison. Lagato tried to bluff it out. Tilting farther back in his chair, his hands still clasped behind his head, he winked at Kelly. "Relax, pal. I'm only trying to be friendly."

Kelly banged his fist on the table, and Lagato sat straight up, no longer grinning. "Nobody in this room wants their name in the paper. So stick to facts." He kept glaring at Lagato as Cully steered him back to the bench.

When the grumbling along the walls died down, Lagato shrugged and said, "Let's have the facts then. Your main beef is the food, right?"

"Definitely not!" Skinny said. "Compared to the other things wrong with this prison, the food is good." He was reaching for a packet of paper in his back pocket when Walkie-Talkie took over.

"The taxpayers are getting screwed!" he cried in the familiar soapbox twang he used in the prison yard to deliver his frequent blasts against the department of corrections. "This is no penitentiary. This is the finest criminal-manufacturing plant in the country. Over eighty percent of the cons in this place are sitting idle. Even those who have some sense when they get here are mental basketcases by the time they leave." His Adam's apple was working like a Yo-Yo. His beady eyes had taken on a fanatical glitter. He was whacking the butchershop receipts on the edge of the table. "It's hard enough for an above-average ex-con to make it in this country, but the ones who leave *this* place are *really* bucking the odds. About all they're able to do is sit in a cage and wait for the chow bell to ring. And who's fault is it? It's the department of corrections' fault! They sit on their asses in the state capitol and talk that crap about rehabilitation—and you guys print it. The big story last month was the new diagnostic and treatment department here. The papers called it a 'giant stride forward.' Well, there it is!" He shook the fistful of receipts at Murry. "There it sits! Our new diagnostic and treatment department. There's your 'giant stride forward.' Since he moved into that mop closet across the hall a month ago, he's been psychoanalyzing fairies. If that's what a diagnostic and treatment department is—" His Adam's apple kept bobbing up and down, but his high-pitched voice was buried under a roomful of laughter.

Murry's face was fiery red. He was leaning toward Lagato, talking a mile a minute. At the opposite end of the table, Fisk was staring at the floor, expressionless, shaking his head.

"It's the damn truth!" someone cried. "Y'gotta be a fruiter."

"Better believe it," said a dark greasy-haired con in sunglasses. "If you're not a rootin'-tooter, you can't get in to see him."

Murry turned and said something to Fletcher. Skinny Burns was waving several sheets of paper, calling for order. The cons along the walls were shouting, "Hold it down! Dummy up!" Walkie-Talkie hadn't even paused for air. He was leaning over the table, haranguing the wire-service man, the youngest of the three reporters, a crew-cut blond with a long hook-nosed face. The man kept nodding, grimacing, eyeing the door.

Shoving past Skinny Burns, Fletcher caught one of Walkie-Talkie's flapping arms and jerked him around. When their voices rose above the diminishing noise in the room, Fletcher was saying, "—bust in the mouth. You don't even know what you're talking about, so lay off. G'wan, sit down."

"I know more about what's going on in this joint than you do. You're in Lockup all the time."

"I said sit down."

"I've been collecting evidence for years. I've got enough to get the whole department of corrections fired."

"Goddammit, man, show some class!" Fletcher gave him a shove. "G'wan, sit down."

"Let him talk," someone said, and the heckling and grumbling broke out again, accompanied by the usual shouts of "Hold it down! Dummy up!"

Cully glimpsed a movement beside him and grabbed Kelly's arm. "Stay out of it, man. Those reporters must think we're all psycho."

Kelly sat down. "Fletcher's turnin' into a fourteen-carat phony," he said. "He's lettin' that headshrinker make a fool of him."

The noise was dying down. Walkie-Talkie had stomped from the room, slinging a shower of butchershop receipts over his shoulder on his way out.

"The warden and commissioner of corrections have a copy of this petition," Skinny was saying, "but we want the main points published so that the public knows what we're asking for."

"By *we*," Lagato said, "who do you mean? The men in this room?"

"He means every swingin' dick in this joint, Mac," Kelly cut in. He tried to get up, but Cully had a hand clamped on his shoulder.

Lagato was sitting about ten feet away. He turned with a weary smile. "Look, friend," he said, "I'm not against you guys. I hope you get everything you're asking for. But I work for a news syndicate, and my job is to ask questions." He turned back to Skinny.

"For crissake, Kelly, get off the man's back," Cully said in an undertone. "We're tryin' to get a decent write-up from these guys."

The air in the sweltering room was entangled in slow-drifting wisps of smoke. A few cons were smoking the smelly two-for-a-nickel cigars sold through the commissary. The jabber sank to a murmur, and Cully listened absently as Skinny began

Joe's shrunken mouth sprang open. "Y'damn right! It's already ruined my looks. When I came in this joint—"

He was cut off by a shirtless cigar-smoking con in the corner of the room, who yelled, "Get that nut outta there! There's more important things to talk about than false teeth."

As Joe slapped on his cap and headed back to the overturned wastepaper basket he'd been sitting on, Gordie Hayes, a cocky young guard hater who was serving a twenty-year sentence for armed robbery, stepped in front of the table.

Hayes operated one of the rickety old washing machines in the laundry. Everyone in the laundry crew, with the exception of the guard and the nearly senile foreman, knew that once a week for more than two years he'd been washing the warden's bedding and table linen, along with the filthy socks and underwear which came in from Cellhouse Five, the prison's skid row. The guards were entitled to free laundry service, but when one was naïve enough to send in a bundle, Hayes would give it his personal attention. He'd steal the socks, starch the underwear, slit the shirt collars, and run the pants pockets through the sewing machine several times, usually with a note inside, saying, "Get back on the freight train you came in on, tramp!" He was also carrying on a note-passing affair with a female junkie in the Women's Quarters. The laundry supplied the Women's Quarters with bleach, and unbeknown to the guard who made the pickup and delivery, the notes were sent back and forth inside the cap on a bleach jug. About the only honest energy he expended on the job went into his own laundry. His dungarees were never without a razor-sharp crease, and his denim shirts were always starched and pressed military-style, three creases down the back. He was dressed in this fashion now and wore a white silk handkerchief neatly folded in the breast pocket of his shirt.

"I keep readin' in the papers and magazines," he said, "about the equal justice in this country. You know, how everyone is treated equal in court. Well, in case you guys don't know it, that's a lotta bullshit. There were two other guys involved in this robbery I'm in here for. One was a three-time loser. He turned state's evidence, and the D.A. turned him loose. The other one got ten years, but he had some juice. His uncle owns one of the biggest hotels in this state. He was paroled after eighteen months. I got twenty years. I've been here over three years already, and I don't get to see the parole board for another two. Well, what I'm gettin' at is this. What if you three guys were livin' next door to each other outside—you know, same kinda houses and everything—and one of you was payin' a thousand dollars a year taxes and one was payin' a hundred and the other one was payin' nothin'?" His eyes settled on Lagato. "Say you were the one payin' a thousand. What would you do about it?"

Lagato grinned. "I suppose I'd write to the tax commissioner."

"Yeah, well, I wrote to the judge who sentenced me, and some jerk out front sent the letter back because the judge ain't on my approved correspondence list. But that's beside the point. The judge wouldn't've done nothin' anyway. The point is this —there's plenty guys in this joint in the same boat I'm in, and we want our cases reviewed."

"That's telling 'em, Gordie," someone said.

"Reviewed by who?" Lagato asked.

"By the parole board."

"That's a mighty big order, isn't it? How is the parole board going to investigate deals that were made in court?"

"The board doesn't hav'ta investigate. The board *knows* what's goin' on in those courts out there. And they better do somethin' about it. The way I look at it is this—the state's screwin' me, and I'm out to screw the state and anyone who does its dirty work every chance I get. That's all I got to say."

As he swaggered away from the table, the cons along the walls began shouting to be heard:

"Be sure to print that about D.A.'s makin' deals with stool pigeons."

"Y'damn right! The thieves are on the streets and the suckers are in here."

"We want that narrow-minded preacher booted off the parole board."

"Yeah, let him do his preachin' in church."

"Knock it off!" Fletcher shouted. "If you got something to say, get up here."

Cully was peering through the smoke drifts above the bobbing heads in front of the windows across the room. The troopers on the wall beyond had bunched up and were craning their necks to see inside the room, their rifles trained on the windows. As the noise subsided, he turned his attention back to the table where Big Al, a Benny-ravaged con in his late twenties, was talking to Lagato. He was taller than Fletcher, perhaps six six, with stooped shoulders, lopsided hips, and a voice like a panhandler's whine. His shirt was frayed and buttonless, and a pair of faded dungarees hung from his hips like an empty sack. Cully had known him for three, four years, only as Big Al, a shifty work-shy wheeler and dealer, who could sniff out a piece of amphetamine-soaked cotton with the unswerving exactness of a bloodhound. His ace in the hole was a partial plate with two gold-crowned teeth—an eyetooth and a molar. Every Benny pusher in the prison had at one time or another held Big Al's partial plate for security. The plate was loose, and he could flip it in and out of his mouth with his tongue. Invariably, on coming up to a huddle of cons thumbing through a girly magazine in the yard, he'd flip out the partial, letting the eyetooth hang over his lip, and say, "Man, I'd give my eyetooth for some of that!" He grinned now, and Cully noticed that he wasn't wearing the partial.

"Like it said in the petition," he was saying, "a guy's worse off when he gets outta here than he is when he comes in. I been tryin' to learn a trade for years, but they ain't teachin' nothin' in here. Since the license-plate factory burned down last year, a guy who hasn't got some money comin' in from the streets hasta sell his soul for a pack of butts. And it's just as bad on parole. The goddamn parole system—"

Kelly sprang from the bench before Cully could restrain him. The wire-service reporter, who was hunched over taking notes, dropped his pencil and threw up a hand as the Irishman's fist banged down on the table.

"You heard what he said!" Kelly cried. "It's the goddamn parole system! Five times I been out on parole, and every time

I get out there, I gotta put up with some snooty, know-it-all college kid tellin' me how to live." He began mimicking in falsetto: "You're not to live with a woman, Mr. Kelly. You've been frequentin' barrooms, Mr. Kelly. You haven't been givin' me an itemized list of your spendin's, Mr. Kelly." His voice shifted to a snarl. "You've been drivin' a car. You've been seen with ex-inmates. You've been doin' this. You've been doin' that. If you don't behave, I'll send you back!" He paused, breathless, glaring around the room. "I don't know anybody but ex-cons out there. How'm I gonna meet people? I'm not suppos'ta drink, drive, or screw. What else is there?"

"What you're saying," Lagato said, "is that the parole regulations are too strict."

"What I'm sayin', Mac, is that this state's had its claws in me for twenty-two years. I came to this state in the Army. I was waitin' to get shipped overseas when I got busted on a drunken stickup. Since then I been on parole five times, picked up three more ten-year sentences for prowlin' some joint for money to get outta this goddamn state, and I still haven't made it back to Iowa."

"Is that your home state?" Lagato asked.

"That's right, Mac."

"Why won't the authorities parole you to Iowa?"

"I got nobody to sponsor me back there. My people are dead."

"I don't quite understand," the wire-service reporter said. "What exactly is your criticism of the parole system?"

"Christ Almighty, man, do I hav'ta spell it out? It's not just parole, it's the *whole goddamn system!* Once a man gets a number on his back, he can't shake it off. There's five, six hundred guys my age and older in here that've been in and out all their lives. Y'think they like livin' in a stinkin' cage? Take the number off a guy's back when he serves his time, and maybe some of us would make it out there. Why keep a man branded the rest of his life? If he breaks the law again, he'll get nailed. There's a cop on every street corner."

Hair was hanging in his eyes. Sweat was streaming down his haggard face. He caught his breath, hitched at his low-hanging pants, then went snarling into the tirade he delivered almost daily from his cage in Isolation: "The four-legged animals got it made. If us convicts had an organization as powerful as the humane society behind us, the public couldn't get away with runnin' a shit house like this. The people out there wonder why seventy percent of us guys come back. Too much time, that's why. Guys are stir simple when they leave here. You think five, six years in a joint like this straightens a guy out? Hell, it's like bustin' a gimp's good leg and expectin' him to walk better. The first scrape with the law makes us third-class citizens for life, and we're suppos'ta take it and like it. If that's the way it's gonna be, why don't the taxpayers wise up and start runnin' these human stockyards like the other ones. Knock us in the head when we come through the door. Put us out of our misery."

Except for Kelly's rasping voice, the room was quiet. Cully had moved to the table and was turning to go back to the bench when Fletcher grabbed his arm and whispered, "Man, get him the hell out of here before he stirs up the other psychos."

Cully started to say, "Do it yourself," but his attention was caught by the silence in the room. He looked over his shoulder.

Kelly was leaning over the table, glaring at Lagato. "What was that, Mac?"

"I said you've made your point. Give some of the other fellows a chance."

"You in a hurry?"

"Look, friend, the press is giving you fellows an opportunity to take your grievances to the public, and all I'm trying to do is hear as many as I can. I honestly hope the story I write enhances the future of every man in here."

"That's a goddamn lie! You newspaper bastards—" Fletcher caught his arm, but he jerked it free and swung back to Lagato. "You bastards who write for the papers go out of your way to railroad an ex-con. He can have thirty years of clean livin' behind him, and you still hang that ex-con tag on him. He's tried and convicted before he gets inside a courtroom. I know, I had—"

Cully had stepped in front of him and was shoving him toward the door.

"Lay off, kid!" He tried to duck under Cully's arm, still

shouting at Lagato: "If I had my way, I'd throw you in The Hole and let you smell those buckets till this is over." He clawed at the doorjamb, his neck in the crook of Cully's arm. The faces behind the smoke drifts along the walls were bobbing like corks. The reporters were perched on the edge of their chairs. "I'd give you guys a taste of this goddamn zoo. I'd—" He made a grab for Cully's face as he was whirled into the hall.

Cully pinned his arms and slammed him against the wall, twisting his hip to ward off the knee aimed at his crotch. No one had followed them from the room. From beyond the door ten feet or so away there came a laugh, then another, followed by a noisy gabble and the usual chorus of "Knock it off! Dummy up!" Cully gradually relaxed his grip. "Man, for crissake, cool off."

Kelly stopped struggling. He was sucking in air, glaring through the hair hanging in his face. "I don't want nothin' more to do with you, kid," he whispered harshly. "You're phony. You put the arm on me in there because Fisk was watchin'. You're buckin' for a parole."

"Cool it, Kelly."

"You showed your true colors. You're phony, kid."

"I'm warnin' you, Kelly."

"G'wan, start swingin'. Lock me up like you did Joe. Go after that parole."

Cully stared into the taunting bloodshot eyes and for a moment everything went blurry-red. He had a vicious impulse to hurt the man, make him crawl, smash the sneer into his teeth. He took a deep breath and turned away. The stir-psycho bastard was sixty pounds lighter, fifteen years older, wasted by more than six months in The Hole. He turned again. Kelly was still standing there, sneering.

"What'sa matter, kid, lost your balls?"

"I wouldn't feel right beltin' a wreck like you. Go get yourself a baseball bat and c'mon back."

"You're not worth it. But I sure hope the Indian buries a shiv in your guts." Still sneering, he turned and started down the hall.

Inside the room, the jabbering was going on again. "Hey,

Red," someone called, "tell 'em about how they screw up our mail."

And Fletcher said, "I don't get mail. You tell 'em."

Depressed, his hands stuffed in the waistband of his dungarees, Cully moved to a window and looked down on the barren courtyard below: an exercise yard for the segregated cons, twice the size of a boxing ring, a square of earth trampled to powdery dirt, a few patches of sun-scorched sod, a rusty drinking fountain in one corner. The gloomy enclosure was surrounded by heavily barred forty-foot-high windows, cellhouse windows—Cellhouse Two on one side, Isolation on the other—and across from where he was standing was the vacancy through which the chow lines passed, at one time Cellhouse Three. The windows were dusty and rain-spattered, but he could see cons moving in an orderly line toward the messhall, and the familiar sight seemed strange to him now. Then, for the first time since he had pounced on Grossman the morning before, the thought occurred that he was in serious trouble, a ringleader in a prison riot. Newscasters all over the country were talking about it. Three newspaper reporters were sitting in the room behind him. For a wild moment he thought of going to the storeroom and releasing the hostages. He'd escort them to the front gate and tell them to go. Who would try to stop him? There was no organization. No one really gave a damn. Why, hell, he'd be a hero! He could end this half-assed riot singlehandedly. Then he remembered Kelly's accusation, and the moment passed.

He turned away from the window and began dragging his feet down the hall, aware again of a sour stomach, listless muscles, the squabbling voices behind him. Now Kelly was down on him, and Christ only knew how many others. Probably half the cons in the joint were calling him a phony behind his back. What a drag! If only he could turn back the time to yesterday morning!

Then, glancing into an empty office and through an open window, he saw the troopers on the wall and was revived by the thought of a guard-abandoned prison, the tunnel in the auditorium, his ten-gallon stash in the kitchen. He swung into the stairwell and galloped down the steps.

# CHAPTER 15

THE kitchen was back in tune. The familiar mealtime slam, bang, and clatter were coming from the scullery. Cooks and messmen were scooting about as if Peek-a-boo Perkins were spying on them through the crack in the pantry door. Beyond the archway, seated in orderly rows in the messhall, between seven and eight hundred hungry cons were loading up on beans and fried boloney.

Cully had just entered the kitchen and was moving past the freshly scoured steam caldrons which a few hours earlier had been bubbling over with eight hundred gallons of raisinjack. The sign which had hung from the canopy as a warning to A.A. members was gone; so was the warden's easy chair. As he passed the hot-storage table, he dropped to one knee, pretending to tie his shoe. The camouflage of pots and pans hadn't been moved. He caught a strong whiff. His stash was still there.

He walked under the canopy and leaned on a caldron, facing the archway, feigning an interest in the activity in the messhall. He'd have to wait. If he dragged the pot out now, every juice-head in the kitchen would be bumming a drink. Hell, ten gallons wouldn't last a hot minute. He decided to check on the tunnel diggers in the auditorium and was about to leave when the head convict cook, Nosy Bains, a bulb-nosed florid-cheeked barrel of fat, came waddling his way.

"I had the boys put your easy chair in the pantry, Champ."

Cully gave him a contemptuous look. "How come you're not in The Hole with the rest of the finks?"

Nosy played deaf. "Are the boys still up there talking to the reporters?"

"Yeah, they're tryin' to get you a medal for all the cooks you snitched off for swipin' chow over the past ten years. You save the state a lotta money."

"Aw, cut it out, Champ. Don't I always take care of the boxers?"

"Big deal! Like it was comin' outta your own pocket."

"Want a coupla pork chops? I got some on the range right now."

Cully grimaced. Just the thought of eating a greasy pork chop made his stomach cringe. "Better go to the neck with 'em yourself. You're wastin' away to nothin'. You must be down to two ninety."

"Two seventy-three," Nosy said, and caught Cully's wrist as he started toward the archway. "C'mon in the pantry and I'll show you something."

"What?"

"Skinny Burns' record."

"What are you doin' with Skinny Burns' record?"

"It was laying on my desk in there."

"Well, burn it. Get rid of it. It's none of your business. And don't be hangin' a bum jacket on the guy. Skinny's a good-head."

"I didn't say he wasn't. All I'm saying is he shouldn't even be in here. His wife had it coming."

Cully started to turn away. He disliked discussing a friend's case behind his back, especially with a two-faced bower and scraper like Nosy Bains, but curiosity overpowered him. "Wha'd she do?"

"She was cheating on him."

"Hell, man, that don't call for the death penalty. It happens in the best families."

"Not the way it happened to him. He was supporting three kids that weren't his. He couldn't have kids—got shot up somehow in Korea. But according to the record he didn't mind that so much—her having kids, I mean. What finally got his dander up shouldn't happen to a dog. She brought him home a dose of clap."

"You been cuttin' this up with other guys?"

"Cutting what up?"

"Skinny's personal business."

"Never! You know me better than that, Champ. Fact is, I just read it a few minutes ago."

"Well, forget you read it," Cully said, and drove a finger into the fat of Nosy's chest. "Y'hear? Burn that goddamn record. And keep your snitchin' mouth shut, or I'll sink a couple in that lard sack of yours." He turned and walked through the archway.

Cons were shuffling up the aisles, leaving the messhall through the rear-side doors. Perhaps from force of habit, no one was using the two doors between the steam tables at the front of the messhall. Bucking the traffic, squeezing his way through the oncoming cons, Cully started that way, surrounded by questions:

"Is Andy Gump still alive?"

"Hey, Cully, when do we eat again?"

"Is it true that Duke Trusdale hung himself?"

"When are you guys turning the joint back over to the screws?"

Cully shrugged, shook his head, nodded. "Beats me," he kept saying. "Listen to your radios."

As he stepped from the messhall, he caught sight of a solitary figure diagonally across the hall-like vacancy. Kelly was hurrying from the rear door to Isolation, head down, arms swinging. Cully watched him pass the shower shed and enter Cellhouse Four. He stood there awhile, thinking of Kelly's parting remark in the hall outside the meeting room; then, snatching the lid from a trash can beside the door, he headed toward Isolation.

The familiar stench of lime-watered excrement buckets met him at the door, and a sickening stink swooped down on him as he stepped inside. The sun had passed over the building, abandoning the Segregation side to gloomy shadows. Carrying the trash can lid by the handle, like a shield, he moved along under the second-tier walkway, crunching over the broken glass and chunks of mortar which littered the lime-splashed floor. A few of the cons locked up for protection were talking in undertones from their cages on the upper tiers.

"Hey, down there, what's goin' on?" It was Duke Trusdale's voice.

Cully ignored him. Earlier in the afternoon someone had started the rumor that Trusdale had hanged himself. Several Isolation cons had rushed to investigate and had returned to the kitchen disappointed.

Near the heavy mesh-wire partition at the entrance to the cellblock, Cully glimpsed the blade of a knife protruding from the second-tier girder ledge, and remembered seeing Bugsy put it there the morning before. He started to reach for the knife, then dropped his arm in disgust. He was pressing the panic button. Christ, if the Isolation gang were to see him! Armed like a gladiator to protect himself against a scrawny psycho who was probably still locked in a cage! Sending the trash can lid clattering across the floor, he walked through the gateway and crossed the dressing-in area in front of the cellblock to the mesh-wire partition on the Isolation side. He stood close to the partition, squinting through.

The lock was still on the Indian's cage door. There was a dim light inside, and a shadow was moving back and forth. The shadow stopped, then approached the front of the cage, darkening the squares in the steel-latticed door. A pair of bony brown hands came to rest on the ledge of the waist-high food wicket.

"Who's out there?"

Cully found an unblinking eye glaring at him through one of the darkened squares in the door. He moved through the gateway in the partition and stopped in front of the cage. The eye moved away from the square and Surefoot's face took shape beyond the door.

"Want some chow, Joe?"

"Have you got the key?"

"Yeah, I got it."

"Open up. I'll get my own chow." His tone of voice was casual, almost friendly, but the grin on his sweaty face was stiff as a grimace and his eyes were wide and glittery.

Cully had an impulse to unlock the door, to release the Indian and let everyone, including himself, look after his own skin. Hell, he was no better than Andy Gump. What right did he have to lock a man in a cage? He was reaching for the key when he thought of the fat chess player he had taken to the hospital. Watching the grin on the Indian's face relax, then stiffen again, he took a step back and stuffed his hands in the hip pockets of his dungarees. "No dice, Joe. I hate playin' cop, but if I turn you loose, you'll wind up killin' someone or gettin' killed yourself."

"Open up. I won't start trouble." His voice had risen. He was losing control. "I've got as much right out there as you guys have. I wasn't bothering anyone. I was minding my own business."

"What about that fat guy you cut over in Eight?"

"He asked for it."

"And what about Andy Gump? You were tryin' to kill him."

"He's got it coming."

"Maybe so, Joe, but if they find one stiff in here when this is over, about thirty-five of us'll be facin' a murder rap."

Surefoot sprang against the latticed door, one eye glaring out. "I'll get unlocked. I've got a friend out there. I can get that lock knocked off any time I want." His high-pitched voice rose to a scream. "You're going to get it, Briston! You and Andy Gump! You're both as good as dead!"

"Fair enough, Joe," Cully said. "But be damn careful. When you come after me, make sure it's from behind." He walked away.

The Indian was still raving from his cage as Cully crossed the dressing-in area. He paused in front of the Control Room door, debating whether to go back up to the press meeting; then, deciding not to, he started back along the Segregation side.

"Hey, you down there, what's goin' on?" Trusdale called.

"Settle down up there, Big Daddy," Cully said. "The queens are gettin' along all right without you."

"That you, Cully? Hey, c'mon up a minute. I got somethin' to tell you."

their T-shirts. A few were wearing shorts. The three most feminine-looking queens, Jackie, Tina and Ginger, and their proud-acting jockers, three jive-talking Reformatory transfers who worked in the laundry, were standing slightly apart from the group, as though they thought themselves a cut above the others. The couples parted now, swinging around to face each other, twisting and pumping their arms as the guitars began twanging and the con on the bongo drum beat out a roll.

"Careful, Bertha!" someone shouted. "You'll snap the poor bastard's neck."

Big Bertha, the first-string center on the prison's football team, a two-hundred-and-twenty-pound queen who could fight as well as swish, had latched onto an onlooker, Groggy Dilbert, a half-punchy lightweight boxer, and was literally yanking him around the floor.

The beat grew wilder, and the onlookers began heckling:

"Hey, baby, one of your knockers come loose."

"Your pants are slippin', dearie."

"Rooty-toot-toot! Rooty-toot-toot! We are the boys from the institoot!"

The queens were darting indignant glances at the crowd.

"Call the cops!" someone shouted. "I think I spot a queer."

Whitey grabbed Cully's arm and said, "If we could get this on television, the taxpayers would close the joint."

"They wouldn't believe it," Cully said, staring. "Lookit those geared-up screwballs! Man, why a judge sends a fruiter to a joint like this beats the hell outta me. It's like punishin' a kid by turnin' him loose in a candy store." He was about to bum Whitey for another cigarette when he glimpsed Ginger leering his way. "See you later," he said and made a beeline for the door.

Outside, in the barred enclosure leading like a cattle chute to the cellhouse door, he had to sidestep an oncoming rush of cooks and messmen. Near the gate, a panting red-faced cook caught his arm and asked, "What's goin' on in there, Cully? We heard the rootin'-tooters are puttin' on a show."

"Yeah, I guess that's what it is. I don't know what the hell else you'd call it," he said and started toward the auditorium.

The two double doors at the front of the building were bolted from the inside. The window shades were tightly drawn. He kicked at the door, waited a few moments, then rattled the knob, and rapped on the window.

At first the shade barely moved; then it was shoved aside, and a sweaty dirt-smeared face appeared. The face grinned as the shade fell back in place; in a moment the bolt was thrown, and the door swung out. The breathing mess of sweat and dirt standing beyond the door was Rick.

"We're under the wall," he said. "If the hole doesn't cave in, we'll be shackin' up in the Women's Quarters tonight."

"Havin' much trouble keepin' the snoopers out?"

"Naw. Whoever's back here just tells 'em to shove off, there's a private party goin' on."

Cully crossed the entrance hall and started down the sloping aisle. The dim wire-caged lights embedded in the bricks along the walls shed a foggy glow over the rear of the auditorium and mingled with the glare of footlights reflecting from the movie screen. It appeared at first as if several bodiless heads were bouncing about on the stage floor; then a dirt-coated form rose, and Cully noticed that the stage floor above the tunnel entrance had been ripped up. Gigolo was visible from the waist up. He was looking out over the footlights, grinning.

"What does it look like out there?" he asked. "Another twenty-four hours?"

Cully shrugged. "They're still meetin' with the press."

"Fletcher still buddy-buddy with the headshrinker?"

"I haven't noticed any change."

"Man, he better not turn the hostages loose, or him and I are gonna tangle. We need at least six more hours. Then he can do what he wants. We'll drag a coupla hostages over to the Women's Quarters and hold out over there."

A grunting con, too smeared with dirt to be recognized, rose up beside Gigolo and heaved a bulging gunnysack on the stage. "Bugsy wants a relief," he said as Coolbreeze Clark crawled from a gaping hole under the stage and dragged the sackful of dirt over the footlights. The hole looked as if it had been made by a torpedo. The orchestra pit beyond was strewn with splintered boards and heaps of rocky dirt. Four more cons, their faces and bodies covered with sweat-smeared soil, had risen up around Gigolo.

"What if we come to an agreement?" Cully said, leaning over the footlights. "We can't very well hold the hostages if the commissioner promises no reprisals and the legislature agrees to investigate the joint."

"Who can't?" Gigolo said, sneering. "Man, I'm doin' life. What the hell do I care about that rehabilitation jive they're askin' for? I'm not comin' to an agreement until I score for some pussy. How about it, you guys?"

A few more dirt-masked faces popped up and joined in a chorus of "You know it! Damn right! You said it, man!"

"You guys look half-dead right now," Cully said. "By the time you get to the Women's Quarters, you'll be too beat to do any good. Those burly Lesbians over there'll boot you out the front door."

"Hell, we're not bustin' our humps," Gigolo said. "We widened the hole enough to relay the dirt out."

"The wider the weaker. That hole's liable to cave in on you guys."

"It's worth the risk."

"Bugsy says he can't breathe," someone called from below the stage.

"Hell, man, he just crawled in there," Gigolo said. Then, ducking his head, he cupped his hands around his mouth and shouted, "If you're afraid of gettin' trapped in there, c'mon out. Otherwise quit bellyachin' and keep passin' that dirt out." He turned back to Cully. "You plan on makin' the trip tonight?"

"Why not? I don't turn the stuff down on the streets, why would I turn it down in here?"

"Well, keep your ears open, and every once in a while let us know what's goin' on out there. We might hav'ta snatch Fisk and Andy Gump. And if you hear anyone talkin' about this, dummy 'em up. There's a coupla cons in here with wives over there and they're not gonna want their ol' ladies gang-banged. They'll try to get word out front."

"I'll keep you guys posted," Cully said, and turned away from the stage, wondering if some juicehead in the kitchen had already sniffed out his stash of raisinjack.

CHAPTER **16**

IT was eight forty-five on the clock be-
hind the range—more than three hours since the newsmen had
left the prison—and Cully had all but given up hope of ever
making his move without being seen by the hungover lushes
who kept prowling the kitchen, sniffing like bloodhounds.

The raisinjack was still fermenting; he could smell it from
where he sat, slouched in the warden's easy chair between the
wall and the pot-storage table, less than five feet and two stacks
of pots away from ten gallons of ripe juice, one gallon of which
would at least ease his throbbing, gnawing hangover. He
wasn't being one-way, he kept telling himself, but if he hauled
out the juice in front of the lushes, nobody would get a buzz,
only a swallow, just enough to want more.

The kitchen crackled with voices. Everyone was on a talking
jag. To avoid being shanghaied into a conversation, he pre-
tended to be asleep, arousing visions of a night in the Women's
Quarters, now and then focusing his ears on a nearby conversation.

"All we've got to do is hang tough," someone was saying.
"If we hold out until the legislature publicly announces an in-
vestigation, there's bound to be some changes."

Cully peered toward the caldrons. The con doing the talking
was in charge of the chapel, a flabby bootlicker serving time for
indecent assault. Since the six o'clock newscast, which had carried a barely recognizable report of the press meeting, many
cons from General Population, the sideliners who had spent
the first thirty hours of the riot glued to their radios with their

cell doors shut, had been strutting through the kitchen talking as if the whole thing had started over conditions in the prison, as if the Isolation breakout had been incidental. The on-the-spot radio reporter had finally convinced them. Now, to hear them talk, the riot had been carefully planned and put into action by seventeen hundred desperate convicts. Except for Fletcher, the Isolation cons had vanished from the scene. Most had joined Gigolo in the auditorium. A few, perhaps from habit, had returned to The Hole to sleep.

"I oughta go upstairs and kick the piss outta Andy Gump," a passing voice drawled sneeringly, and Cully eased open one eye. The sneering voice belonged to a Cellhouse Eight tier tender, who normally spoke in a servile whine—a potbellied check forger who pacified the hardnoses on the tier he tended by scouring their cell toilets once a week. Cully watched him pass. Even his walk was unfamiliar. He was swaggering. So were the three cons with him. All four were yes-men—scorned by the hardnoses, stooges for the loudmouths—exercising their jaws now that it was safe. There was still no real organization, but with the Isolation cons out of sight, the atmosphere, at least in the kitchen, had grown more partylike. Most of the loudmouths had lost interest, and the joint politicians had begun to move in. Several were now in the pantry with Fletcher and Murry.

Keeping his eyes half-lidded, Cully went over the faces scattered in bunches around the kitchen. There was a noisy huddle in front of the pantry, another around the radio in front of the coalroom, and Walkie-Talkie, his knobby elbows flying in all directions, was haranguing a crowd in the center of the room, between the steam caldrons and the range. From a distance, he sounded like a flock of cawing crows.

Kelly was nowhere in sight. Four times in the past three hours, Cully, pretending to be asleep, had watched and listened as Kelly had gathered an audience in front of the caldrons ten feet or so away and, purposely loud, had snarled out his opinion of the press meeting, of the self-appointed policemen who had locked up a solid con like Joe Surefoot, and of a few so-called good-heads who were showing their true colors now that it was time to toss their chips in the pot. Fuming inside,

Cully had kept his mouth shut and his eyes lidded. It would've been senseless to defend himself with words, especially since he had often voiced the same opinions. Besides, the only argument a stir bug like Kelly could understand was a punch in the mouth. And for some reason, probably because he could imagine himself inside the bitter Irishman's skin, he just hadn't been able to get up from the chair and throw a punch. Instead, he had sat within earshot as though asleep, and after Kelly had left the kitchen, he had waited awhile before making a roundabout trip to Isolation to sneak a peek at Surefoot. On his last round, about half an hour ago, the Indian was still pacing his cage.

Cully slouched lower in the easy chair, peering through his eyelashes at Nosy Bains, who was standing on a stool under the canopy, scouring one of the steam caldrons, now and then digging a red bandanna from the waistband of his pants and dabbing at his bulbous nose. Even from a distance, the nose was pain-red and shining like a beacon. Nosy was no longer the head convict cook. He had lost his position and a one-punch fight shortly after the six o'clock newscast.

It had happened in front of the coalroom, where he had made the mistake of announcing, "Regular breakfast menu," to the cooks standing around the radio. Regular breakfast menu meant oatmeal, dry toast—the margarine having been used up in the big steak-and-egg fry the morning before—and skim milk, called Bluejohn, so destitute of butterfat that it gave the appearance of having been diluted with water.

After a round of angry glances had passed among the cooks, Tex Crawford, a rangy fry cook, had asked, "What about the bacon we found in the butchershop?"

"Never mind that bacon," Nosy had said. "I'll make out the menus; you just follow orders. That bacon happens to belong to the officer's dining—"

He had never completed the sentence. He had wound up flat on his back on the floor, blood streaming from his nose, and Tex Crawford had taken over as head convict cook. His first official announcement had been, "We'll fry up that bacon for mainline breakfast."

Cully let his face slump into a more sleeplike expression now as the huddle in front of the pantry parted and Fletcher and Murry came hurrying through, apparently on their way to the front of the prison, their first trip since the press meeting had ended.

"There's entirely too much disorder, Alan," Murry was saying as they passed within a few feet of the easy chair. "The cell-houses should be locked."

Before their voices were lost in the gabble, Cully heard Fletcher say, "Man, that's where I draw the goddamn line! I hav'ta live with these guys when this is over."

Shifting his weight, Cully caught a veiled glimpse of Fletcher's face as he turned through the kitchen archway. The big redhead was scowling. In the past few hours, ever since the Isolation cons had wandered from sight, he'd been acting as if he were tired of playing riot leader, as if he were more interested in the action going on in the auditorium. Twice he had asked Cully to go over there and see how the diggers were making out. Then, an hour or so ago, he had stomped from the pantry, calling Murry a creep and threatening to "tear the whole goddamn joint to the ground" if the governor didn't fire the warden, the chairman of the parole board and the commissioner of corrections by midnight.

As Cully shifted his weight again, he glimpsed Nosy Bains waddling his way. He shut his eyes and let his head hang limp. The drone and cackle of voices grew louder in the darkness. He tried to sense the movements near him, tried to catch the scuff of feet. Finally, curiosity got the best of him. He eased open one eye. Nosy was standing in front of him.

"You asleep, Champ?"

"Yeah."

"Sure got a dirty deal, didn't I?"

"Yeah, you sure did."

"I was gonna fry the bacon. Don't I always hustle extras for the mainline?"

"Yeah, you sure do."

"How about talking up for me? You know, tell Tex I'm not a

bad guy. Tell him—" He waddled out of reach as Cully bounced to the edge of the chair, glaring.

"Get the hell outta here! You're damn lucky the whole crew didn't put the boots to you when you were floppin' around on the floor. You've been beatin' the mainline and pamperin' the bulls for over four years that I know of. G'wan, get outta my face before that tomato nose of yours gets worked over again." He rose from the chair, and Nosy went scurrying back to the caldrons.

Cully stood there awhile, debating whether to drag the pot of raisinjack from under the table and put it up for grabs. He wanted a cigarette but couldn't spot a lighted butt in anyone's hand. No one nearby was smoking, and it was getting almost impossible to bum a whole one, especially a tailor-made. Even the Bull Durham smokers were hiding their sacks. As soon as a match flared up, it seemed as if every nicotine addict in the kitchen yelled, "Save me the butt!"

He glanced around. The sky beyond the dirt-furrowed windows was shading to dusk. The kitchen was crowded, noisy, full of gloomy shadows. Only the lights on the canopy were on. No one had turned on the ceiling lights. Beyond the caldrons Walkie-Talkie was still cawing away at a listless audience.

"Got a smoke, Cully?" someone called.

Cully shook his head and started from the kitchen.

The sun had sunk out of sight, and the heat-wilted troopers on the west wall were fading into the night as he crossed the lawn in front of the auditorium. The shade on the door window rippled as he approached. Before he could knock, the door swung open, and Coolbreeze Clark said, "Got a smoke, man?"

"There's none around. Everyone's snipin' butts," Cully said, and started down the aisle.

The bright-lighted stage area was noisier and more crowded than before. Shirtless dirt-smeared cons, dwarfed by the size of the brilliant white movie screen, were moving about in the glare of the footlights. Heads were bobbing along the trench in the stage floor. There was a huddle at the foot of the aisle: a cluster of cons grinning contemptuously at Bugsy Matthews, who was sprawled in the end seat, his breath coming in gasps.

"He couldn't have got that wasted from diggin'," Cully said as he caught Gigolo's eye, then glanced at the heap of rocky dirt in the orchestra pit. "Don't look like that pile got much bigger."

Gigolo flicked his eyes at Bugsy. "The muscle-bound idiot froze in there. Took us over an hour to drag him out."

"Cave-in," Bugsy croaked. "Got caught in a cave-in."

"Yeah, big cave-in," Gigolo said, sneering. "Coupla pebbles and a teaspoonful of dirt trickled on his back, and he went stone stiff. No jive, man. Y'know how he's always spoutin' that atheist line in The Hole? Well, you should've been here ten minutes ago. He was on his hands and knees in that tunnel—too scared to move—prayin' to the top of his lungs. He knows every prayer in the book."

"Lotta crap," Bugsy muttered. "If I would've moved, the whole thing would've caved in."

"Then how come it didn't? We dragged you out, and nothin' happened. The gang you're suppos'ta be workin' with is in there diggin' now."

"Crawl back in there," someone said. "Start relayin' that dirt out, or you don't get no pussy."

The cons in the aisle began laughing, heckling. "He don't get no ussy-pay! He don't get no ussy-pay!"

Gigolo motioned to Cully. As they met near the stage, he said, "There was a little cave-in all right, but nothin' to panic over. Just enough to slow us down. We won't make it over there now before two, three in the mornin'."

"How many guys in the tunnel?"

"Six relayin' the dirt out and one diggin'."

"Who's diggin'?"

"Rick."

"Why him?"

"Why not? He's the smallest. He can move around better than the rest of us."

"Yeah, but he's only a kid. He's liable to get buried in there. It wouldn't take much. D'you know there's a road between the wall and the Women's Quarters? It could cave in under the weight of a truck."

"Man, nobody's twistin' his arm. He wants to dig. I've been takin' my turn on the shovel, too. Don'tcha think it's worth the risk?"

"It might be for you—you're doin' the book—but the kid'll be out in a year or two."

"I still say nobody's twistin' his arm."

"Okay, forget it."

Gigolo sprang up on the stage and sat there, his legs dangling over the edge. "What's goin' on out there?"

"Nothin', man. The guys that broke outta The Hole are either here in the auditorium or sleepin' somewhere. A few juiceheads are mopin' around the kitchen and the cellhouse creeps finally got up enough guts to come out and take a look. They're ganged up in the kitchen talkin' bad—like they own the joint. Otherwise there's nothin' happenin'. The cellblocks are deader than a doornail."

"Who's runnin' things?"

"No one. But the apple polishers are startin' to get in the act."

"Like who?"

"The politicians. You know, that bunch from the school buildin'."

"What about Fletcher?"

"He's about ready to hang it up."

A loaded gunnysack landed with a thud on the stage, spurting a hail of sand and rocks against the tinny metal hood shielding the footlights. Two cons picked it up and heaved it into the orchestra pit, where another con emptied the sack and slung it back on the stage. The hecklers had moved away from Bugsy. He was still sprawled in the end seat at the foot of the aisle, head back, clutching his throat, breathing loud enough to be heard above the racket under the stage.

Gigolo spat. He dragged a hand over his face and across his sweaty dirt-caked chest. "Maybe we oughta move the hostages over here. That phony headshrinker, too. What if some hero decides to turn 'em loose? The bulls would be pourin' tear gas in here before we knew what happened."

"Punchy's still up there."

"Who's stoppin' *him* from turnin' 'em loose? If he did, he'd be a cinch for a parole."

"Punchy's all right."

"Didn't say he wasn't. But when it comes to a parole, I don't even trust myself. What does he care if ol' Gigolo gets laid or not? Hell, man, I'm desperate. I'll be flubbin' my dub in here for the next twenty years. If I don't make it through that tunnel before this is over, I'm wiped out. I'll be too old to enjoy the stuff by the time the parole board turns me loose."

"You'll only be forty-five or so."

"*Only?* Christ, man, a guy's ready for a wheelchair at forty-five."

Cully grinned. "Not if he lives a good clean life like you're livin'. Get yourself a job in the kitchen, and spend as much time as you can in the freezer. You'll be well preserved when you leave here."

"I'm serious, man. I got nothin' to lose. Believe me, even if I hav'ta cut a few throats to do it, I'm gonna get laid before this is over. That's why I say we should move 'em over here before someone decides to shoot for a parole."

"We? I should help you put a noose around my neck?"

"Just bring Andy Gump. One's enough."

"I'm not bringin' anyone. And neither are you."

Gigolo slid from the stage and stood there straddle-legged, his hands thrust in his back pockets, his dirty sweat-furrowed face set in a sneer. "Who's gonna stop me?"

"Maybe I will."

"You givin' the orders now?"

Cully shrugged.

The sneer on Gigolo's handsome face twisted into a grin. "Look, man, I don't take orders from the warden, so what makes you think I'd take orders from a con?"

"You got more to lose."

"Like what?"

"A reputation. You're suppos'ta be tough, aren't you?"

"So?"

"So you got more to lose. The warden can't wreck your reputation. A con can."

"Is that right?"

"Yeah, that's right, man. All the warden can do is have you
tossed in The Hole—maybe gassed. A con might whip your
ass. There's a difference. You can't win with the warden, and
everyone knows it. But you can with a con, and if you don't,
you're hurtin' because you hav'ta face the boys every day."

They were grinning at each other when someone called, "Our
turn, Gigolo. They want a relief."

"Tell 'em to come out," Gigolo called over his shoulder, then
turned back to Cully. "How about tellin' Fletcher to hold out
at least until mornin'?"

"I'll tell him, but I don't know what good it'll do. The way
he's actin', he's about ready to hang it up."

"Where's he at now?"

"He went out front with the headshrinker just before I came
over here."

"Well, tell him what the score is. And how about sendin' us
a radio?"

"Okay."

"We'll be listenin' to the news. And if it sounds like the bulls
are gettin' ready to move back in, I'm comin' after Andy
Gump."

"Suit yourself."

"I will," Gigolo said, and sprang up on the stage.

The searchlights were on outside, and a silvery mist hung
over the prison. The sky beyond was dark. Cully was momentarily dazzled by the array of lights beaming at him from
the gun walk at the front of the prison. Unlike the night before,
there were no old-fashioned yellow-bulbed searchlights on the
walls; all were of uniform size and gave off a phosphorescent
glow.

What he could see of the prison was quiet, deserted, motionless; not even a shadow was stirring. Imagining himself being
followed by the eyes and rifle bores beyond the lights, he started

through the mist, across the lawn and into the barred enclosure leading to Cellhouse Six.

It was almost like walking into a guard-controlled cellhouse. Except for a few radios on speaker and a few cons loitering on the tier walkways, the sounds were normal, and the scene was in order. Hoping to find someone smoking, he walked through the gateway in the partition and looked into the first cell.

The ceiling light was on inside, and the two double-decked cots against the concrete walls on each side of the four-man cell were occupied. Three of the occupants seemed to be sleeping. The other was sitting Buddha-fashion on one of the upper bunks, ogling a dog-earred girly magazine. On the wall beside his head was a large lithograph of the Sacred Heart, and scrawled across the bottom in what appeared to be black crayon was: TO BILL WITH FONDEST REGARDS—J. CHRIST.

"Got a smoke, Bill?" Cully asked.

The con looked up, squinted for a moment, then pressed a finger to his lips. After making sure the others weren't watching, he slipped a hand under his pillow and came out with a cigarette. He handed it through the bars. "Ain't a butt in the cell," he said loudly, then grinned and winked as Cully palmed it.

"Been catchin' the news?" Cully asked.

"Yeah. Same ol' malarkey. The situation is still grim."

"Grim? Can't be this one. The man must've been talkin' about a riot somewhere else," Cully said, and moved back into the entrance area in front of the cellblock.

A clerk from the school office, whom Cully knew slightly, a husky con in his early thirties, was sitting alone at the cellhouse sergeant's desk, hands clasped behind his head, his legs propped up. He turned as Cully approached, the bare light bulb above the desk reflecting from his horn-rimmed glasses.

"You the wheel in here?" Cully asked.

"Just answering the phone. We have a man on phone duty in all the cellhouses."

"We? Who's we?"

The con unclasped his hands and swung his legs from the desk. "The boys from Isolation aren't around anymore. They broke up and disappeared. Lost interest, I guess. Anyhow, if we're to gain anything from this, somebody has to keep order; so a few of us got together in the kitchen and decided to look after things."

"Kinda late, aren't you? Where were you guys yesterday?"

The con fingered his glasses, twitching a stiff-lipped smile. "Don't get me wrong, Briston. We're not trying to take over."

"Nobody said you were." Cully examined the cigarette in his hand, feeling foolish for having sounded as if he were putting on a one-man performance, as if he begrudged the man a ray of the limelight. He reached for a book of matches on the desk. "Pretty quiet in here. How'd you manage to get these guys in their cells?"

"I didn't. It's quiet all over the place. There's a rumor around that the National Guard is ready to rush in here."

"Anything to it?"

"Could be. Someone over in Seven climbed the water tower and claimed he saw Army trucks parked out front."

"I doubt if they'd try it. Not as long as we're holdin' hostages."

The con shrugged. "It all depends on how much they know out front. There's no resistance in here. In fact, the hostages could walk out if they wanted to. Who'd stop them? There's no one watching them."

"How d'you know? Were you up in the storeroom?"

"About twenty minutes ago."

"Wasn't Punchy Philips up there?"

"There wasn't a con around. The hostages were all alone."

"See you later," Cully said, and hurried from the cellhouse.

The front wall was strung with searchlights, five feet or so apart, spreading a heavy phosphorescent glow over the entire front of the prison. He could hear voices from the gun walk on the wall above the door to the Administration Building and glimpsed a row of ghostlike faces behind the lights as he turned into the Control Room.

Several cons were leaning against the filing cabinets in the screened-in area. One was sitting in Sergeant Gallaway's swivel chair, talking over the telephone.

"Who's on the other end?" Cully asked.

The con palmed the mouthpiece. "Skinny Burns. Why?"

"Where's he at?"

"In the kitchen."

"Tell him to get up to the storeroom right away and stay there," Cully said. He was already moving through the door to Isolation.

The foul-smelling, dimly lighted cellblock was as gloomy and soundless as a tomb. Cully moved quietly to the mesh-wire partition on the Isolation side and peered into the dimness beyond. Most of the doors were hanging open; but the third one down was shut, and the padlock was still in place. There was no light inside the cage. He picked his way over the debris to the edge of the adjoining cage and listened. He could hear someone breathing, evenly, as though asleep. He looked inside. Surefoot's face was discernible in a patch of pale light slanting through the food wicket. Cully moved quietly away, listened again, then headed toward the kitchen.

It was ten fifteen on the wall clock behind the range when he walked through the kitchen archway. He noticed a crowd in front of the pantry and was moving that way when Nosy Bains came waddling frantically toward him, calling, "Hey, Champ, did'cha hear the latest? Coupla guys spotted some Army trucks out front."

"Yeah, and that ain't all, you fink. The Air Force is gettin' ready to bomb the joint."

"I'm not kiddin', Champ. Looks like the National Guard is coming in."

"Don't get your hopes up."

"It's true, though."

"Aw, for crissake, the state troopers are probably sleepin' in those trucks. If the National Guard was out there, you'd be hearin' about it on the radio. What's goin' on in the pantry?"

"They're arguing. Fletcher and the headshrinker. Fletcher's hotter than hell."

Cully brushed past Nosy and shouldered his way through the crowd. In the pantry Fletcher was saying, "Why'n the hell should *you* sweat? You'll be a hero when this is over."

Fletcher and Murry were alone in the room: Murry sitting in front of the paper-littered table, legs crossed, arms folded, a weary smile on his face; Fletcher standing over him. The floor had been swept and the torn cereal sacks restacked against the walls.

Murry rose from the chair, still smiling, the top of his blond crew-cut even with Fletcher's chin. "If you feel that way, Alan—"

"Man, get off that Alan kick. You and I got nothing in common."

"I'm sorry you feel that way, Alan. But if you're convinced I'm not doing my best to help you men, I'll go upstairs. Mr. Fisk can take my place."

"Get off his back, Red," someone called from beyond the door. "Why let personalities enter—"

Fletcher swung around, glaring. "If I want any advice from you jack-offs out there I'll let you know." His eyes lit on Cully. "You know what this phony headshrinker tried to pull out front? He told the warden he'd personally see that us guys who broke out of The Hole would be back in there before the bulls take over again. We're suppos'ta walk back into that stink pit and let *him* lock us up."

"Only temporarily, Alan. Merely a gesture of cooperation. As soon—"

"Man, you can temporarily go to hell! I've done all the co-operating I'm going to do. How about you, Cully?"

Cully had moved to the rear of the room and was leaning against a pile of cereal sacks. He grinned and said, "What difference does it make? Two hours after the bulls take over, every hardnose in the joint'll be racked up."

"Only temporarily," Murry repeated. "The warden has promised—"

"—to review our cases," Fletcher cut in. "Well, he can go to hell. Either every one of us from The Hole—including Joe Surefoot—gets a fresh start in General Population, or we wreck the goddamn joint. And remember, we're still holding hostages."

Cully caught his eye and motioned him to the rear of the

room. When the big redhead was close enough and Murry was blocked from sight, Cully whispered, "There's no way in hell we can come out ahead. But take him back out front and argue some more. The gang in the auditorium needs time."

"Not me. I'm through," Fletcher said, and turned back to Murry. "Better take a hike out there and tell The Man what I just said. Either we all get a fresh start, or we wreck the joint. And if anyone tries to bust in here—like the National Guard— we'll wreck the hostages, too."

One of the cons beyond the door said, "He's not talking for me," and some of the others began voicing agreement; but when Fletcher glared their way, the grumbling stopped.

For several seconds, as though he were asking for help, Murry faced the onlookers. Then he turned to Fletcher. "You're being unreasonable, Alan. You're forcing the authorities to make promises that can't be kept. As concerned as the warden and commissioner are for the safety of the men upstairs, they'd be justified in promising anything."

"In other words," Cully said, moving away from the pile of cereal sacks, "we can expect to get double-crossed. Right?"

"No. Not if your requests are reasonable."

"What's so unreasonable about askin' for a fresh start? If we screw up again, The Hole'll still be there."

"The warden knows this. The warden also knows that he has no control of the prison unless you men show a willingness to cooperate. I'm sure every one of you will be back in General Population within a month."

"Man, you must think we just fell off a hay wagon," Fletcher said. "If we let you lock us up, we've had it. No one listens to a con in a cage."

"There has to be some trust on both sides, Alan. You men were in Isolation for rule infractions before this began. Originally you asked for no reprisals over the demonstration; now you want a complete pardon for past wrongs."

"That's right," Fletcher said. "A clean slate. If we go back to The Hole, we're as bad off as we were—as bad off as we can get. Reprisals or past wrongs, what difference does it make? We'd still be in The Hole for as long as they'd want to keep us there. Man, for a psychologist, you're pretty stupid if you think we'd fall for that trust-on-both-sides routine. We'd be the ones doing all the goddamn trusting."

Murry shook his head, rubbed his brow, stared at the floor. "I suppose we can go back out there and discuss it some more, but—"

"Not *we*," Fletcher cut in. "You. I'm through talking to the warden. Just tell him what I said—a fresh start, or we wreck the joint. And if he wants to send the Army in, we'll go to war."

"Are you putting me on my own?" Murry asked. "Do you want me to speak to the warden alone?"

"Sure, why not?"

"I may not return."

"You'll return. Why, hell, you're a television star. You're getting your kicks, man. You never had it so good. When I offered to turn you loose last night, you acted like I was trying to wreck your career. Besides, who cares if you take off? We got seven more just like you upstairs."

Murry turned to Cully. "Would you escort me out front?"

"I'm busy." He glanced toward the onlookers in the doorway. "Deputize one of the boys from the citizens' committee."

"C'mon, Cully," Fletcher said, and started from the room. "Let's move the hostages."

Cully caught up to him in front of the coalroom. "Where d'you plan on movin' 'em?"

"The auditorium."

"Count me out."

"Why?"

"They're doin' okay where they're at."

"Oh, yeah? What if those jack-offs from the School Building decide to turn 'em loose? Who's going to stop 'em? Hell, man, we're out of business if somebody doesn't keep an eye on 'em."

"Isn't Skinny Burns up there?"

"Yeah, but I don't trust him."

Cully shrugged. "You oughta go up there yourself. Nobody'll try to turn 'em loose if you're upstairs."

"Man, I've had it. I'm going over to the auditorium."

"Go ahead. I'll stick around the kitchen."

"You'll keep an eye on things?"

"I said I'd stick around."

"Yeah, but will you keep an eye on things?"

"Don't you trust me?"

Fletcher grinned. "Why shouldn't I?" He turned and walked away.

Cully watched him leave through the rear-side door, then looked upstairs at the half-open door to the steward's office. There were only a few cons standing around. Not one was watching him. The bunch in front of the coalroom was huddled around the radio—cooks, messmen, the rest mainliners. Not a hardnose in sight. Who could stop him? Who would even bother to question him? Except for the gang in the auditorium, who cared? He could herd the hostages out through the rear-side door and down the shopline to the Administration Building. He'd be a cinch for a parole. Hell, he wouldn't even have to show his face anymore. He could live in the trusty dormitory outside the walls until the parole board released him. He could—

"Wanna coupla pork chops, Champ?"

Nosy Bains, his cheeks bulging like balloons, grease leaking from the corners of his churning mouth, was standing beside him. One pudgy hand held a freshly gnawed bone, the other a metal cereal bowl heaped with greasy pork chops.

"Will you for crissake get that meat outta my face?" Cully said. "I got a goddamn hangover. I'm not hungry."

Nosy stuffed the bone in the bowl and licked his fingers. "Where'd Red go?"

"None of your business."

"Just wondering. Looks like you're the last one left. The last one always gets the blame."

"Don't let it worry you."

"You oughta use your head, Champ." He glanced up at the steward's office. "I sure wish I was in your shoes. I'd do myself some good. I'd turn 'em loose."

"You would, huh? You might get your head caved in, too."

"Maybe *I* would, but *you* wouldn't. You could get away with it." His eyes slid over the nearby cons, and his whiny voice dropped to a whisper, "I'd give you a hand. I could get the guys away from back here. I'll go into the messhall and start hollering that the National Guard is coming in. I mean it, Cully. We could both get a parole out of this."

"Crawl back in the woodwork, you phony bastard."

"What's so phony about helping yourself? Who cares what the guys in here think? We'd get a parole. We'd never see 'em again."

"Get lost! You must think I'm as low as you are." He turned and walked toward the front of the kitchen, feeling guilty, wondering if Nosy Bains had read his mind.

Aside from the huddle around the radio and the congestion in the pantry doorway, there were perhaps forty cons scattered throughout the kitchen. The largest group—a dozen or so cooks and messmen perched like pigeons along the edge of a metal table in front of the range—were tuned in on Walkie-Talkie. A few diehard lushes were still bloodhounding the scullery, and some were sitting on the concrete ridge surrounding the steam caldrons; but for some unknown reason, no one was prowling the area around the pot-storage table, and the warden's easy chair was vacant. No longer in a talking mood, Cully flopped into the chair and went back to feigning sleep.

He caught a whiff of raisinjack, stronger than before, and peered under the table. A foamy puddle was forming on the floor between two stacks of pots, apparently from a bubble over. The juice was still fermenting. He thought of dragging out the pot, of straining off a gallon of two for himself and letting the bloodhounds squabble over the rest; but before he could act, his muscles grew heavy, his eyelids went limp, and the voices nearby began fading into a faraway drone.

He dozed, awoke to the voices, dozed again, over and over, now and then catching drowsy glimpses of passing faces, hearing the shout "News! News!" followed by the scuff of feet rushing toward the coalroom; silence, darkness; then the voices again, cons ganging up in front of the pantry, Murry and two cons from the school office hurrying past, moving toward the kitchen archway. His heavy-lidded eyes found the wall clock behind the range: it was eleven thirty, then twelve fifteen, then one o'clock. Once he forced open his eyes and found Kelly watching him from under the archway, squinting, sort of grinning at him; but before he could rouse his mind, the Irishman was gone, and his eyelids were drooping again. When he finally managed to drag himself from the chair, it was two o'clock, and the crowd in the kitchen had dwindled to perhaps twenty, mostly cooks and messmen.

"What's new?" he called to a sleepy con sitting on a food cart.

The con yawned, shrugged, and jabbed a thumb toward the pantry. "Accordin' to the headshrinker, the warden's suppos'ta give his answer at six o'clock."

"His answer to what?"

"About lettin' you guys from The Hole stay in Population. All but that Indian—the one that's been locked up so long. They say—"

Cully didn't hear the rest. He was moving past the steam caldrons, remembering Kelly, remembering the look on his face.

Isolation was quiet, gloomy, shrouded in eerie shadows. A ragged blue shirt sleeve hung over the sixty-watt bulb beside the rear door. There were a few dim ceiling lights on in the occupied cages on the three upper tiers, but no silhouettes darkened the squares in the latticed doors, no shadows were stirring, and no eyes were peering out.

He moved under the second-tier walkway and started along the Segregation side, hugging the dark and silent cages, breathing the putrid stench of untended buckets as he picked his way over mutilated padlocks and battered bucket lids, listening, straining his ears now as he approached the front of the cellblock. He crossed the dressing-in area and was starting through the gateway in the mesh-wire partition on the Isolation side when he came to a halt.

The Indian's cage door was hanging wide open. A sledgehammer and padlock lay on the floor in front of the cage. There was a light on inside, and a shadow was moving on the wall.

Staying a few yards away from the cages, his eyes on the sledgehammer, Cully moved far enough into the cellblock to see inside the cage. He stopped, stared for a moment, then moved to the doorway.

Kelly was sitting on the sagging bunk inside, head bowed, legs dangling, his hands stuffed between his knees. He lifted his haggard face and looked at Cully. After several seconds he said, "I'm sorry, kid. I honest to God didn't think he was as far gone as he is. I thought if I turned him loose and he settled down in one of the cellhouses, the warden might let him stay there when this is over." He lifted a bloody hand. "I don't know where he got the shiv, but when I told him to use his head, he pulled it out and took a swipe at me."

"How long ago?"

"Just a few minutes."

"Where was he headed?"

"He said he was goin' after you. You and Andy Gump."

# CHAPTER 17

CULLY slowed to a walk as he approached the kitchen archway. The scene beyond was as he had left it: no more than twenty cons, mostly cooks and messmen, some talking in groups, some roaming about, a few sprawled on food carts—no excitement.

He heard a familiar caw as he hurried past the pantry and glimpsed Walkie-Talkie standing inside. Murry was perched on the edge of the table and several cons from the school office clique were sitting on the cereal sacks. Someone called, "C'mon in, Briston," but Cully was already galloping up the steps to the storeroom.

In the yellowish haze of several dim light bulbs dangling from the ceiling on twisted cords, the looted storeroom looked like a soup-and-coffee rescue mission. Someone, perhaps the hostages, had tried to make the place, if not more livable, at least more walkable. The ripped-open cardboard cases had been piled along the wall on the window side of the room, and most of the loose cans had been stacked on the shelves against the wall on the opposite side. A row of lumpy mattresses lined the rear wall. Three were occupied. Sergeant Grossman, Peek-a-boo Perkins, and Dirtyneck Dugan were laid out like corpses, motionless, staring at the ceiling. Hicks, the Isolation guard, and Campbell, the resident parole officer, were pacing the floor. The others in the room, Fisk, Sergeant Gallaway, and Skinny Burns, were sitting on upended cases around a makeshift table.

"See you a minute, Skinny?" Cully said, and moved away from the door, out of the hostages' view.

"Sure glad you came," Skinny said as he entered the steward's office. "I can't stay awake. I haven't closed my eyes since the night before last."

Cully forced a grin. "C'mon, ol' buddy, you can't fold up now. Surefoot's on the loose."

For what seemed a minute Skinny just stared at him, a wanting-to-curse expression on his long homely face. Then he turned and started toward the outer door. Almost there, he stopped and turned again. "I'm finished. I should have my head examined for letting myself get involved in this. No one cares about improving this place, least of all the ones who would benefit most. I've sure come to one conclusion over the past two days —convicts don't deserve decent treatment. At least the ones in here don't. They haven't the brains or guts to help themselves."

"Christ, man, all I'm askin' you to do is watch out for the Indian. Just stay up here until I make one round of the cellhouses. I'll be back in fifteen minutes."

"Why should I? Why should I run the risk of getting knifed?" He glanced toward the storeroom, then moved closer to Cully, and went on in a whisper. "D'you know where the psychos who started this are? They're not a damn bit interested in the improvements we're asking for. They're in the auditorium. D'you know what they're doing? They're digging a tunnel to the Women's Quarters."

"How'd you find out?"

"Fletcher and Gigolo were up here just before you came. They wanted to move the hostages to the auditorium. In fact, they would've done it if I hadn't convinced them that nothing is going to happen before six o'clock."

Cully leaned against the wall. "So what about you and me? What d'you figure we should do?"

"Let's go to our cells and get some sleep."

Cully was about to say, "What about the hostages?" when he heard the scrape of feet beyond the door. Someone was coming up the stairs, already near the top. He spotted a metal rod under a radiator across the room and was moving that way when the door eased open and a foot swung it against the wall.

He was caught bending over, his mouth half open, by a hairy-chested con in a greasy pot washer's apron. The con was carrying a dented aluminum pitcher, full of hot coffee. "Compliments of the management," he said as Skinny maneuvered the steaming pitcher from his hands and carried it into the storeroom.

"What time is it?" Cully asked, his back to the con as he picked up the metal rod and set it on a windowsill, casually, as though setting the rod on the windowsill had been his original intention.

"Two thirty," the con said. "Three and a half more hours. Why they're stallin' out front beats the hell outta me. Everybody's ready in here. Must be red tape. Everything's red tape. They can't even end a lousy riot without goin' through a lotta red tape." He started toward the door. "See ya, Briston. I'm in a domino game downstairs."

"Click the lock on your way out," Cully said.

The con stopped, examined the lock, twisted the doorknob. "Can't, man, the bolt's froze. Somebody jammed it."

The con left, and Skinny came back into the office. "We're asking for trouble," he said in an undertone. "You and I are liable to be left holding the bag. Why don't you release 'em? Escort 'em out front."

"*Me?* Why don't you?"

"I haven't a damn thing to gain, Cully, nothing but a knife in the back. I'm a lifer. I've got a mandatory seventeen years to serve. This prison is my world for the next thirteen years. I can't take a chance on turning the cons in here against me. But it's different with you. You could be on the streets in two weeks —as soon as the parole board meets."

"Yeah, and if it backfired, I'd be the lowest fink in the joint."

"You could ask for outside-the-wall protection. They'd damn sure give it to you in a case like this. You could leave these walls a few minutes from now and never again set foot inside."

Cully walked to the door. He opened it and looked over the pipe-railed stair landing. There was a shadow moving about in the coalroom below, and in front of the cackling radio beside the coalroom door a skinny con was sitting hunched forward on a bushel basket. Farther on, his head just disappearing from sight beyond the ceiling beam which blocked Cully's view of the kitchen, a con in a blue denim work jacket was walking in the direction of the pantry. Otherwise, the dimly lighted rear of the kitchen was deserted. It would be a cinch. Down the stairs and out the rear-side door to the shopline. It was dark out there, dark and deserted. Less than a city block to the Administration Building. He closed the office door and walked back toward Skinny, noticing the anxious expressions on the faces inside the storeroom as he passed the entrance.

"It's the only thing to do," Skinny said, speaking louder now, but not loud enough to be heard in the storeroom. "There's still a chance of gaining something from this. Improving the living conditions in here. But if something happens to the hostages, the public is sure to turn against us."

Cully had crossed the room to an open window. By pressing his face against the bars, he could see the northwest corner of the prison. The auditorium and lawn in front of it were clearly visible in the glow spread by the line of searchlights on the north wall. There wasn't a sign of life. The building appeared deserted. He turned away. "There's nothin' I'd like better than to kiss this zoo good-bye," he said, "but to do it, I'd hav'ta turn against my own kind."

"Who? Fletcher? Matthews? Gigolo? They're not your kind. They were raised in reform school. They're completely dehumanized."

"So am I. I couldn't care less about those hostages in there. If it wasn't for a murder rap—and if the Indian wasn't plannin' to get me, too—I'd help him sharpen his shiv so he could do a good job on Andy Gump. A creep like that doesn't deserve to live."

"I'll go along with you there, but the others are pretty decent guys."

"They're all the same. A bull is a bull. Any one of 'em would blow your brains out if he had a gun and you made a run for the wall—and don't hand me that jive about the man is only doin' his job. Any son of a bitch who earns his livin' sittin' in a gun tower must be dehumanized, too."

Skinny moved closer. "You'll be free one of these days. You can't live by the convict's code out there. If you do, you'll be right back. You'll spend the rest of your life drifting in and out of these places."

"At least I'll be welcome. Out there I'll always be an ex-con. If I screw up on both sides of the wall, I'll be worse off than the Man Without a Country." He turned back to the window and peered again at the bright eerie-still lawn in front of the auditorium. "No, if I took those hostages out front, it would be for no other reason than to worm my own way outta here. And I do mean *worm*."

"That's reason enough."

"Not for me. I'd hav'ta live with it. Right or wrong, I'd be doin' somethin' I'd hate another guy for doin'. So let's forget it. Stick around up here until I get back. Okay?"

"I don't like the idea. If Surefoot comes up here, someone's going to get hurt. I'd rather not be around."

"Look, man, I'm as scared of a shiv as you are, but there's eight of you up here. If he steps in the storeroom, bombard him with can' goods. Anyhow, I doubt if he'll show up for a while. I got a hunch he's layin' for me in the dark somewhere. He'd probably like to get me outta the way first. He didn't make out so good the last time he came up here after Andy."

"Why don't you release Grossman? With him gone, the others would be safe."

"Andy Gump's the last one I'd help. The dog doesn't deserve nothin' but a hole in the ground."

Skinny moved to the steward's desk and rested a hip on the edge. "How are you going to stop him?"

"The Indian?"

Skinny nodded.

"Damned if I know. All I know is I better get to him before he gets to me."

"You mean with a knife?"

"I doubt it. I doubt if I could use a shiv. If I don't let him creep up on me from behind, I oughta be able to handle him with my hands. I must outweigh the puny bastard by seventy pounds."

Shaking his head, Skinny scoonched to a sitting position on the desk. "Go ahead," he said. "I'll wait until you get back. And good luck."

As Cully passed the storeroom, he glanced inside. Grossman, looking as if he had aged forty years in the past two days, was sitting up, gripping the mattress, his bloodshot eyes fixed on the door.

There was a noisy clatter going on in front of the pantry. Cooks and messmen were dropping knives and meat cleavers in a barrel. Murry was standing in the pantry doorway, and the con sitting on the overturned bushel basket in front of the radio was talking to someone in the coalroom. No one looked Cully's way as he descended the stairs and left the kitchen through the rear-side door.

Searchlights atop the front wall and on the rear wall behind the cannery poured a heavy mist of light down both ends of the shopline. He stood on the walk near the cannery end, between the kitchen and the milk house, peering through the mist toward the front of the prison. A con was moving up the messhall ramp toward the side entrance. Two others were perched on the railing near the top. Although fifty yards away and unrecognizable in the hazy light, none of the three resembled Surefoot.

Cully watched the shadowy shop doorways for a while, then entered the lighted milk house. Empty ten-gallon milk cans, usually stacked against the wall, were strewed all over the place, like scattered bowling pins. Smashed and gutted egg cases lay in a gooey heap in one corner. The floor was sloppy-wet and littered with eggshells. Eggs had been smashed against the walls, and the splattered yolks had run in stringy rivulets down the whitewashed concrete and dried there. He sloshed through the mess, kicked open the screen door, and walked out on the asphalt road in front of the powerhouse.

From where he stood, facing a bulwark of bright mist-spreading searchlights atop the front wall more than a hundred yards away, he had an almost daytime view of the buildings, the lawns, and the walks east of the shopline, beyond the delivery-truck road. Only the red-beaconed water tank towered above the bright mist. The spacious lawn below it, caged in shadows cast by the steel tower legs and crisscrossing girders, gave off a pale greenish glow. There was no one on the lawn. He could see the side and front entrances to the guards' dining room, the main entrance to Cellhouse Seven, the rear windows of Cellhouse Eight, and, beyond the powerhouse, the fenced-in area where an outside construction company had begun work on what was rumored to be a new kitchen and messhall. There wasn't a human form in sight, not even a moving shadow.

He turned and faced an unbroken string of searchlights, stretching from what could be seen of the east wall beyond the rear of the powerhouse, right-angling past the northeast gun tower, and continuing on along the north wall to the edge of the cannery, less than thirty yards from where he was standing. There was no one in sight. The loading dock in front of the cannery was crowded with shadows, but not one was moving. He stood there awhile, scanning the top of the north wall, imagining himself being watched from behind the blinding searchlights. Then, distracted by a pounding sound from somewhere inside the powerhouse, he turned again and started down the asphalt road, slowly, watchfully, peering through the eerie light, searching for a suspicious-looking shadow.

Never had the prison seemed so empty and desolate, so hopelessly isolated from the world beyond the walls. Only once had he seen it so destitute of life; but then a guard had been walking behind him, and the sky, veiled now by the misty searchlights, had been sprinkled with stars and beaming a full-faced moon. As he crossed the lawn under the water tower now, he remembered the night more than two years before when a guard had roused him from a dead sleep and escorted him from his cage to the cellhouse door, remembered waiting there for the night lieutenant to pick him up, wondering if some stool pigeon had put the finger on him for breaking a window in Isolation and slinging in a Bull Durham sack full of goofballs the day before, and then, really worried, gnawing on his fingernails, certain that the night lieutenant was bringing a death message, a telegram from Milwaukee announcing his mother's death. And finally, relieved, almost giddy, he was walking toward the hospital, seeing the stars and the moon for the first time since entering the prison, the splayfooted night lieutenant clumping along behind him, telling him of the overturned automobile on the highway a mile away, of the mangled driver who needed his type of blood. He had never learned if the driver had lived, and he wondered now if he himself would be in need of a blood transfusion before the sun came up again.

He stopped at the entrance to Cellhouse Seven and looked back in the direction he had come. The shadows were motionless; the road was deserted. There was no one in sight. Maybe Surefoot had taken Kelly's advice; maybe he had settled down in one of the cellhouses. Not very likely, though. After seven years in a stinking cage, Christ only knew what was going on in the stir-crazy Indian's mind. He shoved open the door and entered the cellhouse.

There was activity in the cellblock area beyond the partition —cons moving along the tier walkways, some standing in cell doorways, a few perched on the tier railings—but most of the cells were dark, and the sliding doors were shut. Only one radio within earshot was on speaker, barely audible, a twangy voice singing, "Good-bye sweetheart, hello Vietnam. . . ."

Cully was moving across the entrance area toward the cellhouse sergeant's desk, where three cons were standing around a faded Army blanket strewn with knives, hammers and straightedge razors. One of the cons had been involved in the Isolation breakout. He was Freddy Phelps, the con who had found the Benny inhalers in Fisk's desk drawer. His eyes were glassy, and from the way he was champing on a wad of gum, he was still loaded. Mashing the gum between his grin-exposed teeth, he said, "Still on your feet, huh, Cully?"

Cully glanced at the potential arsenal on the blanket. "What's goin' on?"

"Where ya been, man? Ain't'cha heard? It's all over but the shoutin'. We're haulin' the hardware out front."

"It's not even three thirty. I thought the warden said six o'clock."

"Yeah, but before then they want all the weapons outta the joint."

"You mean you guys are shakin' down the cells?"

"Naw, just gettin' together a barrelful of odds and ends to take out there. Junk the guys don't want—mostly state-owned stuff. The barbers'll get their razors back, and the res'ta the crap belongs in the kitchen and shops. Ain't a homemade shiv in the lot. At least not in this bunch. I don't know what they got over in the kitchen." He squatted and began helping the other two cons toss the hammers, knives, and razors into a pile in the center of the blanket.

"How'n the hell we gonna carry this without stabbin' ourselves?" one asked.

"Just grab the corners and bundle it up," Freddy said. "We'll drag it over the lawn."

Cully waited until the clatter had subsided; then, casually, he asked, "Has Surefoot been around?"

Freddy bounced to his feet, shaking his head. "Man, ya should've kept that nut locked up. Should've never turned him loose."

"I didn't."

"Who did?"

Cully shrugged.

"I ain't no bull lover," Freddy went on, still shaking his head, "but that nut's too much. Come bustin' in here awhile ago wavin' a honed-down butcher knife. Damn thing was still hot from a grindin' wheel. Wanted me to go over to the storeroom with him and hold off the hostages while he gave Andy Gump the business."

"How long ago was that?"

"Maybe fifteen, twenty minutes."

"Where was he headed when he left?"

"Y'got me. Lookin' for a partner, I guess. Said somethin' about burnin' the joint to the ground. Said he was gonna— Hey, where ya goin'? Give us a hand with—"

Cully was already shouldering open the door. He stepped outside and stood on the walk, adjusting his eyes to the bright haze pouring into the prison from atop the front wall less than thirty yards away. He forced his eyes away from the blinding search-lights and peered past the plumbing shop at the corner of the shopline, toward the heavy steel door leading to the Administra-tion Building. He could make out four cons, cooks or messmen in white pants and T-shirts, standing on the walk in front of the door. On the walk behind them was a flatbed cart on which sat a barrel, perhaps the barrel he'd seen being loaded with knives and meat cleavers in the kitchen. He could hear voices. The cons were looking upward, and one was gesturing, apparently talking to someone on the gun walk behind the searchlights.

He started that way; then, suddenly coming to a decision, he swerved and cut across the lawn, trotting under the water tower, up the asphalt road, past the powerhouse again, through the plundered milk house, and entering the kitchen through the rear-side door.

As he climbed the stairs to the steward's office, he glimpsed several cons standing around the radio in front of the coalroom. "Hey, Cully," one called, "accordin' to the news, the warden's gonna speak at five thirty. Sounds like he's gonna let you guys stay in Population."

"How lucky can you get, Briston?" another called. "That means you'll get to empty your own bucket."

Cully had reached the door and was ramming it with his shoulder. There was a thump, a scraping sound, repeated with each shove, as he forced it open inch by inch. He could see the barricade behind the door: a heavy desk with cases of canned goods stacked on top of it. A case teetered, toppled, crashed to the floor. He saw Fisk and Skinny Burns rushing from the store-room. "Open up," he called. "It's me—Briston."

As he stepped away from the opening, he caught sight of Sergeant Gallaway and Parole Officer Campbell coming through the storeroom doorway. He heard the repeated thuds of heavy cases hitting the floor, heard a screeching scraping sound, and then the door swung open. The hostages were walking back to-ward the storeroom. Skinny was standing inside.

"Was he up here?" Cully asked.

"I'm not sure. Someone tried to get in while we were shoving the desk against the door. Wouldn't say who he was when I asked, so I didn't open up. Have you seen him?"

"I'll find him later. After I get rid of Andy Gump."

He was moving toward the storeroom when Skinny said, "Don't tell me you let Fletcher talk you into moving him to the auditorium."

"I haven't seen Fletcher. I'm takin' the ol' creep out front before the Indian gets a gang together." He sidestepped Skinny and entered the storeroom.

Five of the hostages were hugging the shadows along the window side of the gloomily lighted room. Fisk was leaning against a gouged-up wooden stanchion near the door. Beyond the makeshift cup-littered table, rheumy-eyed and whey-faced under the haze of a sixty-watt light bulb dangling from the ceiling, Grossman was sitting slumped on one of the lumpy mattresses, legs sprawled, arms limp, his back against the wall. He was looking at Cully, his gaunt grizzly-whiskered face twitching and writhing as though he were trying to smile.

"C'mon, Andy," Cully said, "you're goin' for a walk."

Grossman's mouth went slack. His panic-stricken eyes darted to Fisk, and Fisk said, "Where are you taking him?"

Cully started to say, "None of your goddamn business," but suddenly playing the tough-guy role seemed stupid. The deputy warden was looking him straight in the eye. In the gloomy shadows beyond, the hostages' faces were tense with concern. "Out front," he said. "I'm turnin' him loose."

"He's lyin'!" Grossman croaked. "Why me? Why would he turn me loose?" He began crawling over the mattresses toward the other hostages. "I'm only a guard. Take the deputy warden."

Cully turned away, angry, disgusted. "I should worry about a dog like that," he said to Skinny, who was standing in the doorway. "I hope the Indian cuts his throat." He turned to Fisk. "Just remember, Burns and I offered to turn him loose."

Fisk glanced at Grossman, then moved away from the stanchion, closer to Cully, and said, "Perhaps he's safer up here. You might attract a crowd on your way to the front of the prison. Anything could happen."

"I don't know where'n the hell the crowd would come from. Ninety-nine percent of the guys are in their cells."

"What about the men from Isolation?"

Cully dropped his eyes, cast a sidelong glance at Skinny, hitched at his dungarees. For a moment he thought of blurting it out, of telling the hostages to make a run for the Administration Building, that the shopline was deserted, that the only cons who were likely to stop them were nowhere around. Then he thought of the cons in the auditorium, of selling them out, of getting them trapped in the tunnel and tear-gassed. They were solid cons, guys who had cut him in on their Benny and goofball scores, guys who had always treated him right. "Most of 'em are sleepin'," he said.

"And Surefoot?"

"That's why I'm here. I don't know where he is."

Grossman had scrabbled to his feet and was slumped against the stanchion Fisk had moved away from. At the mention of Surefoot he had let out a groaning "Oh, God!" and was now craning his neck to see past Skinny into the steward's office.

"We can protect ourselves against one man," Fisk said and glanced at his wristwatch. "It's quarter to four. Burns tells me that we're all to be released at six o'clock. We appreciate your concern, Briston, but don't you think a false step now is apt to stir up trouble?"

Cully shrugged. "A lot can happen in two hours. Besides, it might not be just one man comin' up here. That ol' creep there isn't exactly popular in this joint. Lotta cons would like to see him get what he's got comin'. And he's puttin' the heat on the res'ta you guys up here. But suit yourselves. I don't care one way or the other. All I want you to do is remember that Burns and I offered to turn him loose."

"The decision isn't ours to make," Fisk said. "It's up to Mr. Grossman."

"Man, forget it! I'm stickin' my neck out for you guys, and you talk like I'm tryin' to start trouble. G'wan, shove the desk against the door and pile up those cases. Sweat it out till six o'clock, I don't give a damn. Just remember, if anything happens to him, Burns and I made the offer." He turned and started toward the steward's office.

"Don't go, boy!" Grossman came scurrying around in front of him, pawing at his arm. "Gimme your word. I trust you, boy. You'll stay with me all the way. You won't—"

Cully jerked his arm away, repulsed by the feel of the man's groveling hand. "You heard what I said. I'll take you to the Administration Building door. If you're comin', c'mon." He brushed past Skinny, entered the steward's office, and hurried to the outer door. Grossman was inches behind him, stepping on his heels, still pawing.

Cully paused in the doorway, listened, then stepped out on the pipe-railed stair landing. Below, beside the coalroom door, a con was dialing the radio. Voices were coming from inside the room. He could see two pairs of white pants legs moving toward the pantry, but from there on, his view was blocked by the concrete ceiling beam. He squatted to see under it, gaped for a moment, then sprang up, bringing a strangled "Oh, God!" from Grossman as he shoved the man back into the steward's office, his heart pounding from the jolt of what he'd seen: Fletcher, Gigolo, and Bugsy Matthews coming through the kitchen archway, hurriedly, arms swinging, heads bobbing.

"What's up?" Skinny asked, and began maneuvering like a matador to block Grossman, who was trying to get back into the storeroom.

"Nothin'," Cully said. "Just playin' it cool." He waited several seconds; then, motioning to Grossman, he moved into the doorway again. The area directly below was deserted. The con who had been dialing the radio was gone. White pants legs were ganging up around the pantry door. Apparently Fletcher and the others had gone inside. He squatted and looked beyond the ceiling beam, toward the front of the kitchen. There were perhaps fifteen cons in sight, all moving toward the pantry. "C'mon," he said to Grossman. "Stay on the wall side when we go down the stairs. Keep in step with me, no faster, no slower.

And take off that goddamn hat!" He stepped out on the landing and started down the stairs.

Four steps down, in full view of the cons in front of the pantry, Grossman froze. "They see me! They see me!" he whispered hoarsely.

For a moment Cully just stood there, his eyes bounding from the pantry, to the steward's office, to the rear-side kitchen door. Then he realized that no one was looking. Not a face was turned their way. "Goddammit, man, *move!*" he said, and snatched Grossman's arm.

Two strides from the bottom of the stairs they were out of sight, hidden from view by the projecting coalroom, only twenty feet from the door. Cully was an arm's length away, reaching for the handle, when the door swung open and Nosy Bains, his stubby arms wrapped around a bushel basket full of cabbages, came waddling over the threshold.

He stopped, stared at Grossman for a moment, then looked at Cully, grinning. "Now you're using your head, Champ."

"You better use yours," Cully said. "Just keep walkin'."

"You know *me*, Champ. I won't say a word."

Still grinning, he stepped aside as Cully steered Grossman through the doorway and into the phosphorescent haze pouring down on them from the searchlights on each end of the shopline.

A tall T-shirted con was moving up the messhall ramp. A hundred yards ahead, two others, barely discernible, were turning onto the walk which ran parallel to the front wall. The kitchen side of the shopline was shadowless; but the doorways on the shop side were dark, and two of the doors were hanging open, casting daggerlike shadows across the lawn. The air between the buildings was muggy, motionless. Only the con on the messhall ramp was moving. Then he disappeared. A door slammed, and it was quiet.

Cully had an impulse to run, to sprint past the dark doorways, but the wheezing half-crouched old man beside him was moving along in spurts, shuffling, stopping, scurrying a few yards, his head jerking about like a wary sparrow's, his visored hat crushed against his chest. They passed the laundry and started past the bakery. There was a light on inside. Charlie Kline, the head con baker, was dumping a sack of flour into the mixer. As they hurried past the lighted windows, Cully glanced at the baggy-eyed face beside him—corpse-gray in the hazy glow of the searchlights—and for a moment he felt like touching the old man's shoulder.

"Nothin' to worry about," he said and was about to add, "We're almost there," when Grossman lunged against him.

"Over there!" he croaked, and flung an arm in the direction of the carpentershop doorway.

The door was hanging open, and the shadow it cast was creeping over the lawn. Someone was standing in the doorway. Cully could make out a moving arm and then the vague shape of a face in the darkness.

"Keep movin'," Cully said, but Grossman was standing a few yards away, stock-still, rooted to the lawn on the messhall side of the walk, watching the carpentershop door swing shut, then open again. The arm reappeared, and then the shadowy face.

Reaching in the waistband of his dungarees, as though ready to draw a shiv, Cully grabbed Grossman's arm and began moving along the messhall lawn. As they passed the carpentershop doorway, less than fifteen feet to their right, the face came out of the darkness, and a familiar hunchbacked form took shape.

Hardnose, the stir-simple old lifer who always spent his summers in Segregation, moved out on the lawn and watched them pass. Although he occasionally mumbled replies to questions from certain old-time guards, Cully had never heard him speak to another con. He gestured wildly now, pointed to the front wall, and shout-whispered, "They're watchin'! They're up there behind them lights."

Feeling foolish, his hand still stuffed in the waistband of his dungarees, Cully waved and nodded as he hurried to keep up with Grossman, who was walking fast now, squinting into the searchlights, his visored hat squarely on his head. At the entrance to the shopline Cully caught his arm and pulled him back between the buildings. The cooks and messmen he'd seen earlier in front of the Administration Building door were moving up the walk toward the Control Room. One was pushing the flatbed food cart, minus the barrel. Behind the blinding searchlights on the wall above the door, Cully could make out a cluster of faces and several rifle barrels pointed into the prison. He waited until the cart and the man pushing it had entered the Control Room; then he released Grossman's arm, and they made a beeline across the lawn to the Administration Building door.

"Hold it right there!" someone called from above.

Grossman shouted, "Cover me! Cover me! I'm Albert Grossman, one of the hostages." He gave Cully a shove. "Get back where you belong, boy! Get away from the door." He began pounding on it.

Ignoring the gabble of questions coming at them from behind the searchlights on the crowded gun walk above, Cully turned his back on Grossman and walked slowly toward the Control Room.

CHAPTER **18**

THERE were three cons in the Control Room. Two were moving away from the door when Cully entered. The other was leaning through the wicket in the screened-in area. "What's goin' on out there?" he asked. "Sounded like Andy Gump."

Cully had started toward Isolation. He stopped and turned to the wicket. "Y'know Surefoot? Scrawny Indian that's been in Lockup for seven years."

The con nodded. "I know what he looks like."

"Have you seen him?"

"Not since yesterday. Why? What's goin' on?"

"Beats me. You guys know more than I do."

"Wasn't that Andy Gump out there?"

"Damned if I know. I'm lookin' for the Indian."

The con took the hint. He ducked through the wicket and sat down in Sergeant Gallaway's swivel chair. The other two cons had moved into the screened-in area and were standing behind him.

"Sure could go for a smoke," one said. "Ya ain't picked up a soggy ol' butt in your travels, have ya, Cully?"

"Are you kiddin'? I'm about ready to throw a nicotine fit myself. Why don't you go out and put the bum on one of the troopers on the wall?"

"I already did. He told me to drop dead. Said it wasn't too long ago they were chainin' guys like me to dungeon walls. Know what I told him? I sez, 'Yeah, Jack, and it wasn't too long before that they were feedin' Christians like you to the lions.'

He told me to go piss up a rope. I told him I would if he'd
smoke it."

The phone rang, and the con in the swivel chair snatched it
from its cradle. After a long silence he said, "Dump it. They got
enough," and then set the phone back in place.

"Who was that?" Cully asked.

"Cellhouse Six. Coupla guys over there collected a boxful of
hardware. They don't want no more out front. We already sent
out two barrels and a blanketful."

Cully moved closer to the wicket. "Have you been callin' out
front?"

"Sure."

"When you call, who answers?"

"Whoever's on the switchboard. Last time it was Lieutenant
Becker."

"Wha'd you ask him?"

"Just told him we had a barrelful of weapons to send out."

"Look, man, why don't you give him another call and find out
when they plan on takin' over."

"I already know."

"When?"

"Six o'clock. Everyone in here is suppos'ta be in a cell at six
o'clock."

"What about the guys who were in The Hole?"

"Same goes for them. They're suppos'ta find a cell in one of
the cellhouses. Everyone starts off with a clean slate—that's if
the hostages get turned loose in good shape."

"Says who?"

"Murry called from the kitchen. I guess he got the information from the warden."

"Don't make sense," one of the other cons said. "Why six
o'clock? Why not right now? Why do they want us to hold the
hostages two more hours? Personally I think they're out there
plottin' some kinda shifty move. Like sendin' the Army in here
with gas guns and clubs."

"Well, if one of you guys see the Indian, tell him Andy Gump
got turned loose," Cully said, and swung open the heavily barred
door to Isolation.

The rank-smelling cellblock was even more desolate-looking than before. Two of the three sixty-watt light bulbs protruding from wall sockets in the dressing-in area were out. Beyond the dusty windows the powerful searchlights flooded the prison with a phosphorescent brightness, giving the lawn outside a frost-covered appearance and intensifying the gloomy dimness inside. The one remaining light bulb, staring from its socket in the gray-brick wall like a bleary jaundiced eye, spread a sickly haze over the shabbiness around it: the littered lime-tracked floor; a battered desk; a cracked rust-stained sink; the sagging steel stairs leading to the tier landings; and, directly in line with the light, rumored to have been put there by a cop killer awaiting the rope, the words carved in the door of the rickety closet-size cabinet in which the dressing-in dungarees were stored—EVERYBODY WANTS TO GO TO HEAVEN, BUT NOBODY WANTS TO DIE.

Cully walked to the gateway in the mesh-wire partition on the Isolation side of the cellblock and glanced along the tiers, his eyes coming to rest on the cage Surefoot had been in. The steel-latticed door was still hanging wide open. There was a light on inside, and he could see the shadow of a head and shoulders. He walked quietly to the door. Kelly, hair hanging in his eyes, his haggard face fish-belly white, was still sitting on the wall-chained bunk, head bowed, swinging his legs, a blood-dripping wad of toilet paper clenched in his hand.

"Better get that gash sewed up," Cully said. "The doc's still over in the hospital."

Kelly looked up, pushed a forearm at the hair in his face, then went back to staring at his lap. "The hell with it," he said. "Maybe if I'm lucky, I'll bleed to death."

"Whats'a matter, man?"

"Nothin'. Just plain fed up."

Cully stepped into the unventilated steel box and leaned on the chain at the foot of the bunk. The steel floor between the bunk and the wall, worn shiny from years of bare- and stocking-footed pacing, was smeared and spotted with blood. There was a dented rust-corroded bucket in the far corner, and the sickening stench of lime-watered urine smothered the already muggy air. "You're weakenin', ol'-timer," Cully said. "Aren't you the one who's always sayin', 'Quit whinin'! I can't stand to hear a grown man cry'?"

"I'm not whinin', kid. I'm just fed up. Disgusted with this rotten life."

"A rotten one's better than none at all. Besides, you can't croak now. You still owe the state a lotta time."

"I don't owe this bloodsuckin' state nothin'. This state owes me."

"Then you better keep those mitts in good shape, so you can steal with both hands when you get out."

"Be a long time before I need these hands. I'll be rottin' in one of these stinkin' cages for the next five years. So will you. They'll give us more time over this, watch and see."

"Not if the warden keeps his word. Accordin' to Murry, all of us involved in this are stayin' in General Population."

Kelly looked up, grimacing. "You don't believe that? Wise up! We'll all be back in The Hole an hour after they take over. I've dealt with these double-crossin' bastards all my life. I know."

Cully whacked the bunk chain. "C'mon, I've got ten gallons of hooch stashed in the kitchen. Let's drink it up before they get in here. Might as well bleed to death in comfort. I'll even let you sit in the warden's easy chair." He moved to the door and looked out. There wasn't a sound or a moving shadow. "C'mon, it's light over there, and I can keep my back against a wall. The Indian hasn't made his move yet."

"G'wan, kid, leave me alone. I just want to sit here and think."

Cully stood there awhile, watching blood drip from the wad of toilet paper in Kelly's hand to the shiny steel floor. He thought of getting the doctor or one of the inmate nurses; then, deciding that the Irishman was in no danger of bleeding to death, he stepped from the cage. "See you then," he said, and started toward the dressing-in area.

As he turned through the gateway, he glanced from the trash can lid he had thrown on the floor the previous afternoon to the girder under the second-tier walkway. The blade of the butcher knife was still protruding. He started to reach for the knife, then remembered an old prison adage: Don't carry a shiv unless you intend to use it. He kept on walking and was nearing the rear door when a hoarse voice cracked the silence.

"Hey, down there! What's goin' on?"

Cully had spun around, crouched, squinting. He waited now until his heart stopped pounding, then called, "Save your voice, Duke. You guys can tell your troubles to the warden in less than two hours."

"That you down there, Cully? C'mere a minute, buddy. Lemme outta here. I got some Benny planted. I'll—" Cully was beyond the door, moving toward the messhall.

The lights were on in the messhall, and three cons were backing along the aisles, swinging mops. Two others were scooting back and forth between the rows of sagging tables, lining up the salt and pepper shakers.

As Cully walked under the kitchen archway, he glanced toward the windows. The sky above the shoeshop roof was turning gray. It was four fifteen on the wall clock behind the range. He moved under the canopy and leaned on one of the steam caldrons, his eyes sweeping the kitchen, searching the doorways and corners for a dark bony face.

There were perhaps twenty cons scattered between the caldrons and the range, some standing in huddles, some sitting on tables, a few strolling about. Loud voices were coming from inside the pantry. Several cooks and messmen were jammed in the doorway. Smith, 19846, apparently exhausted from having spent the day pleading with the troopers from the walk in front of the Administration Building door, was laid out in the warden's easy chair, arms draped over the sides, legs stretched over his cardboard box, his hat covering his face. On the floor beside the chair, looking like a sodden burlap sack, lay his suit coat and, on top of the coat, a wadded red necktie. He was jiggling his white-stockinged feet to the twangy beat of a solo guitar coming from the radio in front of the coalroom.

A cook Cully knew slightly, a dumpy owlish-faced con in his late thirties, was hosing down the drainage area around the caldrons. He turned off the hose now and motioned to Cully.

"Your buddies were lookin' for you," he said as Cully approached. "Fletcher and Gigolo and that skinny Indian you guys carried out of here yesterday. They went out the back door a few minutes ago."

Cully's face went stiff. His stomach seemed to flutter, then tighten. He looked toward the rear of the kitchen. After a few moments he asked, "Wha'd they want with me?"

The con shrugged. "Ask Nosy Bains. He was talkin' to 'em. All I know is they came down from upstairs madder than hell."

"Where's Nosy?"

The con looked around. "He was here a minute ago. Must be around somewhere."

Cully glanced at the clock, hollow-weak inside, wishing he could turn back the time forty-eight hours—or ahead only two. He'd fight if he had to. He'd fight anyone with his hands. One at a time. Hell, he'd settle for a beating right now, but a gang or a knife— Christ! He thought of slipping back to his cage in Cellhouse Four, thought of finding a corner somewhere and lying low until the guards came in. He started toward the rear of the kitchen, past the squabbling voices in the pantry, past the coalroom, where a sprightly voiced radio announcer was chirping, "Happy! Happy! Happy! That's how *you* will feel as you watch your dollars grow. Come to the sign of the Smiling Dollar at five thirty-two East Fifth Street and—"

He plodded up the stairs to the steward's office, aware of his weary muscles, the start of a headache, a sour stomach. The door was wide open. The steward's heavy oak desk set askew in the center of the room, cases of canned goods strewn on the floor around it. Skinny Burns was sitting on an upended case, one side of his homely face red and swollen.

"Did you make it out front with Grossman?"

Cully nodded.

"You're still in one piece. You must not have run into your pals."

"Why?"

"Should've asked for protection, Cully. Should've followed Grossman out the door. It's not only the Indian now; they're all down on you."

"How'd they find out?"

"Not from me. Somebody downstairs must've told 'em. They knew he was gone before they came up here."

Cully stepped over the scattered canned goods cases and slung a hip on the edge of the desk. He could see into the dimly lighted storeroom. Fisk was pacing the floor, his shirttail hanging out, his hands behind his back. The other five hostages were sitting on the mattresses at the rear of the room.

"Christ, could I go for a cigarette!" Skinny said.

"Man, you and me both. What happened to your face?"

"Bugsy took a poke at me. I called him a blockhead." Skinny touched his swollen cheek. "You know, Cully, as out of shape as I am, I honestly think I could take the muscle-bound son of a bitch in a fair fight. In fact, I almost tried him. But not with the others itching to clobber me—and that insane Surefoot standing five feet away with a butcher knife in his hand. I just dropped on the floor and stayed there until they left."

"Did they come up here lookin' for me?"

"They came for the hostages. They were going to move 'em to the auditorium."

"Who stopped 'em?"

"Nobody. That kid—the one you call Jitterbug—he came to the door and said something to Fletcher. The next thing I knew the room was empty."

"They must've made it to the Women's Quarters."

"Be a break for you if they did. It'll get their minds off you."

"I might go over there myself. I like women, too."

"Use your head. Believe me, Cully—"

Shouts came from downstairs:

"News! News!"

"Turn it up."

Cully was moving toward the door. He stepped out on the stair landing and leaned over the railing, looking down as a crowd gathered around the radio. When the commotion subsided, the newscaster was saying, ". . . agreement after two days of rioting in the State Penitentiary. Only minutes ago, not knowing that an agreement had been reached, Sergeant Albert Grossman, a veteran correctional officer held hostage since the rebellion began, broke away from his captors and made his way to the prison's front exit. According to Grossman, the seven remaining hostages were unharmed when he left them, and the prison, except for a handful of inmates congregated in the kitchen, was quiet. The men behind the heavily guarded walls seem to be waiting for six o'clock, the time agreed on for the release of the hostages. Meanwhile, the rebel leaders are preparing to turn the prison back over to the authorities. Weapons, such as sharp tools, straightedge razors, and homemade knives, called shivs, are being collected in barrels and carried to the prison's front exit. When interviewed earlier by Neal Seaburg, our on-the-spot reporter, Warden Sullivan had this to say concerning his agreement with the rebel leaders' liaison, Miles Murry, the prison's recently acquired psychologist.''

A moment's silence, a whir and crackle, and then a heavy, weary-sounding voice broke in: "This is a touchy situation. It requires trust on both sides. Although the men directly involved in this are Isolation cases, troublemakers, what the public refers to as hardened criminals, they're still men, as deserving of a chance to prove themselves as you and I. They're asking for amnesty, a fresh start in what we call General Population. They have from now until six o'clock to remove all weapons from the prison, to return the keys that were given to them when this demonstration began—this was done in hopes of safeguarding the locking mechanisms in the newer cellhouses—and, of course, they must release the hostages unharmed. Also, every man in the prison is to be in his cell with the door closed when—" He was cut off by the familiar voice of the on-the-spot reporter.

"Does this include the men who were in Isolation? Are they to return to Isolation?"

"As things stand right now, they're to find sleeping quarters in one of the cellhouses. Again, as things stand right now, they will remain in General Population and will be treated the same as any other inmate as long as they abide by the rules. This depends, of course, on whether the hostages are released unharmed and assuming no inmate has been killed or injured as a result of this demonstration."

"Loopholes!" snapped a con in the coalroom doorway. "He's leavin' loopholes."

Cully moved away from the railing, scanning the crowd for Nosy Bains. Since the beginning of the newscast, at the mention of Grossman's name, the cons around the radio had been glancing up at him, askance, as if they had heard. He should've known. Of all the cons he might've run into, it had to be a busybody fink like Nosy Bains.

"Doesn't sound like Sullivan," Skinny said from the doorway.

"Voices sound different on the radio," Cully said, and stepped back into the steward's office.

"I don't mean his voice. I mean what he said. The way he said it. Sounds like Murry wrote the script."

"You don't think he'll keep his word? You know, about lettin' us stay in Population."

"Do you?"

"To tell the truth, Skinny, I couldn't care less. You'll probably be the only con in the joint on speakin' terms with me when this is over. I'll be known as the phony bastard who saved Andy Gump."

"You could get a parole. He might put in a good word."

"Hell, man, he's lyin' already. Says he broke out. Besides, I don't want a good word from the creep." He moved back to the doorway. The cons downstairs had scattered. Only two were standing in front of the coalroom. "I think I'll take a hike over to the auditorium. See if they made it."

"You're asking for trouble, Cully. Stay out of sight until—"

"Why'n the hell should I? I'm not ashamed of what I did. Hell, man, that shiv-happy Indian could've got us all charged with murder. He still might. He's liable to cut some broad over in the Women's Quarters."

"And if you go over there, he's liable to plant his knife in *your* back."

"That's where he'll hav'ta plant it—in my back. As long as he comes from the front, I'll spot him a shiv."

"Why don't you forget it, Cully? It isn't like backing down from a fight. Surefoot's a psycho. Let the guards take care of him. That's their job. And it's not only Surefoot now. The others—"

"Fletcher and his clique don't worry me. They're mostly mouth."

"Don't fool yourself. Gigolo's as dangerous as Surefoot. Take my advice and stay away from over there. Why stir up trouble? Ten to one Surefoot's forgotten you by now."

"Are you kiddin'? He's got a one-track mind. Anyway, it's not that I hate the guy—hell, I feel kinda sorry for him—but I'd feel more comfortable if I found him before he finds me."

"Then what? What if you find him?"

"I'll get him back in a cage. Then I'm goin' to sleep. See you, Skinny." He walked out the door and down the steps. No one looked his way as he moved toward the rear-side kitchen door.

The searchlights had been turned off, and the section of wall that he could see at the front of the prison was lined with face-less rifle-armed men, dimly silhouetted against a slate-gray sky. Four cons in white pants and T-shirts were sitting hunched over on the ramp railing in front of the side messhall door. Otherwise the shopline was deserted. As he rounded the rear of the kitchen, moving away from the shopline, he noticed that the guards on the rear wall behind the cannery, their features just barely discernible, were removing the searchlights. He stopped for a moment and was watching the operation when he caught a movement in front of the auditorium, perhaps seventy yards away.

One of the doors had swung open, and a shirtless figure, recognizable only as dark and slender, was stepping into the grayness. He stood there awhile, then descended the steps, and hurried across the lawn, disappearing behind Cellhouse Five as he moved toward Cellhouse Six.

Cully started walking, then trotting, and he was almost sprinting by the time he reached the edge of the auditorium lawn. He could see to the front wall: the barred L-shaped enclosure leading from Cellhouse Four to Cellhouse Six, and beyond, the stretch of lawn between the hospital and Isolation. Except for the line of gray motionless forms silhouetted against the sky at the front of the prison, there was no one in sight.

He cut diagonally across the lawn between the auditorium and the rear of Cellhouse Six, momentarily startled by the line of rifle-armed troopers looming up against the dreary morning sky, starkly vivid now as he approached to within thirty feet of the west wall. The buildings ended there. He now had an unobstructed view. The entire west wall was lined with armed men, strung out several feet apart for almost two hundred yards. He was awed by the sight. A lonely, almost dreadful feeling of insignificance came over him as he forced his eyes away.

He was turning back in the direction he had come when he noticed that the door leading up to the execution chamber at the rear of Cellhouse Six was ajar. Only once had he seen the solid-steel door unlocked. Three years before, he had gone up there on a work detail to sweep and mop. He opened the door now and stepped inside. The second solid-steel door was also ajar. He eased it open and started up the narrow staircase. There was a pale-yellow light coming down from upstairs.

"Hey!" he called. "You up there!" He paused, listened for a moment; then, taking three steps at a time, he tiptoed to the top of the stairs and stopped again.

He was standing in a bare hall, dimly lighted by several frost-coated light bulbs encased in the concrete walls behind squares of thick wire-enforced glass. The place had been viciously defaced. Obscenities, scrawled in red leather dye, covered the whitewashed walls, the letters splotched and runny like splashed blood. The head of a sledgehammer lay at his feet, the broken handle a few steps away. Two heavy metal doors, half ripped from the battered door casings on opposite sides of the hall, hung open and sagged toward the floor. A faint smell of raisin-jack lingered in the motionless air. There wasn't a sound.

He picked up the sledgehammer handle and moved to within a few feet of the closest doorway. The room beyond was lighted the same as the hall. There were splashes of red leather dye on the ceiling, walls, and floor. He could see two cells in one corner and, on the floor near the door, a hauntingly familiar contraption he'd seen three years before—the hanging board. With the leather straps torn off, it looked more like a surfboard. He remembered an old-timer on the work detail telling him that the board was used when the man to be hanged was too wild to handle or too limp with fear to stand on the gallows. Raising the sledgehammer handle, he eased up to the threshold and looked inside. There was no one in the room. He turned and started slowly across the hall, toward the execution chamber.

He stopped a few feet from the sagging metal door and stood there awhile, listening, scanning the area around the doorway for a lurking shadow. The chamber inside was well lighted. The ceiling, lower near the door, was laid out like a checkerboard with squares of fluorescent lights. Some of the squares were dark, the frosted glass shattered, leaving gaping holes in the ceiling. The floor was littered with glass, splinters of wood, and jagged chair legs. The spectators' section had been leveled. The hip-high balustrade had been wrenched from the floor, and the stationary wooden armchairs had been smashed and strewed about. He could see the partially demolished steps to the gallows, the splintered railing, and one of the posts on the platform; but the rest of the gallows was beyond his view.

Whacking the sledgehammer handle against the doorjamb, he lunged into the room and came to a heart-lurching halt. He stood there gaping, his shocked eyes fixed on the gallows. Hanging from the crossbar was a stiff and twisted form in a guard's uniform.

His first impulse was to run from the building; then the impulse died, and he moved closer. He was almost to the gallows before he saw the painted face, the footless legs, the dangling sign. He glanced around the room, sheepishly, as though expecting someone to laugh. The hanging form was a dummy. One of the old guard uniforms found in the Control Room basement had been stuffed, and a brownish cloth sack shaped like a head, with an ugly gap-toothed face painted on, protruded from the coat collar. The dummy wore a badgeless guard's hat. The badge had been pinned to the seat of the pants. And hanging from its chest, printed in red leather dye, was a cardboard sign, reading: ANDY GUMP—THE SORRIEST SON OF A BITCH ON THE FACE OF THE EARTH.

Feeling uneasy and strangely alone, Cully hurried from the room and down the stairs. The gloomy sky was a refreshing sight. Even the rifle-armed troopers looking down from the wall appeared friendly now as he turned his back on them and crossed the lawn toward the front of the auditorium. He was on the top step, reaching out to open the door, when he became aware of the sledgehammer handle still gripped in his hand. He flung it out on the lawn and entered the building.

Even as he started down the aisle, forcing a swagger, his hands in his pockets, he knew he should be running the other way, getting out of the building as fast as he could. There were more than twenty of them, some perched on the edge of the stage, some squatting in the orchestra pit, some sitting on piles of rubble and dirt. All but a scattered few were Isolation cons. Surefoot wasn't among them.

Loud angry voices had dropped to a grumble as soon as he'd been spotted, grew gradually lower, and faded into silence now as he neared the stage. They all were looking at him, hard-eyed, surly-faced. A pleasant male voice, coming from a portable radio atop a dirt pile, was giving the time—five twenty-seven —and the weather—eighty-two degrees under an overcast sky. He glanced over the faces, forcing a grin. No one returned the grin; even Rick frowned and dropped his eyes. He went over the faces again, still grinning. "Thought you guys would be makin' out with the gals by now," he said, and kept his eyes on Rick until the scrawny kid looked up. "What happened, Jitterbug?" His voice sounded hollow, diffident, strange to him.

As though asking permission to speak, Rick glanced from Fletcher to Gigolo, then back to Cully. "There's no women over there," he said gruffly. "They moved 'em to the county jail. We could've got our heads shot off for nothin'."

"That's right," Fletcher said, and moved away from the stage, followed by Bugsy. "Little while ago, the man on the radio said the state troopers took over the building. Sounds like somebody must've tipped 'em off out front. Huh, Briston? You haven't turned stoolie, have you?" He stopped a few feet from Cully and folded his arms, smirking. "You think they'll give you a parole? You know, for being a hero. For turning Andy Gump loose."

Cully could feel blood rushing to his face. He started to say, "Go to hell!" but the words caught in his throat. His legs felt weak, and an itchy trickle of sweat began rolling down his back. He glimpsed Gigolo and Coolbreeze closing in from the side.

Some of the other cons had moved away from the stage and were forming a half circle. He cleared his throat. "Aw, for crissake, Red, you know why I turned him loose."

Gigolo was standing beside him, sneering, his handsome dirt-smeared face thrust out. "Go ahead, man," he drawled, "whine it on out. You been struttin' around here actin' like a goddamn cop for two days now."

"He's the one that dumped the juice," someone said.

"Heavyweight champ!" another muttered sneeringly. "Big deal!"

"Yeah, man," Bugsy said. "We don't fight with cushions on our hands. Huh, Red?"

Fletcher and Bugsy were standing on one side of him, Gigolo and Coolbreeze on the other. He was backed against the first row of seats, and the half circle was getting tighter and tighter. There wasn't a sympathetic face in the crowd.

His mind was functioning now, wildly, desperately. Just the redhead. He'd have to goad the big redhead into making it a twosome. Just the redhead. Otherwise he was in for a gang stomping, maybe even a shiv in the guts. Christ! The thought made his legs feel weaker. A bead of sweat made an itchy zig-zag down the side of his face. There was only one thing to do, and the redhead's chin was less than an arm's length away; but his sweaty hand refused to make a fist. He tried to grin. It felt stiff on his face, like a mask. "You guys sure talk bad when you're twenty against one. You know goddamn well I didn't tip 'em off out front, and anyone who says I did is a lyin' gutless son of a bitch." He looked at Fletcher. "What's'a matter, man? D'you need half the joint to back you up?"

For several seconds no one moved; no one spoke. From the portable radio beyond the motionless half circle, a pleading soulful male voice was singing, *"My love, for-give—me.* I did-n't mean to have it end like this, I did-n't—"

Fletcher sneered and said, "Start swinging, man."

Cully glimpsed a movement from the side: an oncoming fist and, behind it, Gigolo's grimacing face. Instinctively, he rode with the punch and managed to slip it; but before he could set himself, Gigolo had looped an arm around his neck, and the half circle of onlookers, alive and wide-eyed now, began fanning out, yelling, spreading their arms. Then he was on the floor, flouncing on his back, squirming, kicking, grabbing, glimpsing a fist, a contorted face, a clawing hand, hearing the yells:

"Give him the boot!"

"Cream the phony bastard!"

"He dumped the juice!"

"Watch it, Red!"

Somehow he scrambled free of the tangle of arms and legs. He was on his feet, lunging at Fletcher, prying at the arm around his waist. He saw Bugsy, saw the clumsy haymaker coming, and tried to wrench his head away from the smothering hand clamped to his face. There was no pain, only a blinding jolt, and then the yells again:

"His arm, Coolbreeze! Grab his arm!"

"Go ahead, Gigolo, he's got it comin'."

He was in the orchestra pit now, flat on his stomach, his face in the dirt. A searing pain pierced his side, and then another. He twisted, glimpsed a blur of legs, made a grab for a swinging foot, then flung up his arms, and buried his face in the dirt. His head! They'd stomp his head! He burrowed deeper, gritting his teeth, breathing in dirt. He could barely feel the blows now, dull, painless, his mind detached, listless, counting the jolts, waiting for the red-hot sting, the shiv in the back. Then it was quiet, and somewhere nearby the soulful voice was singing, "My love, please kiss—me, *Ar-ri-ve-der-ci a-mo-re*, kiss me—"

His body felt comfortable, his mind adrift, and from a hazy distance he heard Fletcher say, "Cool it, Gigolo. Let the Indian do it. He'll find him here." And from a still hazier distance: "Let's scatter. Find a cage somewhere. It'll take 'em a coupla days to corral us." And then there was one more blinding jolt, and everything went pitch black.

CHAPTER **19**

HE became aware of the grit in his mouth, a million needles pricking his arm, a cramped aching sensation, and then a voice, a friendly voice, unruffled by the darkness, saying, "Believe me, pal, you can't go wrong at Happy Harry's. Drive past on your way to work this morning and take a look at the price tag on today's special under the boulevard canopy—a sixty-five Chevvy Belair, brand, spanking new less than six months ago. And this is only one of Happy Harry's—"

He rolled on his back, gasping as pain streaked up his side, stabbed at his neck, and came to a roaring, pounding mass at the back of his head. He lay there, staring up through a reddish blur at the wavy ceiling, hearing the radio again, remembering the beating, and then, like a blast in the dark, Fletcher's departing words: "Let the Indian do it. He'll find him here."

He raised his head, unleashing the pain again, and struggled to a sitting position, his back against a dirt heap. Gradually, the pain lost its grip, and he sat there awhile staring straight ahead, working up the courage to lift his hand and touch his ribs, his neck, his throbbing head. He could feel a runny wetness behind his right ear and knew it was too heavy to be sweat. He visualized a dirt-infested gash and blood seeping through his hair. He flexed his legs, tightened his chest muscles, slid a hand over his ribs, along his neck, over the stickiness behind his ear. He found the cut in his scalp and traced it with his finger. It wasn't as bad as he'd imagined, perhaps an inch long, no wider than his fingernail. Wincing, holding his side, he staggered to his feet and stood swaying, feeling weak, dizzy.

Then, still lightheaded, he shuffled through the dirt and leaned against the stage.

The movie screen, brilliantly white in the glare of the foot-lights, cast a snowy brightness over the orchestra pit. The floor of the pit was a step lower than the main floor, and the entire area was covered with rubble: rocks and splintered boards, heaps of dirt, and a scattering of stainless-steel cups and long-nozzled coffee dispensers from the kitchen. The portable radio, half buried in dirt, was playing soft music.

He squinted toward the shadowy rear of the auditorium. The aisles near the vestibule were flooded with daylight. He could see the doors leading outside. Both were wide open. There was no one in sight.

Again his fingers examined the scrapes and welts around his ribs, the rawness along his neck, the cut in his scalp. They hadn't done much of a job, he scoffed, considering that at least four had been stomping on him. Hell, he'd been banged up this bad before. He felt the cut behind his ear again. Sooner or later he'd even up the score. He'd get them one at a time. Then he remembered the Indian and tried to imagine himself leaping away from a slashing shiv. He took a deep breath, and pain shot up his side. His arms felt lead-heavy, and his head began to throb again. He leaned against the stage awhile longer, gazing down at the sweaty dirt-smeared bluebirds tattooed on his chest. Then, wincing again, holding his side, he dragged his feet through the dirt and started up the aisle.

Although a shade lighter, the sky was still gloomy and streaked with wisps of low-scudding clouds. He started across the lawn, toward the barred L-shaped enclosure leading from Cellhouse Four to Cellhouse Six, the muggy air clinging to him like a sweaty shirt. The line of troopers on the west wall and on the stretch of wall that he could see at the front of the prison had thinned out. They were standing perhaps five yards apart. He passed within a few feet of the broken sledgehammer han-dle he'd discarded earlier and had an impulse to stop and pick it up, but the thought of bending over made his ribs cringe. He lengthened his stride, suddenly alarmed by the stillness around him, wondering if the guards had already taken over.

He entered the barred enclosure through the open gate at the heel of the L and started along the side of Cellhouse Four, keeping his eyes straight ahead as he passed the towering windows, wondering if the cons inside were watching from the tiers, imagining them muttering, "There he goes. There goes the phony bastard who turned Andy Gump loose." And gloatingly: "Looks like they stomped his ass good. Serves the phony bastard right." The solid-steel door at the entrance to the cellhouse was shut. He swung it open, pausing as a streak of pain shot through him, then stepped inside.

Two cons were standing in the entrance area. One was the cellhouse barber; the other, the head cellhouse orderly, a popeyed flabby-jowled lifer called Froggy. The cellblock area was quiet. Beyond the barred ceiling-high partition on the entrance side of the cellhouse, several cons, including a few who had broken out of Isolation, were on the second-tier walkway, leaning over the railing. Others were standing in the cage doorways, watchfully, as though ready to swing the steel-latticed doors shut.

"Better crawl into your hole, Briston," one of the cons on the second tier called. "It's six o'clock. They're comin' in."

Cully looked up through the barred partition. The con who had called to him was a weasel-faced creep who had always treated him with servile respect. He was smirking now. Apparently the word had got around. Even the creeps were playing him for a stooge. Still looking up at the con, he moved to the gateway and said, "How'd you like to get those buckteeth of yours knocked out?" A painful tightness gripped his side, and he wondered what he'd do if the creep decided to call his bluff.

The weasel-faced con was no longer smirking. He was glancing along the railing, as though looking for help, but the cons beside him were staring out the windows, poker-faced, feigning deafness. "Jesus Christ, Cully," he said, "why blow up at me? All I said was it's six o'clock."

Cully stood there awhile longer, looking up at the cons along the railing, who were still staring intently toward the windows; then, convinced that he was being given the silent treatment, he turned and started across the entrance area, toward the rear door which led to the shower shed in the hall-like vacancy between Isolation and Cellhouse Four.

Froggy and the cellhouse barber were standing near the door. The barber, whose habitual greeting was "Hiya, Cully baby, what's new in the zoo?" turned away. Froggy, his protuberant eyes sliding about as though oiled, said, "Better get in your cell, fella. They'll be rushin' in here with guns any second now. Them hostages got turned loose ten, fifteen minutes ago." His voice was pointedly gruff.

"I'm gonna take a shower first," Cully said, and opened the door, berating himself for having answered the popeyed boot-licker, who normally treated him like royalty.

The cellhouse-size hall was as quiet and desolate-looking as an abandoned warehouse. He could see a patch of slate-gray sky beyond the barred forty-foot-high windows overlooking the segregated exercise yard, the trampled square of earth on which the outcasts, like himself now, were allowed to walk for twenty minutes a day. The two steel-latticed doors through which the chow lines entered the messhall were closed. But the rear door to Isolation was still open, and he could see the entire length of the lime-splashed bucket-strewn cellblock, all the way to the Control Room door. There was no one in sight. Unbuttoning his dungarees, he turned into the shower shed.

There was no electric lighting in the damp dungeonlike room, only fragments of daylight peering through the scratches in the paint-blackened windowpanes and mingling with the gloomy light coming through the jagged hole in the real wall of Isolation—part of the original breakout plan. On the floor below the hole was a scattering of broken bricks and chunks of mortar. From the ceiling hung a sagging network of corroded pipes and rusty shower nozzles. Most of the nozzles were dripping. The sloping concrete floor of the shower, cracked and soap-streaked, was veined with rivulets of water creeping toward the scum-clogged drain. Cully walked to the pipe closet in the far corner and twisted the handwheels on both valves, pain stabbing and clutching his side as his muscles contracted. There was a rainlike patter, then a swash, which grew gradually louder until the whole network of nozzles, perhaps fifty in all, was spraying water.

Holding his side, his head throbbing again, he kicked off his shoes and stepped out of his dungarees. As he started to bend over, pain stabbed his side. He leaned against the wall and lifted one leg at a time, his fingers working gingerly as he peeled the wet socks from his feet. Before stepping under the downpour, he walked to the door and looked out. There was no one in sight.

The water, cool at first, grew gradually warmer, and the pain in his side faded as he kneaded his neck and ran handfuls of water over the cut in his scalp. He kept his eyes on the door and his ears alert, listening for sounds beyond the swash and spatter around him. It would be impossible, he knew, to hear the Indian's approach, and even if he did, he was in no condition to face a shiv, especially naked in a slippery shower. But the thought of going back into the cellhouse, of walking along the tier to his cell, past the silence, past the accusing eyes behind the latticed doors, was even more disturbing than the thought of Surefoot leaping into the room. A guard's face, any guard's face, would've been a welcome sight. Never, at least not since the day he had entered the prison, had he felt so alone in the world. If only he could turn back the time two lousy days, he kept telling himself, he'd play it all different. If only he had known about the breakout, he would've kept his mouth shut in Fisk's office, and he sure as hell would've never laid a hand on Andy Gump. No doubt about it, he had screwed up but good. The raisinjack. Punching the Indian. All the way down the line, The Man, playing the role, throwing his weight around, strutting around giving orders like a fourteen-carat chump. Aw, Christ, it was always the same, looking back, always looking back and regretting, the goddamn story of his life. He stepped from under the swashing downpour and, dripping wet, slipped into his dungarees and shoes.

Leaving the water running, he walked into the hall and stood there awhile, between the open door to Isolation and the rear door to Cellhouse Four. Froggy was hunched in the fan-shaped wicket, looking out. There was no one else in sight. He started toward Cellhouse Four; then, wondering if Kelly was still brooding in Surefoot's cage and curious about what was happening at the front of the prison, he turned and entered Isolation, careful as he wormed his way through the clutter on the floor, not wanting to attract the attention of Duke Trusdale, who he imagined was tuned in with both ears at one of the cage doors three tiers above. He was halfway along the Segregation side when he saw a movement beyond the mesh-wire partition at the front of the cellblock. Someone was coming through the Control Room door into the dressing-in area, just moving into the dreary light slanting through the windows.

He stopped. Pain gripped his side, and his heart gave a lurch. Surefoot was standing in the gateway, less than forty feet ahead, a grin on his face, a honed-down butcher knife in his hand.

Cully had an impulse to wheel and run; but his legs felt mushy, and the thought of a shiv in the back kept him from turning. He glimpsed the trash can lid on the floor against the wall, glimpsed the knife blade jutting from the girder ledge under the second-tier walkway twenty feet ahead, and took a step closer. So did the Indian.

"I'm warnin' you, Joe! I don't want trouble, but I'm not backin' down." His side was aching. He kept telling himself to act calm. "One of us is gonna get hurt, Joe. I'm warnin' you!"

"That you, Cully?" It was Trusdale's voice. "What's goin' on down there?"

The Indian closed the distance by another step. So did Cully.

"For crissake, Joe, use your head. None of us hav'ta go back in The Hole. You're gettin' a chance to start off with a clean slate." He took a step closer to the knife on the girder ledge. "We can settle this some other time. Get in one of the cellblocks before they come in, and they'll let you stay there. The warden gave his word."

Surefoot made a spitting sound. "They never keep their word. We'll all die in The Hole. All but you." Holding the butcher knife like a candle, his back against the cage doors, he began sidling closer. He was almost under the knife on the girder ledge but gave no indication of knowing it was up there.

Cully forced his eyes away from the Indian's knife, forced himself to grin. "Okay, Joe," he said and reached into his pocket as though for a shiv. "Mine's smaller, but my arm's longer." He took a step forward, took another as the Indian hesitated; then, lunging to the side, gasping, pain searing and clawing his ribs, he snatched up the trash can lid with one hand and a heavy padlock with the other. "C'mon," he muttered and dropped into a crouch. "C'mon, you crazy son of a bitch!" He held the metal lid by its handle, like a shield, and kept acting as if he were going to throw the padlock, pain streaking through him every time he raised his arm.

Surefoot had sprung away from the cages. In the open now, still holding the butcher knife like a candle, he began making a cautious roundabout approach.

Above them someone rattled a cage door, and then another rattled, setting up a loud familiar clank and clatter. "Hey, Cully!" It was Trusdale again. "Y'down there, buddy? What's goin' on?"

Cully glimpsed a movement in the dressing-in area, near the gateway in the mesh-wire partition, and darted a glance that way just as a shadow-darkened face swung from sight around the edge of the locking lever box. He heard the tramp of rushing feet and a cracking sound; then a cage door above rattled again. He kept telling himself to stay calm, keep talking.

"Come a little closer, Joe," he muttered and raised the padlock, still in a crouch, only vaguely conscious now of the pain in his side as he maneuvered closer and closer to the knife on the girder ledge. He was on the verge of making a lunge for the knife when he saw Kelly coming through the gateway with what looked like a broken shovel handle in his hand.

Surefoot glanced over his shoulder at Kelly, then turned back to Cully, grinning, circling again, motioning with his knife for Kelly to close in from the opposite side. "You can't get us both with that lock, Briston," he said, and was turning again, as though to see if Kelly had followed directions, when the metal grip end of the shovel handle swished past his face and ripped the butcher knife from his hand. He flung himself to his knees, hugging his wrist.

For a moment, apparently unable to believe it had happened, he just knelt there, gaping at Kelly. Then, yelling, "I'll kill you both!" he began scrambling after the still-spinning knife.

Cully had dropped the padlock and trash can lid, and he, too, was moving after the knife. His foot came down on the blade just as Surefoot stretched himself out in a belly slide and seized the handle. Cully's free foot was planted beside the Indian's face. "Let go, Joe," he said. "I swear by Christ I'll kick your teeth out."

The cage door above rattled again, and Trusdale shouted, "Hey, Cully! What the hell's goin' on down there?"

Kelly, gripping the shovel handle like a harpoon, was standing straddle-legged over the Indian's bony back, shreds of blood-soaked toilet paper hanging from one of his hands, blood dripping on the Indian's neck. "Can't talk sense to a guy like this," he said, and smashed the grip end of the shovel down on Surefoot's hand.

There was a strangled yelp, a snarling commotion of arms and legs, and then Kelly was kneeling astride Surefoot's chest, hunched forward, bearing down on the shovel handle, choking him, crushing the Indian's windpipe. "Get one of those cages open," he gasped. "Grab his legs and drag him inside."

As Cully caught hold of the skinny ankles, aware again of the pain in his side, someone behind him said, "Gimme one of them legs, man. I'll help ya."

Smith, still wearing his gray felt hat, his dress-out suit looking like a trampled burlap sack, set a coffee pitcher on the floor and snatched one of Surefoot's ankles. He smelled of raisinjack, and his eyes were glassy. "I'll have this goddamn suit wore out 'fore I get outta here," he said as they dragged Surefoot into the cage.

The Indian made no attempt to resist. Even as they stepped over him on their way out of the cage, he just lay there glaring up at them.

"Now what?" Kelly said, after clamping a lock on the door. "We might as well lock ourselves up, too. We'll be right back in one of these stinkin' boxes as soon as they get in here."

"Maybe not," Cully said. "Don't you look for the warden to keep his word?"

"Hell, no. He couldn't run this pen with us on the loose."

Smith had picked up the coffee pitcher and was holding it out. "Have a snort. Stuff's got a pretty good kick."

"Where'd you get it?" Cully asked.

"In the kitchen. I found ten gallons stashed under the pot table. C'mon, there's plenty left."

"Too late, man. They're on their way in."

"Naw, I just looked out there. Ain't nothin' happenin'. C'mon."

As they left Isolation, a cage door rattled again, and Trusdale shouted, "Hey, Cully, for crissake, have a heart. What's goin' on down there?"

CHAPTER **20**

"MAYBE we better take another look out front," Cully said. "It's ten to seven. Didn't take 'em this goddamn long to occupy Japan."

He was stretched out in the warden's easy chair, a quart mason jar full of raisinjack in his lap. The jar had just been filled for the fourth time, and a familiar to-hell-with-everything feeling was beginning to creep over him. His side no longer ached, and the thought of being put on silence by the prison hardnoses seemed too remote right now to brood over. Now and then in the past half hour cons had passed through the kitchen or had looked in at them from the archway, but except for an occasional warning or wisecrack, the three of them had been left alone. Smith and Kelly were sprawled on the floor beside the easy chair, their backs against the greasy tile wall.

"They're makin' a million-dollar production outta this two-bit riot," Kelly said, flapping the boxing-glove-size bandage on his hand. A cook's apron had been torn in strips and wrapped around the deep gash across the heel of his hand. He, too, was on his fourth jarful. "They're playin' it up for television. Wouldn't surprise me a goddamn bit to see the warden come ridin' in here on a white horse."

"Horse or no horse," Smith drawled drunkenly, "he better get his ass in here pretty damn quick. If I ain't outta this dump by noon, I'm suin' this crummy state." He belched. "Hell, man, I'm a citizen. Been one for twenty-four hours now." He belched again. "How's the juice holdin' out, Cully?"

"No sweat. There's enough here to wipe the three of us out
—and then some."

"Lousy slop gives me heartburn," Smith said, stifling a belch.
"I oughta be out there drinkin' that top-shelf stuff." He set his
jar on the floor and shoved his rope-bound cardboard box under his head.

"Wha'cha got in that Oklahoma suitcase?" Kelly asked.

"Personal property, man."

"Like what?"

"Clock, toilet articles, coupla sweatshirts. You know, personal
stuff."

"Oughta chuck it. Box like that is a dead giveaway. People
see you with it, they know you just got out."

"How'm I suppos'ta carry my stuff?"

"So you got two bucks' worth of junk there. Leave it here.
Have somebody hold it till you get back."

"I ain't comin' back, man. I've had it."

"Yeah, I heard that before. Y'got a job to go to?"

"No, but I'll find one."

"Forget it. They don't hire ex-cons out there. Believe me, pal,
I been through it three times."

"I'll make it."

"Got a place to go? You know, family or friends."

"Naw, I'm on my own."

"Got any dough on the books?"

"Just the twenty-five bucks I got comin' from the state."

"Yeah, that's some bankroll all right. Hell, you can sit on
your ass for a whole day before you hav'ta start stealin'."

"C'mon, Kelly, it's not that bad," Cully said. "Some of these
guys stay out."

"How many? Three out of ten?"

"Those aren't bad odds. Better than the Irish sweepstakes."

Smith had lumbered to his feet and was dipping his jar
into the ten-gallon pot. "This is one guy that ain't comin' back,"
he said. "If worse comes to worse, I'll hold court in the street."

"Yeah, that's somethin' else I heard before," Kelly said.
"When the wagon comes, you'll climb in just like the rest of
us."

Smith's ruddy bleary-eyed face stiffened and turned a shade redder. "What's with you, man? You tryin' to put me on a bum kick or somethin'?" As he started to set his jar on the floor, his hat fell into the pot of raisinjack. He snatched it out, slapped it against his thigh, and clapped it on his head. The hat was still dripping and splattered with foamy scum. "I said I'll make it out there. And if I don't, I'll hold court in the street. Wanna make somethin' of it?"

Kelly flapped his bandaged hand. "Sit down before you fall down. Another jarful, and you won't even make it out the front door."

A con looked in at them from the archway, grinned for a moment, then said, "You guys better scatter. Radio says they're on their way in."

"Radio said they were on their way in a half hour ago," Kelly said.

Cully moved to the edge of the easy chair. "Let's take the juice to the Control Room. We can watch the front door from there."

"Hell with 'em," Kelly said. "Let 'em drag us to The Hole from right here."

"If we're in a cell when they come in, we might not be goin' to The Hole. Maybe the warden'll keep his word."

"You're dreamin', kid. Every one of us who was in The Hole when this started is screwed with a capital S. Believe me."

"Okay, I believe you. But let's take the juice to the Control Room anyway. We can watch 'em come in."

"Yeah, let's go," Smith said. "Soon as they open that front door, I'm gone." He picked up his cardboard box by the rope and grabbed one of the pot handles. "C'mon, let's roll. Free world, here I come!" He stifled a belch and let out a howl.

Carrying the sloshing pot between them, Cully and a rubbery-legged Smith, raisinjack still dripping from his hat brim, made a seesawing shuffle the length of the messhall, diagonally across the hall, and through the rear door to Isolation.

At the scuff of their feet, Duke Trusdale called, "Who's down there?"

Kelly, grumbling along behind the pot, shouted, "Dummy up, you loudmouth fink!"

They passed Surefoot's cage in silence. He was standing at the latticed door, one eye glaring out, his hands gripping the food wicket ledge. One hand was swollen and discolored. Cully had an impulse to stop and offer the Indian a jarful of raisin-jack, but the glaring eye decided him against it. They entered the Control Room and set the pot on the table behind the opening in the screened-in area. Then the three of them walked to the door and looked out.

The black heavy steel door to the Administration Building was shut; even the peephole shutter on the inside of the door was down. There were perhaps twenty rifle-armed troopers in jungle helmets and brown short-sleeved shirts strung out along the two-hundred-yard-long front wall, but on the gun walk above the Administration Building door there was a crowd. Brass-insigniaed state trooper officials and portly civilians in shirts sleeves and suit coats were looking over the wall, talking, gesturing. Farther down, near the center gun tower, three television cameras were pointed inside the prison.

"Watch it!" Cully said and backed from sight as one of the cameras swung in their direction. He closed the door and moved to the barred window beside it. "What the hell they waitin' for? If they don't get in here pretty soon, the guys are liable to come outta their cells and really start a riot."

"Christ knows what they're doin' out there," Kelly said. "Those civil service lame-brains can't do nothin' right. Might've lost the key to the door."

They filled their jars and returned to the window.

"You really think the warden'll renege?" Cully asked. "You know, about everybody startin' off with a clean slate."

"He's got to," Kelly said. "How'n the hell is he gonna settle this joint down with all the stir bugs runnin' loose?" He looked away self-consciously. "You might get a break, though."

"Why me?"

Kelly shrugged. "Andy Gump might put in a good word."

"Are you kiddin'? He'll bury me."

"Might fool you. Bein' a hostage might've made the dog do some thinkin'."

Smith belched, hiccuped, belched again.

"Better take some bakin' soda out with you," Kelly said. "Enough to last a coupla days—till you get pinched again."

"Man, get off my back. You won't see *me* in jail again. If I don't make it out there, there ain't a cow in Texas." He drained his jar, belched loud enough to be heard outside, then shuffled back to the raisinjack pot.

Cully, feeling the euphoric effects of five jarfuls, his aches and worries buried under a warm blurry contentment, was on the verge of going for another refill when he noticed activity on the wall above the Administration Building door. The crowd on the gun walk parted, and Warden Sullivan, a tall heavyset man with a ruddy bold-featured face and a headful of wavy gray hair, leaned over the wall and looked down as the heavy steel door below swung open and Lieutenant Becker stepped into the prison, a sawed-off shotgun in his hands. He stood there for several seconds, his head moving slowly from side to side; then he took another step forward and spoke over his shoulder.

Two abreast and armed with rifles, the state troopers began pouring through the doorway, then peeling off single file, hugging the wall on each side of the door, moving along in a crouch, swiftly, like infantrymen encircling an objective. Cully moved closer to the window, staring as the troopers kept pouring into the prison, moving in opposite directions along the front wall, the string of rifles growing longer and longer, winding along the east wall and then the west wall.

"I'll be go to hell!" Kelly said. "They're surroundin' the joint. Look at 'em! Nobody's makin' a goddamn peep, and they're chargin' in here like there's a war on."

Smith had picked up his cardboard box and was swinging open the Control Room door. He lurched, swayed for a moment, then staggered outside.

"Hold it, man!" Cully said, and reached the doorway just as Lieutenant Becker leveled his sawed-off shotgun at Smith, shouting, "Get back in there, boy! One more step, and I'll blow your goddamn—" He broke off as the warden called down to him from atop the wall; then he lowered the shotgun and went on in a milder tone, "Better get back in there, boy. We're through foolin' around with you people."

The troopers had bunched up in the doorway and along the wall on both sides of the door. The lines began moving now, briskly, still hugging the wall.

"C'mon, Smitty, get inside," Cully said, but Smith slammed his cardboard box on the sidewalk and sat on it.

"Go to hell, Becker," he called. "You're done givin' me orders. I'm a citizen."

Kelly was walking toward Isolation. He turned in the doorway and said, "C'mon, kid, the party's over. Let's grab ourselves a cage near the front. They don't stink as bad."

"Not me, man. I'm not lockin' myself in The Hole. There's still that one chance in a million that the warden'll keep his word."

"*You* might have a chance, but not the rest of us. Believe me." Flicking his bandaged hand, he crossed the dressing-in area and turned through the mesh-wire partition on the Isolation side.

Cully closed the Control Room door and walked to the window. Smith was still on the sidewalk, sitting on his cardboard box. The troopers were now straggling through the Administration Building door, and a huddle of gray-uniformed prison guards had formed around Lieutenant Becker. The party was over all right, he told himself, and suddenly felt exhausted, depressed, forlorn. He walked to the raisinjack pot and filled his jar. If only he were blind and deaf and dumb! Gagging, he gulped the soupy sickening-sweet liquid and filled the jar again. He drank half, held his breath to keep from retching, then dropped the half-filled jar into the pot, and walked into Isolation, moving along the Segregation side, past the Indian's glaring eye, out the rear door, and through the rear door to Cellhouse Four.

The cellblock was quiet. There wasn't a con in sight. He climbed the worn steel stairs and started along the second-tier walkway, past the hands in the food wickets, past the unfriendly eyes behind the steel-latticed cage doors. No one spoke.

No one moved a hand. A gust of smoke billowed across the walkway, and he wanted a cigarette, suddenly needed one; but as he passed through the smoke drift in front of the door, a pair of familiar tattooed hands withdrew from the wicket, and the face turned away. He reached his cage and stepped inside.

"Who was that?" someone hissed from the tier above.

And after a moment: "Briston."

And then: "Screw the ass-kissin' bastard!"

He stretched out on the wall-chained bunk, his stomach bloated, his head reeling, telling himself to hell with everything, to hell with everyone. The cage seemed airless. He caught a sickening whiff of watered lime from the battered metal bucket in the corner. Maybe there would be no reprisals. Maybe the warden would keep his word. His head stopped reeling. Hell, Andy Gump might even go to bat for him. Anything could happen. A parole! To hell with the hardnoses! He'd never see them again. He heard the familiar grate of a locking lever, the thud of a doorstop bar swinging into place, again and again. They were securing the cellblock. He flopped an arm across his face, and his thoughts began to flounder.

At first the sounds were meaningless: murmuring voices, the scuff of feet, a clinking sound. He heard the grate and thud of a doorstop bar being lifted, faraway, insignificant, and then a snarling voice came at him through the darkness: "Get on your feet in there!"

He rolled on his hip, gritting his teeth, squinting to focus his eyes. Pain gripped his side, shot up his neck, and came to a throbbing mass at the back of his head. He dragged himself up on his elbows. Through the fast-clearing blur he saw the badge on the hat and then the scowling baggy-eyed face under the visor. Sergeant Grossman, looking as belligerent as he had two mornings before, was standing in the doorway. Three troopers and a prison guard were standing on the tier walkway behind him. The guard had a tear-gas gun in his hand. The troopers carried riot stick and handcuffs.

"Get your hands behind your back," Grossman said as Cully slid from the bunk. "Turn around. Move closer to the door." Then, less harshly: "Better cuff him up. He's a bad one."

He heard a clink and a string of clicks and felt the handcuffs bite his wrists; then Grossman's liver-splotched hand caught his arm, and the fingers dug into his biceps. "Get movin', Briston. You know the way."

As he stepped past the troopers, he heard shouting from the opposite side of the cellblock and recognized Fletcher's voice: "Hey, you guys! It's a double cross! Don't let 'em get—" The shouting stopped as though smothered by a hand.

He started down the tier walkway, head throbbing, sick to his stomach. The cages he passed were dark inside. There were no eyes at the doors, no hands in the food wickets. He glanced toward the dust-furrowed windows overlooking the courtyard where the buckets were emptied and could see a gloomy patch of sky above the messhall roof. They'd replace the broken windowpanes in Isolation and paint them black again. It would be a long time before he'd see the sky. He turned past the locking lever box and started down the stairs.

A familiar voice was coming from a portable radio on the cellhouse sergeant's desk: ". . . quiet and completely under control," the warden was saying. "Except for a few recalcitrant diehards who refused to comply with the agreement and had to be placed in Isolation, the entire inmate body has—"

The rear cellhouse door was open. A trooper was standing beside it. Across the hall-like vacancy two more were standing beside the rear door to Isolation. Beyond the door, halfway down the Segregation side, a shirtless handcuffed con was walking between two prison guards. His head was bowed, but the muscular back was familiar. The con was Bugsy Matthews.

As he passed the shower shed, Cully noticed his wadded socks lying on the floor near the door and remembered the locking-up procedure. Andy Gump would take his shoes, and he'd have to pace the worn steel floor barefooted until he could connive a pair of socks.

He felt the fingers dig into his arm again and heard Grossman say, "Step it up, boy!"

He jerked his arm away and entered Isolation, glaring, walking slower.

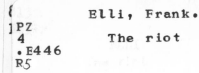
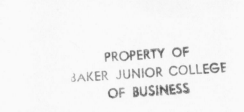